THE PALE S'
BOOK ONE OF TH!
TRII

C000150349

Robert Ryan

Copyright © 2018 Robert J. Ryan
All Rights Reserved. The right of Robert J. Ryan to be
identified as the author of this work has been asserted.
All of the characters in this book are fictitious and any
resemblance to actual persons, living or dead, is coincidental.

Cover Design by www.damonza.com

ISBN: 9781790890200
(print edition)

Trotting Fox Press

Contents

1. The Runes of Life and Death

Horta chanted, and there was magic in his words. He felt it buoy them with life. Yet such magic was dangerous. None knew that better than he, but he was dangerous also, and he gathered his power about him.

The sound of his voice was harsh. But the language he spoke, the tongue of his people who once contended to rule the world but were now scattered, was a harsh speech. He thought it fitting, for they were a callous people. The *Kar-ahn-hetep*, the Children of the Thousand Stars they called themselves. A pretty name for a race whose ancestors' swords dripped blood.

Horta raised his chanting to a higher pitch. His people were as nothing now, no more than a tattered race haunting a petty kingdom in the forgotten south, but he would raise them up as once they had been. He would make them great again, and all the blood his ancestors spilled would be but as a drop compared to what was to come.

He chanted, the power of his magic one with the words. His disciples, his *Arnhaten*, chanted with him. And the hidden roof of the cave mouthed their words back at them hollowly like the voices of their long-forgotten ancestors. And well might it be so, for the magic he invoked summoned the dead.

The stale air of the cave grew ice-cold, and the fire of the burning torches set against the walls gutted erratically. An acrid odor rose, though from smoke or some otherworldly origin Horta did not know. Nor did he care.

The magic was everything to him, and with a final surge of determination he loosed the last words of the spell.

He ceased to chant, and the Arnhaten fell silent with him. The magic surrounded him, drew on his strength and gave form to his purpose. He sat still, eyes open but gazing at the sandy floor of the cave before him. What he had summoned was not visible, but he felt its presence.

There was a whisper of sound behind him that should not be, and he turned to look. One of the Arnhaten groaned softly and slumped to the ground. It was Asaba, the weakest of them all. He had fainted, or perhaps his heart had stilled. No matter.

Horta shook the small pouch that hung from his slim cloth belt ten times. It was the ritual, and it existed for good purpose. But though he fulfilled it dutifully, still impatience gripped him.

Slowly, carefully, he dipped his right hand into the pouch and felt the dry bones gathered there. Finger bones. The bones of dead men, magicians all. One, that of his own master, who having taught all he was able Horta had slain. These were the *Kar-karmun*, the Runes of Life and Death.

His fingers slid through the rasping bones, and he was careful to grasp only some of them. To hold and cast all at once presaged ill-fortune of the highest order. He would not permit that, though the spirits of the dead that surrounded him, the possessors of the bones in life, anxiously awaited such an accident and he felt their ill-will like a cold exhalation on the back of his neck.

He drew forth the bones, and with a quick but sure jerk of his hand cast them onto the sandy floor before him.

The Runes of Life and Death rolled and scattered over the ground, then stilled. The future he sought to foretell was now laid bare and revealed by the agency of the summoned spirits. And though they wished his death, or worse, the force of his magic constrained them to obey.

A sense of uncertainty settled over him. Four bones had fallen, and the runes were never wrong for he possessed true power, but he saw things that he had not expected. Strange things.

He must study the casting carefully. But the presence of the dead was unsettling. It seemed to him as though they looked over his shoulder with anticipation. This was distracting, and he needed them no more, so he chanted again, this time only a few short words of command.

The spirits were released, their work done, and the power that summoned them now forced them away. One of the torches flared and then snuffed out as they resisted, and Horta felt their hatred rage in the shadowy cave. It was of no concern, for they must obey. Momentarily, the air seethed and roiled about him with invisible forces, and then they were gone.

Away in the distance the cave mouth moaned as a rush of air was expelled from the earth. And then silence fell, deep and profound. Horta turned his mind once more to the runes and studied them.

Small beads of sweat broke out on his forehead. He wiped them away with the back of his hand. Behind him, he heard Asaba groan. The man had fainted rather than died. A pity, for now a way must be found to kill him. He was too weak to learn more of the mysteries. Yet he knew some, and that was his death sentence. A little knowledge was more dangerous than mastery, and returning him to Kar-fallon in shame would see him killed anyway. His family would arrange that, for his failure would taint them.

A frown creased Horta's brow, and he realized he was prevaricating. He turned his mind to the runes and their meaning. Destiny would be what it would be, and he would accept it.

He read the runes from top to bottom and left to right. The first was *Hotep*, and it showed the Change aspect of the rune in ascendancy. Cut into the bone and then filled with blood that dried within the symbol, the stark lines showed dully. Better if it had landed on its reverse aspect, Quiescence.

Horta considered the rune's meaning. It was true that, as the lore of the Kar-karmun taught, it was the nature of the world that things existed in a state of flux. The wise man looked for opportunities that arose from turmoil, and so he must do. But that this rune landed above the others signaled a time of great change, and that was disconcerting.

He turned his attention to the next rune. It had landed a little lower and to the right. This fingerbone was older and yellowed, but the symbol cut into it remained clear: *Orok-hai*. It was The Hanged Man – or The Fugitive. In this case the rune had landed showing the fugitive aspect. But this was difficult to interpret. Did it signify that he himself would have to flee? Or the king he served? Or that the man he knew was returning to the realm from exile had finally arrived? He took it for the last, because it was against the threat of this man's coming that he had cast the runes.

Next, he looked at the third rune. This was *Fallon-adir*, usually interpreted as Soaring Eagle and Roosting Sparrow. It had fallen upon the sparrow aspect, and this was a clear warning.

It was universally acknowledged that eagles were birds of nobility, creatures of majesty that wheeled in the sky and rode waves of warm air with grace. Meanwhile, the sparrow chattered raucously in shrubbery. Yet, in truth, eagles were opportunistic feeders that hunted or scavenged carrion as circumstances dictated. The one was no nobler than the other, and the warning here was to beware false assumptions. He, and the king he served, were sure of their power and secure in their unchallenged strength. But circumstances could change. The threat of the man who was coming was real, and must be acknowledged as a danger.

He turned his attention to the last rune. *Karmun*. This disturbed him most. Its aspects were Death and Life, yet the bone had fallen on its side and showed neither clearly. The lore of the Kar-karmun dictated that this indicated uncertainty. But *whose* fate was uncertain?

Horta stilled his mind. His wishes, hopes and plans were irrelevant. He must not allow them to color his interpretation of the runes. The truth, the destiny revealed, was all. And much as he disliked it, the clearest reading was that uncertainty applied to all parties involved. Destiny had not yet been set. Brand, the man who was coming, could live or die. So too the king, and most importantly himself.

It was a shock to him that it might be so, but his own death would not matter so long as he had achieved his great purpose before it occurred. It was for this that he lived, and he must let nothing interfere with his fulfilling of it. The runes indicated that fate was uncertain. So be it. Yet he now had the advantage of foreknowledge, which his opponent did not, and he would ensure that uncertainty turned to certainty, that his own possible death turned into his enemy's.

His mind made up, he quickly gathered the runes and returned them to the pouch. They had served their purpose, and now he would accomplish his. Nothing would stop him.

Horta stood, and the Arnhaten rose with him. It was time to leave the cave and enter the world again. Much needed doing, and many plans required putting in place.

"What did the runes reveal, master?"

Horta turned his gaze to the Arnhaten who spoke. According to the lore, it was within the man's right. Nor should he be told a lie, no matter that Horta wished to keep things secret until he had resolved the uncertainties. The man, along with the others, had taken part in the sacred ceremony.

"This is what the Kar-karmun revealed," Horta answered. "Change comes, and the man we are cautious of is he who will bring it. We are warned to be wary of false assumptions, which I take to mean the man is a greater threat than expected." He paused, and the other man's eyes narrowed. He knew there would be more. "And death shall walk among us, though if it be our own, the king's or the man who comes is yet to be decided."

"But *someone* shall perish?"

"It is so," Horta replied. "But forewarned, we shall ensure it is our enemy."

Horta led them out of the cave now. It was not his way to answer questions. He had told them all they needed to know. Too much perhaps, for he heard the whispering of their fear in the dark passages as they trailed after him.

He did not judge them too harshly though. He himself felt the shadow of doubt upon him. This person that came was known to them by rumor of his deeds. Brand. Rightful heir to the realm, and a dangerous man. The runes were not needed to tell him that. And Brand came for just cause. King Unferth had killed Brand's parents and sent assassins to hunt him all through his childhood. Unferth ruled now from the high seat in which Brand should sit.

Horta sighed. He did not blame the man for coming, and in another time and place he would have ignored him. But for the moment, Unferth was necessary to further, even if unwittingly, the great task of Horta's life. Therefore Brand must die.

8

They neared the cave mouth. It would be best to see what Unferth did first. That was regrettable, for the man was small and petty and incapable of understanding the great game that was afoot. No doubt, he would try to kill Brand, as he had always tried. But if he underestimated him and did not take the proper steps, then it was time to act himself. And that meant magic. The thought of it sent a shiver up his spine. Magic was to be feared, and yet he loved the sense of danger it brought. But it came with risks that could not be ignored. The game was finely balanced however, and the one thing he needed most was time. But it was the very thing that was running out, and every step Brand took toward Unferth cut it shorter. The man *must* die.

He walked from the cave, and felt the lush green grass beneath his sandals. Below lay the Duthgar, the land of the Duthenor tribesmen whose king he now served. Immediately, the chill breeze of this northern land cut through him. It was spring, approaching summer, yet it was colder than the bitterest winter in his homeland. The simple linen *shenti* he wore, what these northern barbarians called a kilt, was not warm enough. He and the Arnhaten had been forced to wear a portion of bearskin over their normally bare shoulders. This was barbarous beyond description, but it *did* keep the cold at bay.

How he hated this land, so cold and damp and chilly. But the inhabitants loved the greenness of it. It seemed unnatural to him, for he remembered the beauty of the arid wastes of his home and the struggling tufts of grass and the vultures circling in an azure sky devoid of cloud. He remembered them, and yearned for them. But his loss was nothing against the great task he had set himself.

He strode down the hill, determined. The Arnhaten followed behind. They passed through crude farmland, fenced by hedges and scattered with fields of green grass grazed by fat sheep and sleek cattle, lustrous-coated and beautiful even after winter. But neither would survive in his homeland under the hammering sun and the moisture-sucking air. The people though, they were tough. They would adapt to such an environment. But that was not their fate. Destiny promised a different future for them: one they would eventually embrace. Or they would die.

The hall of Unferth was not far away. They came soon to a track and then a road which passed through a hamlet. The buildings still amazed Horta, for he was used to stone and mudbrick constructions. These were village huts, often of wicker and round in shape. Others were small cottages built of sawn timber.

The youths playing in the dirt ran when they saw the procession come. Horta had never been good with children, but it distressed him every time to see this. The adults noticed him too, but they went about their tasks as though he and the Arnhaten were not there. This was of no concern. They did not like him, nor he them. But it did not matter. He had cultivated Unferth's trust, and that was all he needed for his purposes.

It did not take long to reach the hall. They climbed a hill toward it, for it was set at the highest point of the land round about except for the hills that Horta had just descended.

The road came to an end. Smaller tracks veered away to right and left toward stables and storehouses. Ahead, where the road led, commenced a flight of broad stairs segmented by wider platforms where people could rest. At least this was built of stone, and well-crafted too.

Horta climbed the stairs, his disciples behind him as was proper. He was old, very old indeed, though he did not look it. He spurned the resting platforms, though it irritated him that his left knee began to ache with the strain imposed upon it. It had been injured of old and rheumatism had set in. He put the pain from his mind and walked faster.

In a short while he reached the top. A platform was set here, broad and wide. To each side stone benches were placed, and hall guards sat there, the naked steel of their drawn blades resting across their thighs. These men were warriors, and they were not positioned here for show. They would kill intruders swiftly, for Unferth was a man of many enemies.

The hall guards stood. They came to him, one man at their front.

"Are you bidden to this hall, master Horta?"

Horta looked up into his eyes, cold and blue. There was no friendliness there, but despite the drawn sword the man carried, and the swords of his men behind him, there was fear.

"I am bidden."

A moment the doorward gazed at him, weighing him up and assessing him. He wished to refuse entry, but that would cause his own death. Either by his lord or Horta himself, and he knew it.

"I shall tell the king of your coming, and he will bid you enter. No doubt."

The man turned and entered the hall. His men remained at guard, a wall of cold steel and colder eyes.

Horta waited patiently. Their enmity meant nothing, and he told himself that the wise man rose above insult and animosity. He thought of his great task, so long in the making, so close now to fruition. Patience here was but a small thing.

The doorward returned. "The king bids you welcome. You may enter, and one of your … assistants also."

This was not unexpected. It was a slight, one of many, but Unferth knew no better. None in this backward land understood the customs of his people and that a magician

11

kept his Arnhaten about him. It was not kings alone who needed protective guards. Quickly, he gestured to a man in his retinue and that disciple stepped forward. Together, they followed the doorward toward the hall entrance.

The hall was large, larger by far than any other buildings in the district. The broad gables were decorated, and the long sloping roof steep to shed snow. The doorward opened the great doors, huge constructions of oak slabs bound by black iron.

They entered the dim hall. Light came from wooden louvers high in the timber-paneled ceiling, and from a fire that burned in a long pit in the middle of the floor. The scent of smoke lay heavy in the air, and the aroma of food and mead from the previous night lingered.

The doorward led the way. Down the long aisle they passed, massive timber pillars carved with the strange legends of the Duthenor upheld the high roof. The fire warmed the room, casting flickering shadows into the recesses where mead benches were set and beyond them private rooms.

On the walls woven cloths hung, bright in the shadows, and the footsteps of the three men on the timbered floor echoed loudly. Here and there men sat, warriors all, their eyes grim in the shadows, their long-bladed swords by their sides and their war-scarred hands close to the hilts.

Horta gave them no heed, but he felt their eyes on his back as he passed. After some while they approached the high seat where Unferth, King of the Duthenor, sat. A king he styled himself, but rather was he a chieftain of a barbarous and wild people, quick to anger and quick to laugh, dressed in trousers and tunics and wearing boots. They had clothes, and habits, and a temperament that Horta did not like nor understand. But he knew well enough, despite all the strangeness, what motivated

Unferth. Greed and fear. Like all men, whatever their origin and customs, he was easy to manipulate.

"Hail, Unferth, king of the Duthenor," the doorward proclaimed. "I bring Horta, guest of the realm, into your presence."

Horta gave a bow, but his eyes never left Unferth, sitting high and proud upon his carved seat of black walnut. The doorward left, his footsteps hastening back to the entrance. He had no wish to stay.

"Welcome, Horta," the king greeted him. "Do you bring news?"

"Indeed sire." He looked about at several others seated near the king. These were his close advisors, men from his own neighboring tribe rather than the Duthenor. The king trusted them, but Horta did not.

Unferth noticed his concern. "You may speak freely in front of these men. Hold nothing back."

"Very well. You asked me yesterday to consult the Karkarmun." His gaze flickered to the king's advisors, many of whom would not be familiar with the term. "The Runes of Life and Death," he added for their benefit.

"And have you done so?"

Horta detected eagerness in Unferth's voice, though the king tried to hide it.

"I have. The divination was difficult, and the results not easy to interpret. Yet this much is clear. Brand returns to these lands, as our information already suggested. He is a dangerous man, and he brings change with him. Not only change, but the runes revealed the mark of death also."

Unferth leaned forward. He was close to fifty, yet still a man in his prime and the sword belted at his side and the chainmail he wore were not for decoration. But always there was the shadow of fear in his eyes, and it fanned to life now.

13

"*Whose* death?" the king asked.

Horta did not hold back. The truth would serve him best here. "It could be yours, sire. Or mine. Or Brand's. That he comes is certain, and that also with him he brings great danger. But the consequences of his coming? Fate yet hangs in the balance. But forewarned of danger, we can turn it aside."

Unferth sat back in the high seat. The black walnut was one with the dim shadows of the hall, but the swirling, intricate designs upon it of gold inlay gleamed brightly.

"He cannot come unobserved," the king stated.

"Sire," said one of his counselors. "The crossing of the river is guarded night and day, as you have ordered. He cannot return, nor has yet attempted to do so."

The king nodded slowly, but Horta sensed his doubt and attempted to spark it to life. "Perhaps. But our enemy is a canny man. At the very least, he will not come openly."

"There are men at the crossing who know him by sight," the king countered. "One is on duty at all times."

Horta nodded. "So I have heard, sire. And your precautions have been wise. Yet the last time these men saw him he was a youth. Will they recognize him now?"

"They had better," Unferth said. "No man changes that much."

Horta capitalized on the slight doubt in those words. "They should, but they may not. Nor is the crossing you speak of the only way to enter the realm."

"The Great River lies between Brand and us," another of the counselors said. "It's called great for a reason. It's wide and deep and cold. The currents are strong also, and only a fool would seek to swim it, with or without a horse."

"That is true," Horta replied. "Yet swimming is not the only way. As I have heard the tale, he escaped this realm long ago by crossing the river when it was frozen."

14

Unferth shook his head. "That was in winter, and far to the north. Besides, against that possibility, or the chance of boat, I have set men to patrol the river border all the way north into the mountains from which it issues. He will not come that way, and if he does he will be marked and killed."

Horta gave a slight bow. "Even so, I suggest you send more men to guard against his coming. Even, though this would be inconvenient, I advise closing the river crossing to trade temporarily."

The king pursed his lips and thought on that. But Horta knew before Unferth answered what decision he would make. Too much tax was raised from incoming merchants, and the king loved gold. He needed it to maintain the loyalty of his men.

"I think that unnecessary," the king announced at length, and his counselors vigorously nodded their agreement. "Brand is a dangerous man, and I accept that he will try to enter the realm. And also that he has proven difficult to kill in the past. But is he a god to defy all the measures I have set in place against him? No, he is not. When he comes, one way or another, his threat will be eliminated. Permanently."

Horta disguised his chagrin. It would serve no purpose to press the matter futilely. "As you wish, sire. I am but a humble servant."

The king smiled. "You speak humbly enough, yet there is enormous pride in you, Horta. I like that. And you have served me well. I have learned that your runes are worth listening to, and your counsels also, but you are wrong to fear Brand." He paused. "Nevertheless, I will send an extra ten men to the river crossing. He shall not pass, and live."

Horta bowed again. "I live to serve, sire."

"I do not think so. You are a secretive man, as well as prideful. Your goal, whatever it is, remains your guiding force in life. I do not hold that against you, but see that it does not cross my purposes."

"Of course, sire."

"You may go now." The king gestured to one of his men who handed Horta a pouch. It rattled with the dull clink of gold coins.

"Thank you, sire." Horta took the pouch and turned to walk back through the long hall, his assistant one step behind him.

He had not gone far when the king's voice halted him. "It seems to me that you wish Brand dead as much as I do, magician. Why should that be?"

Horta went perfectly still for a heartbeat, the blood in his veins turning chill as the air of this land he hated. And then he slowly turned, his face a mask. He must reveal nothing.

"I serve you sire, as I have these last several years. I think only of your interests, and Brand's death best fulfils that purpose."

Unferth laughed, and then stroked his uncouth beard, black and silver. Horta was disgusted. Why did so many of these northern barbarians not shave? But the king, for all his vulgar ways, was not stupid. He fixed him with his pale eyes.

"I do not think so. And yet you have served me well. Best that you do not falter now."

It was a threat. Veiled, but still a threat, and Horta felt anger rise within him.

"I shall not falter, sire. I serve, and I give myself to that service, in life and in death."

The king waved him on, and Horta turned and kept walking. He allowed himself the hint of a smile. He had not said *what* he served.

16

As he walked, the smile faded. Still the men in this hall gazed at him with their pale eyes, full of enmity. They mistrusted him. And that thought nearly made him smile again. Unferth saw much, too much perhaps. But at the same time he did not see enough. The men in this hall, as with many of the men who held power throughout the realm, were not Duthenor tribesmen. They were from a neighboring tribe, Unferth's tribe. They were his hold of power on this land, subduing the Duthenor. But the Duthenor were like dry grass waiting to be fired. They could rise at any time. And the king's own men ... they did not like him. Under the right circumstances they could turn on him too. Unferth saw the first danger, but was oblivious to the second. The wolf dreamed only of the fatted sheep, not the tearing fangs of other wolves.

He went on, the scuff of his sandaled feet loud in the dim hall. The bag of gold he placed within one of the pouches that hung from his cloth belt. Gold? It was an insult. Did Unferth think he was a dog whose loyalty could be purchased with throwaway scraps? Time was when he dined off gold platters and drank from gem-encrusted goblets. Servants tended his every need and dark-haired women with bright smiles massaged oil into his skin and eased away the day's care. He had wanted for nothing, and those days would come again. He must just bide his time a little longer.

He and his assistant exited the hall, and the Arnhaten waiting gathered to him, following him down the stairs. They all sensed his mood, but the assistant he had taken with him knew the cause and spoke when they were out of earshot of Unferth's guards.

"What now, master?"

Horta came to a stop and took a deep breath before he spoke. "Now, we ensure the death of Brand. He is a threat. The king cannot see past his hatred, cannot see his enemy

17

as anything but an exiled man. The precautions he has put in place should work. But they may not. Brand is greater, more dangerous and touched by a higher purpose than the king dares admit to himself. Therefore, I will take my own steps."

"Magic?" his disciple whispered.

"Indeed. Magic of the darkest kind. Brand will *not* survive it."

2. That Sort of Man

Brand endured the lash of the whip in silence. Seven times it streaked across the skin of his back. Seven times he gritted his teeth and rode a wave of pain that tore his flesh, churned his stomach and set fire to the marrow in his bones. And seven times he swore vengeance. Silently.

The head guard of the merchant caravan enjoyed whipping the junior guards. Brand was not junior to him in any way, shape or form. Yet just now, in this time and place, he was. Fate had willed it so, and Brand knew he must endure. But not for much longer.

He felt hands upon him then, deft hands undoing the rope that tied his arms around a tree. Brand had allowed himself to be bound, had accepted this punishment for a misdemeanor. It was necessary to his purposes. But he would not forget. Not ever. And the man who whipped him, who decided his punishment and enjoyed meting it out so much, he was marked for death.

The tight-bound rope fell from his arms and Brand staggered away from the tree. His legs were weak, and light-headedness threatened to see him fall to the ground. He fought it off, and those same hands that unbound him now gripped his shoulder. They held him steady and helped keep him upright. There was kindness in those hands, and he would not forget that either.

The world seemed to swim before his vision for some moments, and then he realized that the hands belonged to several men. He saw their faces now, concern in their expression and the glint of anger also. Not at him, but at the head guard. Yet they were careful that only he saw it, and not the head guard himself.

The pain began to recede, and Brand felt the sting of splashed vinegar flare it to life once more. Yet there was honey in the mixture, and this took some of the edge off the sharpness. This too he endured, for it was the standard preventative of infection, and he could not afford to succumb to sickness. Too much needed doing, and too many people depended upon him.

A moment later the guards began to ease his tunic back on, and he raised his arms to help them. The movement sent new spasms of pain through his body. He gritted his teeth once more, desperate for the agony to cease. It would pass, as all things passed, and he strove for a sense of serenity amid the turmoil that wracked his mind and body.

He did not quite attain the mental state that he sought. But he needed no help to stand, and he kept his hand away from the hilt of the sword belted at his side. Now was not the time, and if he could not rise above the urge to kill, he would never fulfil the purpose that he was needed for. Yet still, a cold gleam of hatred burned in his eyes as he slowly turned and faced the head guard.

The man stood a dozen paces back. The whip was still in his hand, the cord trailing along the ground before him, a satisfied smile on his face. Yet that smile faded as Brand stared at him.

Laigern stared back. The smile was gone, and his massive frame seemed taut and ready to explode into action. His muscles rippled and flexed as he began to fidget with the whip. He sensed the threat in Brand, the unspoken menace sparking through the air between them.

"Do you want more, boy? Turn around and get back to your duties."

Brand held his ground. "I did not know that looking you in the eye was also a misdemeanor."

"It *is* when you look at me like that."

The two men glared at each other, and tension filled the air.

"Enough!" called another man. This was the merchant. "You take offence too easily, Laigern. You just whipped the man. Have done with it."

The head guard turned to where the merchant sat in the driver's seat of one of the wagons, seemingly impatient to get underway again.

"You need guards," Laigern said. "Any time you feel like interfering with *my* men, and how I discipline them, just let me know. There are other caravans and other merchants."

The merchant shook his head. He was an old man, thin and scrawny, his hair and beard silvery white. But his eyes were shrewd and bright.

"You're the best, Laigern. I know that. Your caravans never get attacked by outlaws, but trouble will find you one day, mark my words."

Laigern grinned at him. "I eat trouble for breakfast, old man." His gaze flickered back to Brand. "Don't get any ideas, boy. If you think to try something against me, you'll get a sword in your belly. Do we understand each other?"

"Perfectly," Brand answered. He understood also that the reason Laigern's caravans were never attacked was because he bribed the outlaws and fed them information about other merchants, their whereabouts, schedules and the goods they carried. He was a robber as much as the outlaws.

Laigern turned away, coiling the whip and stowing it back in the saddlebag of his horse that was tethered nearby. Brand only took his eyes off the man when he heard footsteps approach him from the side.

21

Tinwellen walked up to him, all curves and dark hair and deep-brown eyes that swallowed a man whole. How the merchant had fathered a daughter like her, Brand did not know.

"You're a fool, city boy," she said while she shook her head. But the words were not meant unkindly. "There are no town guards here, no king's rule. If he were to kill you, there would be no one to stop him. Best let him be and forget about it."

Brand knew her words came out of concern for him. It was all she would say openly, but he had felt her eyes on him for days now. Her father had seen it also, but said nothing.

"Would *you* forget about it?" he asked quietly.

For a moment her eyes flashed, and he glimpsed her fiery side. "I would if someone as smart as me gave me the same good advice. At least until I was in a position to do something else."

"Ah, well, now that *is* good advice. I shall bide my time."

Brand guessed well enough that any man who raised a hand against her would wish he had not. Especially when one of her many daggers slipped across his throat. She would not be one to delay retribution a moment longer than necessary.

He decided to shift the conversation. "Why does your father put up with him?"

She frowned. "I don't know. Sometimes I think he's scared that Laigern would rob him if he were dismissed. He's a bad man. You're not the first one that he's whipped, nor will you be the last."

"Don't bet on that."

She held his gaze, and there was worry in her eyes. "Don't take him on. He'll kill you."

"Perhaps."

She ran a hand through her hair. "I can't make up my mind about you. You seem so smart. You seem like you've been far more than a caravan guard in your time, but you can be stupid too. Very stupid."

Brand did not answer that. There was nothing he could say at the moment.

She dropped her hand. "Come to my wagon when we stop tonight," she said, "and I'll rub oil and special herbs into your back to ease the pain."

Without waiting for an answer, she left him then, all dark hair once more and a purposeful stride. She had fire in her, that one, and he liked her. But she would be trouble too.

The caravan would not stop just because of the whipping of one man, and Brand had used whatever time had been allotted to him to recover. He must ride now, and more depended on it than the merchant's schedule.

He went to his horse, a sleek roan mare that had drawn the eyes of all the guards when he joined the caravan days ago and signed on. Gingerly, he mounted.

One of the twenty guards drew close to him, his own mount nearly as fine. He was older than most of the group, his bushy moustache silver, and Brand had sensed his experience and skill at this business from the first day.

"You should have cried out," the rider murmured. "Laigern has you marked now. You challenge him, and in his mind he must break you. That's how he thinks. He'll be looking for an excuse to whip you again."

Brand shrugged, and regretted it. Pain flared in his back once more. "You're right. But he doesn't need much of an excuse. He didn't have one just now."

The older man looked at him knowingly. "You're right. Dismounting to help up an old man who had tripped and fallen on the road as the caravan passed isn't much of a misdemeanor. But Laigern is like that. He has his rules, and the old man could have been a ruse to distract us while an attack was launched by outlaws."

"Maybe so," Brand said. "But what others were there? The old man's wife and grandchildren? And there was no cover for an ambush."

The older man let out a sigh, but did not reply.

"You're right," Brand continued. "His rules may be stupid, but I should have known better than to break them."

"They *are* stupid, but it's best not to talk that way. You're new with us, and he likes to make sure that new starters understand right from the beginning who is in charge."

Brand wondered if the man had cause to remember his own introduction to Laigern, but he did not ask about it. They fell silent. Around them, all the other guards had now mounted, their expressions grim. They looked neither at him nor at Laigern, and Brand realized they sensed trouble brewing. He sensed also that they wanted no part of it, for Laigern was feared.

The lead wagon gave a sudden lurch, and then began to roll forward. The merchant sat high in the driver's seat, looking straight ahead and ignoring all around him. He did not like what was happening either, but Brand knew he had given him as much time as he could to recover. More than Laigern would have wished.

Another four wagons followed the first, packed tightly with valuable goods. Around them the twenty guards nudged their mounts into a walk, Brand likewise, and the caravan began to move forward once more. They were heading toward the Duthgar, the land of the Duthenor. It was a wild land, populated by wild tribesmen.

City boy, Tinwellen had called him, but she did not know the truth, nor any of the others. He had traveled further than she had, further than her father, and though he had come from the city and acted as such, he was born in the Duthgar. And he was returning home. But trouble would come of that, and a whipping was the least of it.

Ahead, leading them all, rode Laigern. He sat his horse like a king on his throne, but he turned from time to time, and his dark eyes, sullen with menace, found Brand on each occasion. Brand stared back. And trouble would come of that, too.

The caravan had started in the great city of Cardoroth. That was where he had signed on. They did not know who he was nor his history, and that was the way he wanted it. Laigern had looked him over gruffly and accepted his word that he was good with a sword. He had been forced to, for he was short of recruits. Word of his fondness for the whip had obviously reached the ears of many.

The merchant had gazed at him shrewdly, seeing through some of his guise, seeing that despite appearances he was more than he seemed, even a man of wealth and influence. That old man said little, but saw much. Still, he did not guess the truth. Had he done so Brand would have seen shock in his eyes. What he saw instead was curiosity, and a mind that gnawed away at mysteries. That was dangerous too, for the old man might eventually work out who he was.

The great city of Cardoroth was not his true home, if he even had one anymore. It was a haven for him though, a place of exile that he had come to love. But all things ended, and as they did something new began.

He was returning home now, the land where he had grown up, and yet where he had been pursued as a boy by assassins and hunted from place to place and farm to farm. Only now, coming home, he was a greater swordsman than he had been, a better strategist. He was older, wiser, more confidant. And, though none in this caravan knew it, he possessed the use of magic. These were not small things, and they would stand him in good stead. Yet his enemies were powerful, and still they would seek his death. And coming back to the Duthgar, where their power was greatest, placed the advantage with them.

Dusk came and the wagons drew to a stop. Camp was set, horses fed and rubbed down, fires lit and meals cooked over the embers. Night fell, the stars sprang into the sky and music from pipe and drums and voice filled the darkness. Brand liked it all. There were worse fates in life than traveling with a merchant, seeing new ground every day and camping at leisure under the stars. But it would not be his fate, not for long.

By dawn the caravan was rolling again. Not long after, the river came into view. Not just any river, but the Careth Nien, the great river that divided the continent of Alithoras. Trees lined its winding path, hiding much of it, but here and there the glint of silver and wide stretches of water showed. And soon the crossing came into sight. It was here that the caravan must pass, and here that the first great danger lay. Brand looked ahead with determination.

3. The River Crossing

They came to the crossing before mid-morning. Nothing special marked the place, except a small group of cottages. Why this place had been chosen, Brand did not know. It was the same as any other stretch of the river. Yet even so, his instincts flared to life. There was danger here.

The crossings were not a ford or a shallows of any kind. Perhaps the two banks were closer together, but they were still hundreds of feet apart. Between lay the river, beautiful but deadly for man or horse that attempted to swim it.

Men came out of the cottages. Laigern and the merchant went off to speak to them. They would negotiate the fee for the crossing, and while they did so Brand studied how it would be achieved.

His eyes were drawn first to the barge. It lay anchored in the river. It was a boat, of sorts, but very wide and flat in order to carry the livestock and wagons over the water. Large as it was though, there would need to be two trips to get all of this caravan across.

At least the barge was on this side of the river at the moment. That would speed things up. Also, the men that had come out of the cottages were men from Cardoroth. The danger, if danger there was, would come from the other side. There would be Duthenor there, but how many and who Brand did not know.

Would his enemies be waiting for him? It was possible. The crossing would certainly be guarded and there would be men with his description there, even men who had once known him. That was the greatest danger of all. He had taken precautions against the first, but against the second there was little he could do.

He removed his hand from his sword hilt when he realized he was touching it. It was a sign of nerves, and nothing would give him away swifter than that.

The merchant soon returned with Laigern. The old man muttered something about being overcharged, and Brand smiled. Merchants always thought anytime they had to pay something it was too much. But they each charged as much as they could for the goods they carried themselves.

Laigern called most of the guards forward. Brand was not one of them. These, and the first three wagons moved forward and were loaded on the barge. Eventually, it began to move across the river. It would be a long wait here with the last two wagons.

Brand looked about. He saw that his friend had been left behind too. The older man approached, his expression slightly amused and his mustache almost twitching.

"It seems that we are both out of favor," he said.

"You spent too long talking to me, it seems. I'm sorry about that."

The older man laughed. "To be sure, that wouldn't have helped. But Laigern and I have never seen eye to eye. A pox upon him and his type."

"Likely enough," Brand replied, "he sells information to outlaws about caravan movements. But I've a feeling his day is done."

The older man looked at him thoughtfully. "You see things quickly, especially for a man that's new to this guard business. It's almost like you've done it before. But if you had, I'd know you. I've been at this a long time."

Brand said nothing, but the older man looked at him not unkindly. "We all have our secrets, I guess. And what you say about Laigern is probably true. There've been rumors for years. But this much I'll tell you for a fact. He's killed men. He's dangerous, and I've seen none better with sword, knife or fist. Stay clear of him. Let your anger go, and live. Push him too far, and he'll leave you lying by the side of the road for the crows to eat."

The older man did not wait for an answer this time. He had given his advice and now he wandered off to idle away the boring break they must endure before the barge returned.

Brand liked him, and he considered his advice. But it was hard to forgive or forget a man who had whipped you for no good reason. His back still felt raw, and he remembered the agony of the lash and the rising torrent of hatred that overwhelmed him. It had receded a little now, but not much.

Everyone seemed on edge, for the caravan and the guards had been split into two groups and should an attack by outlaws occur each group would be isolated and vulnerable. This only added to Brand's concerns. But he remained still, casually observing the river and trying to see what was happening on the other side without looking anxious. But it was too distant to tell much, other than that there were men there, and this he already knew.

Eventually, the barge returned. It was now the second group's turn to cross. The wagons rolled onto the barge first, and then the guards followed with their horses.

Brand led his roan mare over the landing. Her hooves clattered dully on the timber platform, and he saw flashes of the river between planks. Then they walked over the barge ramp and onto the boat itself. He kept to the rear of the wagons, not wishing to be seen any earlier than necessary when they made it to the other side.

"Cast off!" yelled the captain when all were ready.

"Casting off!" responded the crew.

The ropes holding the barge were untied and straightaway Brand felt the boat shift as the river current took hold of her.

Quickly now the crew worked, and they retrieved long poles and moved to the downstream edge of the barge. The poles speared into the water and found the river bed. The barge steadied. Then they withdrew the poles and began the arduous task of propelling the craft forward.

The current was slight at first, but then it grew stronger as the minutes passed and they ventured further out. The opposite shore remained distant. The current took hold of the barge, let her go and then gripped her again. Brand was glad that he had not attempted to swim, even with the horse. It may have been possible, but neither he nor the horse had the training for it. They would likely have died. He looked across to the far shore and wondered if he still might.

Not for nothing was this called the Careth Nien, the great river. It was wide and it took a long time to reach the shallows. But eventually they did, and the poles splashed through the water and hit the bottom quickly.

With a bump that thrilled through the deck beneath Brand's feet, and then a grinding noise, the barge came alongside the landing on the far bank.

"Tie her up, lads!" came the shouted command of the captain.

Some of the men ran to secure the boat, while the rest remained where they were, holding the barge steady in the water with their poles.

When the boat was securely tied, a ramp, this time at the front, was let down. The wagons rolled onto the landing and the guards followed them.

Across the timber landing they went. But soon there was ground beneath them once more.

Brand felt a strange sensation pass over him. This was home. He walked once more on the land in which he had been born. He felt pride and fear and love and hope all flow through him at once. He had returned from exile, had returned to right a great wrong done against his people, and the world would never be the same again.

This moment had been long in coming. He had so much to achieve. But it could end now, before it began, if he were recognized and killed. His great enemy would be sure to have the borders watched.

The wagons rolled forward to join the tail end of the first three. Soldiers were everywhere. And on this side of the river they were Duthenor warriors. No, he changed his mind. They were Callenor tribesmen, men of a neighboring land. Men who followed Unferth and who, by their strength of arms, had allowed him to usurp the chieftainship of the Duthenor and maintain it.

The soldiers moved among the wagons, checking their contents and assessing the value of all goods. This would be used to calculate the taxes Unferth charged. But at the same time the men searched the wagons carefully. This may have been for contraband, but he knew they were also looking for him. Better to hide in plain sight, he thought.

Even as he casually watched the men search, his stomach sank. Several tribesmen were also coming through, looking at the guards one by one. And Laigern was with them.

They came to him, and his stomach sank further. Among the Callenor soldiers was a Duthenor; one that he knew of old. Yet he had been but a child then, and had changed much and now spoke differently. Would the man recognize him? Perhaps. He had recognized the man.

Brand looked as casual as possible, merely checking the tightness of the girth strap of his mount when they approached. He made no attempt to hide his face and looked up when they neared.

The men paused and looked at him. He felt their eyes burn into him, and saw a frown appear on the face of the one he knew.

"And who are you?" the man asked, his eyes searching.

"Conmar," Brand answered, giving the same name he had given Laigern and the others.

The man did not take his eyes off him, and Brand tried his best to look bored.

After a moment the man turned to Laigern. "Is that so?"

The head guard grunted. "That's his name. Leastways the name he gave me. He signed on recently."

The man seemed to be interested by this. "Then he could be the one we're looking for."

Brand looked surprised. "Why would you be looking for me?"

"Where were you born?"

"In Cardoroth city. Midwinter night it was, and the howl of the wind was so loud my father said that—"

"He's not interested in the wind, idiot," Laigern interrupted him.

The other man's eyes were still on him, and the surrounding soldiers were growing uncertain. This was taking longer than it had with the other caravan guards, and he felt their eyes on him, weighing him up.

"An idiot, am I?" Brand said to Laigern. "Is that what I get for working day and night for a pittance. Is that—"

"Enough!" Laigern yelled.

Tension hung in the air between him and the head guard. Brand hoped it was enough. No man trying to hide would draw attention to himself in that manner. Yet still the Duthenor's eyes were on him.

"Pay no attention to this one," Laigern said. "I'll sort him out afterwards. He's a troublemaker his is, for sure. But I'll sort him out."

Brand felt the threat in those words, but the Duthenor warrior spoke again. "A troublemaker, is he?"

"Aye. The worst kind. I had to whip him yesterday."

The Duthenor looked at Brand once more, and then slowly shook his head as his eyes lost interest. "He's not the man we're looking for. That one wouldn't allow himself to be whipped."

They walked away, but Brand saw Laigern look back at him, his eyes smoldering pits of hatred. If he had known the truth, he would have turned Brand in quicker than blink and enjoyed the consequences. But he was blinded by his sense of superiority to the possibility that one of his junior guards was more than what he seemed. Brand was amused by the irony of that.

Not long after the caravan began to move again. The guards mounted and rode beside the wagons.

"Keep a sharp lookout!" Laigern ordered.

Brand knew why. They had now entered the Duthgar, the land of the Duthenor, but this was a wild region. It was a shadow land, ruled in name by the Duthenor king, but it seldom saw its supposed leader. Instead, it was a haven for outlaws. Most came from other Duthenor lands, but not a few from the kingdom of Cardoroth far to the east. Brand did as instructed, and kept his eyes open. But he did not look just for signs of outlaws, but also for friends; two in particular, and he would be glad to see them.

As they traveled, the land rose slightly away from the river. But they had not gone far when by chance Brand rode a little fast and passed some of the wagons. He drew level with the lead one, and felt the eyes of the old merchant fix on him. There was speculation in them, and more curiosity than had been there before. The old man knew that the soldiers at the crossing had been looking for a man. And he had guessed it was Brand.

Brand slipped back to his regular place as fast as he could without making it obvious. He should have known that the merchant would have figured things out. But he had guessed only half of it yet. That was half too much, and it was high time that Brand extricated himself from the situation. He did not think the merchant would say anything, but if Laigern got wind of things then anything was possible.

The ground rose more steeply, and the beaten track they followed shifted left and right always seeking the easiest incline. Wagons had been coming this way for years beyond count, and the best path had long been discovered.

About them rose a countryside of small hills and winding gulleys. Patches of forest ran across it, sometimes chocking the gulleys or covering the sides of a hill. At other times the land was bare, save for green grass. It was a haven for outlaws because at one and the same time it offered concealment and good lookout spots where the progress of a caravan could be watched and its guards assessed for their numbers, competence and routines.

In truth though, or at least so Brand believed, outlaw attacks were rare. There were too few bandits, and they seldom acted in unison. Also, the merchants always traveled with sufficient guards.

They moved higher into the hills. There were no farms here, though there were signs that farms once existed. It was not an area of the Duthgar that Brand was familiar with. But he knew there were settlements not too far away. Not of outlaws, but proper farms and villages. He was looking forward to talking to his own people again, and to seeing how they reacted to him. He had been away for many years.

He kept an eye out for his two friends as he rode. They would not have been troubled at the crossing, for though they were men coming from Cardoroth they bore no resemblance to him and would not have been bothered by the soldiers. Especially without him there.

But there was no sign of them. He had not expected to see them though. Not yet. But when the caravan stopped for the day he would leave it. Then he would head north into the hills. That was what they had arranged, and his friends would find him there. And though he could not see them now, he knew they were there somewhere, watching.

The track was dry and dusty. It was spring, and there had been rain, but the flow of traffic over the rutted lane was constant, and this kept it as it was. A cloud of dust rose up about the plodding hooves of the horses and the churning wagon wheels. Brand tried not to breathe it in, and thought as he rode.

He remembered the night his parents had been killed, murdered by Unferth and his men. It was long ago now, but the memory of that night and the days that followed haunted him. By chance, he had not been there and had escaped. He remembered the long years growing up, hidden by family after family who had been loyal to his parents. And why should they not have been? His parents were well loved, for they had ruled the Duthgar well and wisely.

His father was the chieftain, and Brand was the true heir. But he had escaped, and Unferth could not tolerate that. Brand's life must be a constant reminder that his rule was earned by spilling blood and treachery, and doubt would gnaw at him for fear that Brand might one day begin a rebellion and claim his own. For that reason

Unferth had sent the assassins after him. Over and over, again and again. But he had lived. He had endured. He had grown strong as a warrior, and later as a captain of men in Cardoroth's army. He had even risen to … but none of that mattered now. It was all dust on the wind. Those days were passed and new days had begun. At *last*, they had begun, and justice was coming after the long wait.

Despite all that had happened to him, it was some of his earliest training that would serve him best now. His father had taught him the warrior's ways, as well as strategy and diplomacy. After that, he had learned from some of the greatest fighters in the Duthgar. And he would need all the skills he had learned, of blade and mind both. He was about to start a fight, and he was badly outnumbered. At the beginning, it would be him and his two friends against the might of Unferth. But he had plans to change that disadvantage. But first, he must leave the caravan and deal with Laigern.

The day wore on. The caravan covered many miles, and the crossing of the Careth Nien was far behind. The sun set in the west, straight ahead of them, in a blaze of red and orange that streaked the sky and shot the scattered clouds through with crimson. Crimson like blood. And blood there would be, Brand knew. Soon.

His job would be to serve as a figurehead. He must get the people of the Duthgar to rally behind him. He must grow an army from nothing, and he must do so knowing that Unferth would be seeking to destroy him. No small task for one man alone with the aid of a few friends. But two friends was a beginning. If he could rally one person to the cause, he could rally fifty. And if fifty, a thousand. And if a thousand, an army. But Laigern was his obstacle now, and it was time to deal with him.

The caravan approached a small creek that ran down from the higher hills. Trees lined it, and it was a pleasant spot. But it was not where Brand would spend the night.

"Halt!" ordered Laigern. "Set camp!"

Brand nudged his horse toward the head guard. Laigern watched his approach, his eyes dark pits of hatred. He would be even more unhappy when he learned what Brand had to say. There would be trouble. Oh yes, Brand thought. There was big trouble coming. Laigern was that sort of man.

4. Sword or Knife?

Brand came to a halt before Laigern. The other guards were nearby, setting up a picket line for the horses. He did the polite thing and dismounted. He would talk to Laigern man to man, not from atop his horse. It occurred to him though that deep down he wanted to fight this man, to provoke him. And the head guard would not attack him while he was mounted.

"This is where we part ways," Brand said. He made no effort to speak quietly, and the other guards stopped what they were doing and watched. The merchant and Tinwellen were close by also.

Laigern smiled, but there was no humor in the big man's expression.

"No," was all he said though. Yet he said it with assurance.

"It's not your decision, Laigern. I'm leaving, and I'm leaving tonight. I'm just giving you the courtesy of notice instead of riding off into the night."

"You're not riding off anywhere, tonight or any other time. You'll do what I say, when I say it, for the rest of this trip. Or I'll whip you again."

Brand felt his temper slip. His back still hurt.

"You've whipped me once, and that will *never* happen again. Now, I'm going."

"If you make a move to mount that horse, I'll break your legs, boy. You signed on for the trip, and you're coming with us even if you have to crawl."

Brand looked Laigern in the eye. "Actually, I signed on for my daily fee. That was our agreement, and you know it."

"To hell with the agreement!" Laigern yelled. He was angry now, and his dark eyes shone with malice.

Brand stood his ground. More than that, he pushed it further.

"Pay me my day's wages, and be done with it."

Laigern shook his head like an angry bull. "No."

"Then I shall take it from you."

The head guard looked at him as though he were stunned by the idea, and then a slow smile spread over his face.

"You? A trifling man such as yourself, take something from me?"

"Yes."

Laigern's grin split his face, and it was not humor but an anticipation of inflicting pain. "Then what shall it be? Sword or knife?"

Brand felt his own hatred rise. This man had whipped him, and taunted him afterwards. He was a bad man, and the world would be better off without him. Yet should he be killed for that? The temptation was there, a strong pull, and it would be justified, to a degree. The man was asking for it. Yet for the very reason that it was a temptation, he must resist it. If he did not, would he not slip down the same slope that Laigern had? He had to do better than that, had to be a better man.

"Neither," he said at length. "We'll fight man to man, fist to fist. I have no wish to kill you, which I would with a blade."

Laigern chuckled. "You're sure of yourself, boy. I'll give you that. But nothing else." He removed his tunic, his great arms bulging. His upper body was thick and hairy, but corded with muscle.

Brand unbelted his sword and placed it on the ground. He was giving away an advantage here, for he was a better swordfighter than anything else, yet he did not regret it. He wanted to kill Laigern, and he must prove to himself that he was better than his baser instincts.

Suddenly Tinwellen was beside him, dark eyes flashing. He had not gone to her wagon last night, and she had avoided him since.

"Don't be a fool, city boy," she said.

"A man is no man who doesn't stand up for himself."

"That may be, but a live man is better than a dead man. At the least, he'll cripple you in some way. Just look at him, fool!"

Brand turned his gaze to Laigern. The man stood there, a picture of confidence. Brand was a large person himself, but the head guard stood six inches taller and weighed much more, most of it muscle. Scars showed on his arms and chest too, evidence that he was not all talk and bluff but had survived many dangerous fights.

With a shrug, Brand turned his gaze back to Tinwellen. "Thank you for caring, but this is something I must do. And besides, I'm going to win."

She looked at him, her expression incredulous, but whatever she had intended to say she never had the opportunity.

"Quit talking, boy." Laigern said. "There's no point in delaying this any longer."

Brand turned and walked toward him. He breathed deeply of the air and settled his nerves. He sought the mental state of the warrior. *Stillness in the storm*, his father had called it, though it had many names beside.

The world faded around him. There was only himself, and the huge man before him. Time seemed to slow, and his body moved with smoothness and ease. He was ready.

Laigern did not hesitate. He stepped in and jabbed with his left fist. It was a swift blow, and powerful despite the shortness of the movement. He was no common brawler rushing in and swinging wildly.

Brand shuffled back a pace. He moved with ease, sure of himself. But the big man moved faster than someone of his size had a right to.

Laigern followed with a right cross. Brand swayed to the side and let loose a right at the man's midriff. There was a satisfying thud as his fist struck flesh.

Brand moved away again, content to take his time. Laigern stepped after him, grinning. The blow he had taken had no effect on him. Brand was not really surprised. A well-muscled man, used to fighting, could take punch after punch to the body. The head, however, was another matter.

With a few quick steps Laigern bridged the gap between them. But he did not throw a punch. Instead he dropped and his leg swept out, trying to topple Brand.

Nimbly, Brand avoided the leg sweep. It had come as a surprise though, for its execution had been swift, and that was not easy.

They circled each other for a few moments. Brand saw an opening and jabbed with his left. The big man was swift, but the jab still took him square on the nose and blood began to flow.

Brand moved back. It was not his normal way of fighting, but his opponent was too big and too strong to take down swiftly. Patience must serve him here and not aggression. Laigern seemed unaffected. He ignored the blood and stepped after Brand.

The big man drew close once more and drove a left jab followed by a mighty right cross. Brand avoided them both and landed his own right to the man's body again before backing away.

None of Brand's blows seemed to hurt his opponent, but they would over time. Especially another one or two to the head. But if they were not hurting the big man yet, they were annoying him. He was hit and bleeding, but he had not touched his opponent. It made him look inferior, and that was the one thing Laigern could not tolerate. It burned his soul, and Brand knew it would. Fighting was a mental battle as well as a physical.

Laigern dropped his head and charged. Brand expected it, and his left jabbed out followed by a right that cracked into the other man's skull, opening up a cut and drawing blood above the eye. It did not stop him.

The breath was knocked from Brand as his opponent crowded him and an uppercut took him in the stomach. This was followed by a stomp towards Brand's foot, but despite the blow he received he was still nimble. He moved to the side, crashing an elbow into his enemy's midriff as he passed.

Laigern followed him, unleashing a succession of blows. Some took Brand in the head and body, but he avoided most of them. Just as well. The big man put power into his punches.

Brand feinted with his left. Laigern moved slightly to the side, straight into a hard right that sent him reeling backward. Brand moved in, sending a swift flurry of punches at the other man and then striking his neck with the blade of his hand.

The head guard had survived a hundred such fights though. He was bleeding and bruised, but not beaten.

A left cross struck Brand in the face, and he felt his enemy's fingers scratching and seeking his eyes. He dropped his head – directly into an uppercut that rocked him back and made his legs weak.

Brand stepped away and swayed. Laigern leapt in for the finishing punch, but Brand had also endured many

42

such fights and the swaying was illusory. He seemed to stagger, then as he dropped low he sprang up again driving a massive blow under the other man's chin.

Laigern toppled and crashed into the ground. But then he rolled and was up on his feet again.

Brand cursed silently as the two circled each other with wariness. Would this man not just give up? But at least he was not smiling anymore, and his breaths came in great heaves of his chest. The longer this fight went, the more he would be disadvantaged.

As they circled, Brand had a vague impression of the watchers in the background. Tinwellen stood perfectly still, her face a picture of concern. Her father was beside her, frail and old but his eyes bright and alert. The guards watched carefully, aware that they witnessed a fight of two highly skilled protagonists.

Laigern charged again. This time he did not punch, but moved to sweep Brand within the grip of his great arms. If he did so, the fight was over, for Brand could not counter the other man's enormous strength and weight.

With a smooth motion, Brand retreated, but he hammered a left jab into his opponent's already bloody face. Yet Laigern kept coming, and one hand found an unrelenting grip on Brand's tunic. Brand fended the other one away, but it sought to grab him also.

A moment they stood thus, and then Laigern surged forward with his greater strength and smashed a headbutt into Brand's face. The world turned dark and pain shot through him. Dizzy, he began to fall, and he heard the cries of the watchers.

His legs buckled. Searing pain tore at his skull, and he felt Laigern loosen his grip. No doubt his boots would take up the attack when his opponent lay on the ground.

But letting Brand go had been a mistake. Expecting him to fall had been another. It was not the first great blow

Brand had taken to the head, and he rode the pain and weakness in his legs, and then surged back catching his enemy by surprise.

Brand caught him with a swift left jab, and followed it with a pounding range of combinations to Laigern's body and face. The big man reeled back, shocked and hurt. Not fast enough to counter the blows, they rained upon him in succession until his legs gave way and he fell to the ground himself. He tried to rise, but then slumped once more, beaten.

Silence fell, broken only by Brand's deep breathing. He felt blood ooze from the whip marks in his back, and the pain from them flared to life once more. He looked down on Laigern, and there was no pity in his gaze. The man had brought this on himself, yet still Brand was glad that he had not killed him.

He bent down, wary that his opponent might try something, and untied the money pouch from his belt. Then he stood, opened it, and removed the coin owed to him. Then he dropped the pouch beside Laigern.

"It would have been better to have just paid me," Brand said quietly. The big man groaned and tried to rise once more, but then slumped again.

A few of the guards came over and helped the fallen man. They did not like him, but these were good men and they did not like to see people suffer.

All the while Brand felt everyone's eyes on him. He had done what none of them had expected. Laigern had seemed invincible to them, and now they looked at the smaller man, the junior guard, who had beaten him.

The merchant studied him, his eyes glittering. He did not like Laigern any more than the others.

"Stay on," the old man asked him. "I'll make you head guard in Laigern's place. A man like you, with your talents, can rise high … very high indeed. Even to the top."

Brand grinned at him. The man may have worked out who he was, but if so, he was not saying it in front of the others, which was for the best.

"Thank you," Brand replied. "But being a guard, of any sort, is just not for me. I have other duties."

The old man raised his eyebrows. "Ah well, never mind. Thank you for your services here. You've been entertaining, to say the least."

Tinwellen came forward. "You're more than what you seem," she said. It was almost an accusation.

Brand shrugged. "I'm just a man passing through."

"What man, though? And passing through to where?"

The merchant glanced at her. "Leave it alone, daughter. All men are entitled to their secrets."

She looked as though she would argue, but then thought better of it. "As you wish, father."

She came to Brand then. "Best of luck, city boy. I don't know who you are, or what your task is, but we'll meet again. I have a feeling about that." She hugged him quickly, and then went to her wagon and disappeared inside.

Brand would miss her. But he saw no way that they would meet again. He turned to the merchant once more.

"May I offer a final bit of advice before I go?"

"Of course," the old man replied.

"Dismiss Laigern. But then change your schedule."

"Aye," the old man replied knowingly. "I think it was time I did just that. Best of luck to you."

"And to you," Brand said.

He mounted his horse. Dusk was falling, but there was still a little daylight left. The guards, quiet until now, cheered him and wished him well as he left. They were glad that he had beaten Laigern, and even happier that the man would be replaced.

45

He rode higher into the hills. The sun dropped below the horizon, but to the north two riders appeared and angled toward him.

5. By Sword and Magic

Horta was in the old woods, the woods sacred to the Duthenor. Their dark trunks marched away out of sight, their limbs creaked and scratched. The men he sought to avoid, the Duthenor themselves, came here but once a year. Now was not the time, and he and the Arnhaten would have the solitude they required for what now must be done.

That the woods were sacred meant nothing to Horta. Yet it was a strange place, and it gave him an eerie feeling. Especially now, at night, with the stars blocked out from above. That was not natural, not what he was used to. Even the snow was better than that, for the stars had shone on his people for millennia. By them they navigated, under their influence they cast auguries, by their light they hunted and feasted and sang their songs of power.

Even so, cut off from the nighttime sky, he still felt power about him. Not for nothing had the Duthenor designated this wood as sacred. There were places in the world where the magic of creation still ran strong, and this was one. Best of all, he had need of such power now and it would aid him in what he did.

A bonfire burned before him in a clearing. The Duthenor would not light flame in a place such as this, nor bear steel blades. Horta shook his head at their ignorance. Superstitious fools. They did not understand the true powers of the world, had no knowledge of the beings who ruled it, did not know their names nor their functions and even less upon whom to call in times of need.

But he did. He knew the lore. Bitter had been his life to gain it through long years of servitude. And many had been the enemies along that journey. He shifted position where he sat cross-legged on the grass, and he heard the Runes of Life and Death rattle in their pouch.

The bonfire had caught swiftly, nor would it last long. The timber used was pine, and though there were trunks in it, they would not burn till morning.

"It is time," Horta said to the Arnhaten.

They stood. Slowly they began to circle the fire, casting on green branches broken down from the sacred trees. The sap-filled needles smoked heavily, and soon the forest meadow lay under a pall of seething, roiling smoke.

Horta gestured, and his disciples started to chant. It was an old ritual, laden with memories of his homeland, and it reminded him that he missed it and of how much he hated his self-imposed exile in this cold, damp northern land.

They continued the slow procession around the bonfire. Each time Horta reached the northern end, he cast a pinch of special herbs onto the flames. The herbs were a mixture of hallucinogens, and he was careful not to use too much. But likewise, he must use enough. But this too was part of the ritual, handed down over the eons and tested. He followed the ceremony to perfection. There was little room for error, and none in what was yet to come.

He breathed in of the air, and he felt his mind steady. Nervousness left him, though in the back of his mind fear still lurked, even if it seemed a separate thing from him. So too his conscience. He was about to unleash terror and death into the world. Brand would be the focus of it. A part of him did not wish this, for the man was no personal enemy. He was merely in the wrong place at the wrong time, but this was a weakness he must overcome. Morals

48

and regrets had no place in the great task that he must accomplish. He must rise above such frailties to serve a greater good.

Horta removed a single leaf of the *norhanu* herb from one of his pouches. This too was hallucinogenic, and he was wary of it. Yet it broke down the barriers of the mind and aided the release of a magician's powers. He slipped it into his mouth, tasting the bitterness of the waxy leaf but not chewing it. That would have too strong an effect too quickly. Moreover, it might kill him.

The night grew darker. The pall of smoke lessened as the fire burned. They cast no more green leaves upon it. Yet it was time now for the next part of the rite.

Horta stood still now at the northern end of the bonfire. The Arnhaten circled until they drew near him, and then they also stood still, gathering to each side of him. From another of his many pouches he gathered powder, and cast a small handful into the flames.

The fire roared to life. Red sparks shot up into the smoke-laden air, followed by trails of green. A stench wafted to him, but he did not hold his breath against it or falter. Now was not a time to waver or show weakness. Twice more he cast the powder, a little more each time.

Now, he began to chant, his words rising up with the smoke and heat-shimmer of the fire, up into the night and toward the hidden stars. The Arnhaten chanted with him, intoning the ancient words that he uttered as an echo.

Upon the gods he called, the old gods that ruled air earth and sky. The gods that existed before humankind and would endure beyond the fall of civilizations and the descent of man into oblivion once more.

Horta chanted, his voice resonant with power, not summoning a specific god, but beseeching their aid and asking that one would appear and hear his request.

And in the play of twining flames a form took shape. Vague it was, though it grew more distinct. It was manlike, but where a human head should have been was a flaring mane and the regal head of a lion, eyes sparking fire. And the eyes seemed human.

Horta recognized the god. It was Hathalor.

"Hail, great lord!" he exclaimed. "I beseech thee! O Master of the Hunt, Ruler of the Wastes, Voice of the Night. I beseech thee! If you are willing, lend me of your power."

The lion-headed god roared. Fire was his breath and thunder rumbled through the sacred woods.

"Hear me!" Horta continued. "Hear me, O Father of the Desert, Stalker in the Silence, King of the Hunt."

The god raised his arms toward the heavens. The trees leaned, the boughs bent to an otherworldly breeze, and the stars glittered in the now open patch of sky above.

"I beseech thee, Hathalor. Lend me of your power!"

Horta ceased to chant, and bowed his head, waiting.

"I hear you, Horta," answered the god. "Speak."

Horta did not waste time. Time was precious, and the god could grow bored at any time and leave.

"Great lord. A man comes. He is mortal, but he has power. He threatens all I strive to achieve. I beseech thee, crush him with the shadow of your thought. Let the dark eat his mind and the crawling worms devour his body."

The god looked at him, his gaze a window into other worlds.

"And why should I do this thing?"

Horta could not hold the gaze of the god, but he answered swift and truthfully.

"Because I serve the gods with loyalty and devotion. I would rebirth them into the world of men once more. Not just in white-walled Kar-fallon, but in Alithoras from shore to shore, atop all mountains, within all woods, across all lands and in the hearts of all people."

The god looked at him, the weight of his gaze as a mountain.

"The old gods you would rebirth into the world, as well as a new. Is that not so?"

"It is even as you say, great lord. The old gods I serve, as have my kind since the stars first arose, but the new god calls also. And the Kar-ahn-hetep shall once more conquer by sword and magic. And in conquering, the old gods and the new god shall walk among men together, for knowledge of them shall pass wherever sword slashes and the travails of battle pass."

The lion-headed god pinned him with his eyes that turned red and green like the fire in which his visage stood.

"You take much upon yourself, Horta."

"I am called to do so."

The god considered that. "It may be thus. Therefore, I will send hunters after this threat you fear, this man called Brand. But first they must feast on human flesh."

"It shall be so, great lord."

The fire died down, the image of the god flickered away and the Arnhaten gathered close around Horta, uncertain. Yet the hallucinogenic smoke they had inhaled dulled their sense of fear. He looked at them, glad of the old rituals. Nothing in them was done without purpose, and the old masters anticipated the will of the gods. Yet in this case, the smoke alone would not be enough.

He dipped into his pouch once more with strangely steady hands, and withdrew a norhanu leaf. This he passed to Asaba.

"Consume it," he said. "It will calm your nerves."

The Arnhaten took the leaf and sucked upon it. The disciples moved closer to the fire, but it was dying swiftly, dwindling to ash and embers. The night was old about

51

them, and the sacred woods of the Duthenor alive with power.

But something else stalked the woods also. Wolves. Horta glimpsed their gray pelts and the glinting of their eyes.

He turned to Asaba. "I have a task for you."

The disciple replied, his voice slurred. "Yes … master. What shall I do?"

"Do you feel magic run through your veins?"

"I do, master," Asaba answered softly.

"Then swallow the leaf. It will enhance what you feel."

Asaba seemed to struggle to focus on him. "But is that not dangerous?"

Horta placed a hand on his shoulder. "It is dangerous to the weak, but you are strong, are you not? Do you not feel strength thrumming through your body?"

Asaba seemed confused, and he did not answer. Yet as Horta watched the man chewed and swallowed the leaf.

"Ah," the magician said. "Such power. With it you shall ride the night and destroy our enemy. You are the first and greatest of the Arnhaten."

No answer did Asaba give, but he sighed dreamily. And his eyes were now black.

In the woods, the wolves began to howl. Horta studied the darkness hemming them in, and when he returned his gaze to Asaba he sensed the magic surging within him, wild and unpredictable. The Arnhaten trembled, and he swayed rhythmically from side to side. White foam frothed at his mouth, but the man did not seem to notice.

"It will be soon now," Horta said. He took his hand from Asaba's shoulder and stepped away. "Stay clear of him," he instructed the others. "Be still. Watch, and learn. For the power of one of the old gods is loose in the world this night. Do not move, and you shall survive it."

The wolves came into the clearing on padded feet, their eyes alert and their long snouts sniffing. No one moved. All was still, except for the gentle swaying of Asaba. The wolves sniffed at him and growled.

Asaba slowly straightened. A dozen wolves circled him, drawing close. He raised his arms, and power flashed in his black eyes. Not for nothing had he been chosen to join the Arnhaten, but his courage was raised by the norhanu leaf. Without it he would have fled. Yet standing still or running, the result would have been the same. Horta watched dispassionately.

Several of the wolves leaped at him. Some tore at his legs, but one jumped high, its jaws snapping and gnawing at his throat.

Crimson blood sprayed. Asaba tried to scream, but his voice was torn away by the frenzy of the wolf. He staggered, clutching at his throat, and the rest of the wolves went for him, dragging him down into their scrabbling midst.

The wolves swarmed over the thrashing figure beneath them. The struggle soon ceased, and the wolves tore into the body, snarling at each other with reddened snouts. Bones cracked and blood spilled onto the ground, visible even in the dim light of the fire.

When the frenzy of feeding died down, the wolves began to howl. They had eaten of human flesh, but they had absorbed something more also. In their howls was something not quite wolf-like. There were words in their baying, something human, some form of communication amongst themselves. They were now more than wolves, for they had taken up some of the nature of the human they had devoured, and the touch of a god was upon them.

Horta looked at their eyes, and he saw that the amber they should have been had a tinge of blue. Like Asaba's had been. And they returned his gaze as though they knew who he was and what he had done. One of them, the leader no doubt, had the touch of the god more heavily upon him. His eyes were completely blue, and a fierce intelligence shone in them.

Then, as though each wolf caught the same scent of prey simultaneously, they turned as one and padded away into the woods, passing out of sight.

It was silent for some moments. No one looked at what was left of Asaba, but one of the Arnhaten eventually spoke.

"What did we just witness?" he asked.

"The power of a god," Horta replied. "And the beginning of a hunt that will end with the death of Brand."

6. The Touch of Magic

The two riders headed toward Brand, and he watched them carefully. It paid to be cautious in the wild.

They came closer, and he knew beyond doubt who they were. One was a short man, but he would stand tall beside any hero of the land, past or present. He was boisterous, swift to speak his mind and too fond of wine and gambling. Brand liked him anyway.

The other was taller, green-eyed and with pale, slightly freckled skin. He rode like a king, though there was hardly a drop of aristocratic blood in him. When he spoke, it was quietly. He rarely offered opinions, but when he did, Brand listened. He was a man to listen to, and he had served his land with the same courage as the other, could stand beside any hero of the ages.

And they were his friends. His sword brothers. No two men were ever more different, and no man had ever had better friends.

They pulled their horses up when they reached him, and they looked him over.

"I'd hate to see the other man," the first said.

"You'd hate to fight him too, Shorty. But he's not of concern any longer."

The second man raised an eyebrow. "You fought him hand to hand by the looks of it. Why? The sword is your best weapon."

"Yes, well, I didn't really want to kill him. Though he deserved it. And it's nice to see you too, Taingern."

The other man bowed his head slightly, but it did not stop him raising his other eyebrow.

55

"None of it matters now, my friends. What's done is done, and the future lies ahead of us."

"Right now," Shorty said, "the future holds a warm campfire and some hot food. At least, that's the one I'm looking forward to."

"Then let's start," Brand said. "This is as good a place to camp as we'll likely find before nightfall."

His two friends grew uneasy. "Not here," Taingern said.

"Definitely not here," Shorty agreed. "Not in the open. We've found a better place, not too far away. It's a small cave at the side of a low hill."

Brand's instincts suddenly flared to life. There was something out of place, here.

"What's wrong with camping in the open? Outlaws?"

"Let's talk as we ride," Taingern suggested. "It's growing dark quickly, and the cave is a little way off."

They nudged their mounts into a trot, and Brand followed them. These were men who knew what they were about, and if they wanted to camp in the cave then the cave it was.

Shorty let his mount fall in close beside Brand's. "We're just being careful. You warned us about the outlaws, though as yet we've seen no sign of them. But there are other things in this land. There are … wolves."

Brand was surprised. "There have always been wolves here. Same as back in Cardoroth. In neither place do they attack people."

Shorty grunted. "So I've always believed. But the wolves of the Duthgar are different, or else they've changed since last you were here. These ones might."

Brand was worried. These were not the sort of men who would be scared of wolves, either four or two legged. But neither of his friends seemed talkative, and he guessed that they were intent on getting to the cave. He would find out more when they reached it and had set up their camp for the night.

The three of them rode across the green grass of the hillsides as the light of the sun faded and night seeped over the land around them. The stars kindled in the sky and the air turned chilly. It was spring, but summer still seemed far away.

It was not long before they came to the cave. It was not a hidden entrance, but it was narrow and easily defendable by even one person. Brand approved of it as a place to hold against an enemy, and he wondered how different he would be if he had not been forced all his life to make such considerations. He could not guess, for that was all he had ever known.

The cave was more spacious inside. With difficulty, they led the horses in and tethered them to rocks on the back wall. After rubbing them down and giving them grain, they started a fire in the center of the floor. Shorty and Taingern had previously gathered dry timber for it. Rocks were positioned here in a circle, and they were blackened. This was a place used many times over the years, but most recently the occupants were likely to have been outlaws. This did not concern Brand overly, but his companion's reticence to speak of the wolves disturbed him.

When they had got the fire going to a point that they could separate away some embers and commence cooking a stew of meat and vegetables, Brand broached the subject as they sat around the warming flames.

"Tell me about the wolves," he asked.

There was silence for a moment, and his two companions exchanged glances. It was Shorty who answered though.

"You'll hear for yourself, soon enough. It started last night about this time. There was a great howling, but not from a pack together. They were all spread out, as though searching for something."

"And what else?" Brand prompted.

Taingern answered him this time. "They sounded like wolves, but not quite. If I did not know better, I would have said that it was men imitating wolves. There were words within the howls…"

"Outlaws, perhaps?"

"We don't think so," Shorty said. "We spoke with a wandering tinker also. He was scared out of his mind. Said that he'd seen a wolf with blue eyes, and that it spoke to him."

"What did it say?" Brand asked a little flippantly.

Shorty grunted. "Joke about it if you want, but you'll see."

"So you believed the tinker?"

"I believe *he* believed it."

Brand looked over at Taingern. "What do *you* say?"

"I wasn't there. The tinker was. And I have no reason to disbelieve him."

Brand thought about it. The news was disturbing to say the least. But he saw no direct threat, and Unferth possessed no magic nor was in league with a sorcerer. At least, he had never heard so.

"Well, this cave is a good place to camp. And if there's trouble, we're prepared for it."

The two men seemed relieved that he took the situation seriously.

"Speaking of trouble," Taingern said. "If it comes, you will want these."

He rose and went to the horses. When he returned, he held two objects out to Brand. One was a helm, the fabled Helm of the Duthenor that had long belonged to Brand's family. And the other a white oaken staff. These were objects of power, objects that he was known to carry and that the soldiers at the crossing would have been looking for. Shorty and Taingern had offered to take them across themselves, and they had gone separately. That way they had avoided recognition.

Brand took them. "Thank you. Had I been carrying these at the crossing, there would have been trouble. I was nearly recognized anyway."

Taingern fed the fire another dry branch. "Unferth is looking for you. He knows you're coming, and he's worried. There will be other men in other places too, and your return to the Duthgar will be noticed quickly."

Brand knew it was true. What he was going to attempt was risky, and he had none of the resources he had enjoyed in Cardoroth. But that was not his home. His exile there had served its purpose, more than its purpose. It had originally been just a place to live, free of assassination attempts, but it had become so much more. First a soldier, then a captain, then bodyguard to the king himself. Then regent for the crown prince until he came of age.

He could have made himself king, had he wanted to. King of a realm far, far greater than the Duthgar. Yet that was not what he wanted, nor would he have displaced the rightful heir. But he missed the resources at his command. With the army of Cardoroth, he could have swept through and deposed Unferth in just a few days. It was not Cardoroth's war though, and he was no longer regent. That part of his life was over, and he must start anew.

Shorty gave the stew a stir. The smell of it gave Brand hunger pangs. It had been a long while since lunch.

"What now?" Shorty asked. "As Taingern says, your coming will be marked soon."

It was true, and Brand knew it. "I can't remain hidden, and I can't achieve my aims by trying to hide. So, the best way forward is the opposite of hiding. I'll make my presence known quickly, spread word, and build an army."

Neither of his two friends seemed surprised. They would have given the question thought themselves, and probably arrived at the same answers.

"And how will you gather an army?" Shorty asked.

Brand placed the Helm of the Duthenor upon his head. To his people it served the function of a crown. Long ago it had been won by one of his ancestors through the performance of an act of high courage. The immortal Halathrin had given it to him, and it was crafted with their skill and their magic. It was worth more than all the gold in the Duthgar, but to the Duthenor it was a symbol, a talisman of everything that they were or yet could be.

"I'm the rightful chieftain, or king as Unferth now styles himself. And the Duthenor, I think, will rally to me. Slowly at first, and then swiftly as word spreads."

Taingern looked thoughtful. "It may well be as you say, but Unferth will not stand by idly while you gather an army."

"True. But the philosophy of a warrior is to turn your enemy's strengths into weaknesses. I'll send him a message, one that despite all the advantages he holds will cause him anxiety and increase the fear that's gnawed at him all these years. In this way, I may prompt him to act hastily, or do the opposite of what he should in a show of pride to prove that he's *not* anxious."

"A dangerous path to tread," Shorty said. "It may cause him to come against you with all he has and try to crush you before you even begin."

Brand shrugged. "That's possible too. All life is a risk, is it not? Nothing is certain."

They offered no answer to that, nor gave any advice. They knew the risks as well as he, and if they had a better plan, they would have suggested it. But good plans or bad, they would stick with him anyway. They were the best of friends, and danger was no deterrent to them.

The stew was ready, and Brand dished it out to them on wooden platters with a chunk of old bread each. He had rarely tasted anything better, but hunger was the cause of that rather than the food itself.

Shorty looked over at Brand while they ate. "You could have stayed in Cardoroth, had you wanted to. You may have stepped down as regent … but afterward you could have done anything. You have wealth, lands and business interests there. You could go back still, if you wanted to. Are you sure you want to go ahead with things here?"

"You mean why do I want to come to this backward and forsaken part of the world to risk my life?"

"That's what I just said," Shorty grinned at him.

"Because it's home. My heart is here, and it always was. And my people need me."

"All true," Shorty agreed. "But you left Arell behind as well."

Brand gazed into the fire. No matter what he did, he could not please everyone, least of all himself. He had no wish to be separated from Arell, and he felt a void in his life without her.

"She wasn't happy at my going, but she understood. More or less. She offered to come with me, you know. But the sick and injured of Cardoroth need her. Her fame as a healer continues to grow. Now, it's not just the ill who come to see her but other healers also, from all over Cardoroth. They want to learn from her. That's where she belongs, doing the work she's good at."

They fell silent as they finished their meal. The cave was getting darker as the fire died down, and the air was full of smoke. It hung heavy just below the roof, but there must have been cracks there that slowly let it out too. It was into that quiet that the first howling of a wolf came, and it sent shivers up Brand's spine.

The call was taken up by a second, and then a third. In moments the whole pack voiced their beastly yowling, yet they were spread out over the land and not in one place. Brand sensed that they hunted something, sought for some trail. But it was not game they were after. It was him. He knew it with certainty, just as he sensed the touch of magic also. There may have been words in the eerie sound as his friends had suggested. These were wolves, but magic infused them and gave them life and purpose. But it was magic of a kind that he had never felt before.

The three men looked at each other in silence. The howling faded away, and the silence after was alive with menace. Brand was glad to be in the cave, and he added more timber to the fire.

A long while they waited, but there was no further sound. The pack had moved their hunt elsewhere, for the moment.

"It will be a long night," Brand said.

His two friends nodded grimly in the flickering light of the fire, and they also added more wood to the hungry flames. There was enough to last through the night, though whether these wolves would be scared of fire was another matter.

They did not set a watch. But they slept on the other side of the fire, keeping it between themselves and the entrance. The horses would give alarm if they scented a wolf approach, and Brand trusted his instincts to wake him if something was wrong.

The night passed. The men slept. The fire died down, and the smoke in the cave swirled in slow eddies, gradually escaping through the cracks above.

When at last something woke Brand, it was dawn. There was light in the cave, but it was more from the slanting rays of the sun than the near-dead fire. And in the cave entrance a figure moved, but Brand could not see it clearly for the light of the new day streamed in around it.

Brand leaped to his feet, sword in hand. Taingern and Shorty, woken by the sudden movement and sound, did likewise a few moments later.

7. Deep and Dark

Brand felt the weight of his sword balanced smoothly in his hand, the instincts of a warrior lending his slightest motion deadly grace. Yet he remained near still, and his other talent, magic, surfaced. It told him that something of great power was before him, something as deadly dangerous as ever had lived in Alithoras.

It was no wolf though. The figure was that of a man. And a tall man at that. A sense of recognition began to infuse him, but he did not lower his sword.

"Hail, Brand of the Duthenor. Warrior that was. Regent that was. Lòhren to be. Greetings, and well met."

Brand knew that voice. He lowered his sword, but did not sheath it. He still could not see the figure clearly. But the man sensed his uncertainty. Slowly, so as not to cause fear, he moved into the cave.

He was a tall man, white-robed and silver-haired. He was old as the hills, yet his face had a perfect complexion. His eyes missed nothing, seeing right through whatever they saw, weighing and assessing, finding the measure of every man and every situation in a glance. Yet they were eyes that had seen terrible tragedies, and sorrow and compassion lay behind them.

Brand let out a long breath and sheathed his sword. "Hail, Aranloth. The days have been long since last we met."

It was a formal greeting, but Aranloth was not just any man. He was greater than kings, more powerful than armies, deadly as an enemy but the greatest of friends to those in need.

Aranloth grinned at him. "It's good to see you."

"And you, too. Much has happened since we spoke last, but it seems that you're well informed of events."

The old man walked further into the cave. "I hear much. The land tells me what I need to know. Sooner or later, one way or another."

Shorty and Taingern sheathed their swords as well. The old man turned to them. "I should have expected as much. You two are never far from Brand. Or he is never far from you. And just as well. Trouble has a way of finding you all."

They shook his hand, and Brand did as well. His grip was strong as steel sheathed in silk.

"Speaking of finding things, how did you find *us*?" Brand asked.

"Ah, well, that's interesting. I didn't find you. I wasn't looking for you and this is a chance meeting, although there are some who don't believe in chance. I was just passing through, and I sensed the wolves. I knew they were hunting something, and I put them off the trail."

Shorty and Taingern exchanged a look. "We thought it strange that we only heard them howl once last night."

Aranloth looked thoughtful. "There's much about this whole thing that's strange, the wolves especially. They're more than wolves, and the shadow of dark magic is upon them. That was what raised my curiosity. Who were they hunting? For if the hunters were so unusual, so too must be the quarry."

"Well," Brand said, "no one has ever accused me of being normal, so the wolves are after me." He had felt that last night, and nothing had happened to change his mind.

"No, you've never quite been normal. Not since the day we first met," Aranloth said. "You draw trouble to you like no man I've ever seen. And the trouble of the wolves is not over. I put them off the trail, but that won't last long. You must be wary of them, for they'll find you soon."

Brand knew it was so, but he was not looking forward to it. He trusted in his skill as a warrior, and the sword he carried. He trusted less in the magic he possessed, but he might need it against the wolves. He retrieved the oaken staff he had long carried, and handed it to Aranloth.

"This is yours," he said, "and I thank you for the lending of it."

Aranloth looked at him keenly. "You have the magic. The staff is an aid to that. But it's more. It's a symbol of being a lòhren, a wizard as we're known here in the Duthgar. Do you seek to escape that fate, to be seen just as a warrior? Is that why you offer me my staff back?"

Aranloth always knew. Those eyes of his missed nothing, and his sharp mind even less. In truth, some of what he said was correct. Brand had no wish to be a lòhren. Yet he had accepted it was so, whether he wished for it or not. But he would be lying to himself if he did not admit that a part of him, now coming home to the Duthgar, did not want to reclaim his old life.

"I offer it back simply because it's yours. And I understand better what it is, and what it represents, better than I did when you first lent it to me. A staff is earned by a lòhren, given to him at a time of need by the land itself. That's how the magic works. And this staff isn't mine."

Aranloth reached out, and slowly he took the staff. Brand saw relief on his face, for it truly *was* the lòhren's, linked to him by magic. But he saw worry also.

"I don't doubt that you're a lòhren," Aranloth said. "Yet I find it strange that you've not found your own staff yet. One way or another, and each of us in a different way, a lòhren discovers his staff. The land itself sees to that, the land which we serve and protect."

"Maybe it will not be so with me," Brand said.

66

"It is *always* so. Yet, perhaps, it will be different for you. Time will tell."

Aranloth gripped the staff and ran his hands over it. "Truly, it's good to have this back. I've had it a *very* long time. It may even be that while you carried this, you could not find your own true staff. Perhaps. The ways of the future are often unseen, and even when we plan them out ahead with precision, thinking to leave nothing to chance, yet still things turn out quite differently than we expect."

The lòhren's sharp eyes fixed him for a moment, and Brand knew there was a warning in his words. But then he seemed uncertain, which was not like him at all. He gave a slight shrug, as if to himself, and then spoke again.

"It may be, in this case, that your duties as heir to the chieftainship of this land and as a lòhren are one. For while a chieftain or a king must first think of his own people, a lòhren must think of *all* the land. The two concerns rarely match. Yet, just now, in this time and place, they may for you."

Brand did not quite like that. The words signified that there was more going on than what he had thought. It tied in with the wolves. Magic was at play, and forces that he did not yet know or understand.

"What do you think is happening?" he asked Aranloth.

The lòhren pursed his lips. Another sign of uncertainty that he rarely showed.

"I don't know. But I have seen things, heard words in the wind and seen messages in the starry sky. The earth murmurs of it in the quiet of the night, and birds of the field call it out in flight. It is there, and yet not there. Call it intuition, if you like. Perhaps even imagination. But I have listened to the land for years beyond count, and know its ways. Something stirs."

Brand knew it was more than imagination. He had felt it with the wolves. There was a power abroad of which he knew nothing, except that it existed.

"What do you think it is?"

Aranloth leaned on his staff. "Trouble. That's what it is. And it's old, old and patient and wise in the ways of evil. Men will serve it, wittingly or unwittingly. Sorcery is at its heart, deep and dark. A power is waking, or being woken, that has long slumbered. Almost I recognize it, but not quite. It has the feel of something that long ago I knew, but it cannot be that."

"I'll watch for it," Brand said.

The lòhren straightened. "It watches for *you*. That much is certain. Who sent the wolves? And why? When you discover that you'll have found the power that stirs to life in the Duthgar, or whoever seeks to wake it. And whoever, or whatever, aids Unferth. For in this the enemy who you know, and the one which is hidden, are working together for a common purpose."

Brand felt a shiver work its way up his spine. That was all he needed. Two enemies when he thought to confront only one.

The lòhren seemed to sense his thoughts. "Worse, I'm not able to stay and help. I'm needed in the south of the land … I would stay if I could, but it cannot be. And I must hasten away even now."

"I know, Aranloth. There's a dark shadow over all Alithoras, and evil stirs to life everywhere. I wish you luck."

"And luck to you also."

Aranloth studied him a moment, his eyes keen and sharp. "Be wary Brand, just now you ride the breath of the dragon."

It was a term that Brand had not heard before, and his confusion must have shown on his face.

"Forgive me!" Aranloth said. "I forget sometimes. That's an old, old saying. It means though that you ride the winds of fate."

Brand did not much believe in destiny or fate, but he knew the power of being in the right place at the right time. He felt that he was *meant* to return to the Duthgar just now.

"I know what you mean. There's a sense of fittingness to what's happening. But fate, if there's such a thing, is a two-edged sword."

"Indeed it is. When the dragon's breath falters, and it never lasts forever, you could end up in serious trouble."

They clasped hands, and Brand sensed the good wishes of the lòhren wash over him almost like a blessing. He truly would stay if he could, for he held grave fears for the Duthgar. The wolves had disturbed him more than he had said aloud.

"Take care, old man," Brand said.

Aranloth grinned at him. "You too, boy. And if you do, you might just live to be my age."

He glanced at Shorty and Taingern. "Be careful lads. The Duthgar isn't like Cardoroth, but it's just as dangerous. More so now, for something is coming after Brand. And if you're with him, that means it'll be coming after you too."

Shorty grinned. "We're an army of three. We'll teach it to fear us instead."

"Let it be so! And farewell!"

The lòhren glanced once more at Brand. "Remember, you begin a battle now against Unferth. But there's another player to this game, greater and more dangerous. Beware of him." Then he turned and left.

Brand was sorry to see him go. He was not just a lòhren, but the *leader* of the lòhrens. But what would be would be. And whoever this other player was would be revealed. In time.

8. Eye of the Eagle

The morning passed swiftly, and Brand and his companions made good time. The hilly country did not hinder them greatly. Each slope they climbed had as its opposite a downhill incline. What they lost on the first, they mostly made up on the second.

It was a wild land, and beautiful to Brand's eye. But he was born in the Duthgar. Taingern and Shorty looked around them, thinking the hills unfit for all but sheep. It was certainly true that it was good sheep country, as was most of the Duthgar, but the soil was more fertile than it looked. When cultivated, it produced good crops, and there was water to be found, sweet and good to drink for those who dug wells.

There was evidence of farming about them too. Here and there were patches of land that once had been ploughed. Remnants of small orchards survived. Now and then, there was even an old cottage to be seen, though long abandoned.

"Why did the people leave here?" Taingern asked.

Brand sighed. "There was war. The Duthenor have many rivals, for there are quite a few tribes covering this region of Alithoras, shifting back and forth with the ebb and flow of food, famine and politics. We are all closely related, but we fight amongst ourselves. Some hundred years before I was born the Duthenor were attacked. We held the Duthgar, but it cost many lives. There are other regions such as this, where the people left were too few to farm it. They died out. And the Duthgar was only beginning to recover when Unferth usurped the chieftainship. He was chieftain of a neighboring tribe. So far as I know, he remains so. Perhaps that's why he styles himself as king now."

Shorty was in the lead, and he slowed. "It looks like here at least is one village that didn't die out."

Brand drew level with him and looked downslope toward the cluster of buildings that lay in the middle of a shallow valley. "It's small, even for a Duthenor village." He looked closer, and frowned. "But the patches of cultivation are full of weeds. They've not been ploughed since well before winter. And there are no fires from any of the chimneys."

They rode down, warily. They did not draw their swords, but each of them was ready to unsheathe their blades at a moment's notice. Brand led them, and the other two fanned out some distance behind and to either side in a staggered manner. It was standard practice when going into a dangerous situation. If there were an archer or ambush, it would make it harder to kill them all at once.

Brand studied the village as they drew close. It had the feel of something abandoned, and he did not sense any danger. Yet something had caused the villagers to leave. Or killed them. It was not a place to take chances.

They came to the main street. It was dusty, and no weeds as yet grew in it. But the thatched houses seemed untended, and here and there were signs of fire.

Brand drew to a halt. Before one such house lay the remains of several men. They had been picked over by scavengers and the bones spread out. But there were swords too. Rusted now and pitted by weather, but that they had been drawn and used Brand did not doubt.

"Outlaws?" Taingern asked.

"Perhaps," Brand answered. "Certainly there was fighting. But whatever the cause of it, no one buried the bodies."

72

Shorty grunted. "Outlaws would not trouble to bury their victims."

"That may be so," Brand agreed. "Yet word would have spread, one way or another. I would expect Unferth to send soldiers to hunt the outlaws, and whether they found them or not, they would still have buried the dead."

He nudged his roan onward. There would be no one here, else the bodies would long since have been buried, and whatever danger there was had passed. He felt a sense of shock creep over him though. The Duthenor were called barbarians, but whatever crime had been committed here had gone unpunished, and that was not the Duthenor way at all.

They left the village and moved up the slope opposite. They did not look back or speak. There was nothing to be said. But leaving the village behind did not reduce Brand's unease. Had the Duthgar changed in his absence? Were the Duthenor not the people he had grown up believing they were?

The path they followed was a track, of sorts. There were signs that wagons and horses had used it, though rarely. And none recently. It led them through some timbered country, and they moved warily, watching all about them with a sense of being scrutinized back. But they neither saw nor heard another person.

Somewhat later the countryside opened up again. The trees grew sparse and the land leveled.

"There's a farm ahead," Shorty observed.

Brand had not seen it. He had been deep in thought. But looking up he noticed it straightaway, and saw also that it had the same abandoned look to it as the village. Yet there were a handful of sheep in a paddock behind the large homestead.

"There's a well there, close to the path. We might as well water the horses."

They moved along the path, well-used here for this farm had evidently once been quite large and a central gathering place for smaller farms nearby. There was a barn behind a stand of trees and stone-walled enclosures behind that separating off fields for cultivation and livestock.

Brand dismounted first. He hauled up the bucket, and tasted the water. It was cool and good to drink. The others stayed mounted, alert to the surroundings. The three of them rarely spoke of such things, but they were all careful men who thought alike and did these things by second nature. With many other men, Brand would need to give a command for a watch to be kept. Not so with them, and that was the way he liked it.

There was a wooden trough near the well, and this Brand filled again and again with the bucket. He had just brought another one to the surface when he heard a quiet warning from Taingern. He let the bucket go, and drew his sword from its sheath in one swift movement.

A man had come from the barn, and a sword was in his hand. Brand moved away from the well in case he needed room to move. Then he studied the figure as it approached. It was not a man, but a boy of perhaps fifteen summers, though large for his age.

"Be off with you!" the boy commanded. "I'll not have your type here, and if you come back again you'll end up with an arrow in your guts. That's more warning than you deserve."

Brand did not lower his sword, boy or no boy. "A strange greeting for travelers," he said. "It's been some while since last I came to the Duthgar, but it seems hospitality is not what it was."

For the first time, the boy showed signs of doubt. "It's customary for travelers to ask permission first." While he spoke his gaze flickered over the three horses and the

74

accoutrements of the men. They were better quality than any he had ever likely seen, and a long moment his glance rested on Brand's sword.

"I apologize," Brand said, giving a slight bow but not lowering his sword nor taking his eyes off the boy. "You are correct, and we should have gone to the homestead first. Only we've passed through the village and saw that it was … empty. And we thought the same of this farm. No harm was intended."

The boy studied him, his uncertainty growing. "Then you're not outlaws?"

"Indeed not," Brand said. "Just travelers, passing through."

A few more moments the boy scrutinized them, and then he sheathed his sword. "I'm sorry then, please go ahead and use the water. You're the first people, other than outlaws, that I've seen in months. I thought you were more of them, but their kind don't apologize. Or have horses like those."

Once more the boy looked at Brand's sword, and Brand slid it back in its scabbard. At the same time, he saw Shorty and Taingern surreptitiously sheath the daggers they had drawn, ready for throwing. He was not sure if the boy noticed that. Otherwise, he had handled himself remarkably well for someone of his age.

"What's been happening around here?" Brand asked.

The boy looked grim. "There's not much to say. The outlaws rode through and killed everyone in the village. The outlying farmers thought they would be safe – farmers don't have much worth stealing – but we were wrong." He paused and gathered himself, showing little of the emotion he held in check. "They destroyed every farm in the district, so far as I can tell, including this one. I was out hunting, and when I returned … it was all over. I buried my family and I've been getting by since."

75

Brand looked at him, taking in his gaunt frame and threadbare clothes. He was surviving, but only just. Yet that alone was impressive. It was no easy thing to deal with such a trauma, and then go on living. Especially by yourself.

"Didn't Unferth send soldiers? Surely word must have reached other districts."

The boy spat. "Someone somewhere around here must have escaped. Unferth knows, but he does nothing. A pox upon him."

Brand felt a slow anger creep through him. Unferth was a murderer and usurper, yet still he had a duty of care as leader of the Duthenor. And he had done nothing.

The boy kicked the ground with a worn-out boot. "I'm Sighern," he said. He held out his hand and Brand took it. They shook the warrior's way, wrist to wrist.

Brand indicated his companions. "The short one is best known as Shorty. The freckled one is Taingern."

The boy shook their hands one at a time. "Taingern? That's not a Duthenor name."

"No. We're from Cardoroth. At least we two are. Our illustrious leader over there," he pointed to Brand, "is from hereabouts though."

The boy looked them over again, assessing them. "I'm sorry I took you for outlaws. You have the eye of the eagle about you, but there's a kindness to you as well."

"The eye of the eagle?" Shorty said.

"The look of a warrior," Brand said. "It's a saying around these parts."

Brand gestured to the water trough, and his two friends dismounted and watered the horses. They also filled the water bags.

"What now?" Sighern asked.

"Now we ride away. We have places to be and things to achieve."

The boy looked at him, nodding slowly. "You never said what your name was."

Brand had a feeling that question would come. The boy was not only courageous but swift of thought. And he had looked with interest at Brand's sword. He would not have seen its like before, but he would have heard stories about blades of that kind. And who they belonged to.

"I'm Brand."

Sighern eyed him again, but there was little surprise there.

"You really are, aren't you?"

"I am. Brand, son of Drunn and Brunhal, and the rightful chieftain of the Duthenor."

Sighern looked at him long and hard. "If you're Brand, who I have never seen, but of whom I have heard stories, that sword you carry will be your father's and your father's father's deep into the history and legend of our people. Let me see it again."

Shorty laughed. "I like the boy! He doesn't have much trust for strangers, and that's a good quality."

Brand lifted the sheath of his bade slightly for the boy to see. It was an ordinary scabbard such as any warrior would have. But the sword it hid was another matter. He drew the blade slowly, and the music of the steel sliding free was the hiss a warrior loved.

The blade came free, and it glittered in the sun. Halathrin wrought it was, with all the skill the immortals had acquired over long, long years of life. The blade was silver, shimmering with pattern-welding, the light shifting and swirling along its length, the edge so sharp as to nick other blades yet never blunt itself. The steel strong as an ancient oak tree, yet pliable as a whip, but for all its flexibility able to withstand the mightiest blow of any enemy.

Sighern looked at it keenly, noting its every aspect and feature. This was a sword that tales told of, that everyone in the Duthgar had heard a hundred times. And the boy knew it. Brand saw it in his eyes when he looked up from the blade.

"And the ring?" the boy asked.

Brand slid the blade back into its sheath. Then he lifted up his right hand. A ring glittered there, and a design upon it of stars gleamed. It was the twin constellation of Halathgar. "This," Brand said, "I obtained in Cardoroth in service to a great queen. It is a treasure beyond compare. But this also I hold dear, dearer even, for it is as old as the sword and has passed through the same hands, was worn by my ancestors each in their turn."

He lifted up his left hand then. Upon the index finger was a smaller ring, less well-crafted but still beautiful. It was cunningly designed so that the band of gold looked like a coiled snake that ate its own tail. Yet where head and tail met a sapphire gemstone glimmered like a winter's sky. He had hidden it in his boot at the river crossing; otherwise it would have identified him even more surely than the sword.

Brand lowered his hand. Sighern looked him in the eye, and then did something Brand had not expected.

The boy knelt on one knee, but he did not drop his gaze. And he voiced the oath of loyalty that had come down through the ages and was remembered in story and legend.

"Lord. My sword is your sword. My heart is your heart. As the great dark descends, we shall light a blaze of glory against it."

Brand could not quite believe a farm boy knew the loyalty oath, but the Duthenor were a surprising people who loved their history.

"Rise, Sighern," Brand said.

The boy stood, his gaze unwavering, and he surprised Brand again. "Take me with you."

Brand knew he should have guessed what was coming before the boy spoke. But he had not, and though he liked him he could not let him come. His two friends came up beside him, listening intently.

"You know who I am, and what therefore must come of that since I've returned to the Duthgar. Everywhere I ride now, danger will be with me. Unferth *must* stop me, and he will try his best. Everyone with me is in as great a danger. You're safer here."

Sighern shrugged. "That much I know already. But though I'm surviving here, there's no future. I'd rather take the risks with you."

Brand was impressed, but he just could not risk the boy's life. "There is another danger too. There are wolves hunting me. There's sorcery about them, and though I cannot be sure who sent them, I know they come for me, and that they will not give up. They, or whoever sent them, may be more dangerous than Unferth."

There was a look of recognition on Sighern's face. "I have heard the wolves. They passed close by last night, or some of them did. They did not sound like any I've ever heard before, and I don't doubt they hunt you. It's rumored that Unferth has a magician in his service. He must have sent them. But still, I would go with you if you will allow it. I can fight as well as a man, and I'm good with a bow. I can track, ride and swim. I'll not be a burden to you."

Brand understood what they boy wanted, and that he was willing to take risks. But he could not allow it. He spoke slowly, and reluctantly.

"I understand everything that you say. And I know you would not be a burden. But … but," he could not get the words out. When they came, they were not the one's he intended. "Very well. You may come, and may fate have mercy upon me."

The boy looked at him with excitement. "Do you mean it? Really?"

Brand did not hesitate this time. "I mean it. Quickly now, go and get whatever you would bring with you."

Sighern turned and raced away. Brand and his companions stood in silence a moment, watching him run to the homestead. Then Brand felt the gazes of his two friends turn to him.

"I like the lad," Shorty said. "He has courage. Great courage. But he's only a boy. What on earth are you thinking?"

Brand had no answer. He could have said that he had a hunch the boy would prove useful. But it would mostly be a lie.

"I just don't know. I was going to say no, but what came out was yes. I can say no more than that."

His two friends seemed puzzled, but they said nothing. Brand was puzzled too. And yet now that the decision had been made, there was a sense of rightness to it.

"It starts with one," he said. "Perhaps it always does."

"But the nation is still to come," Shorty replied.

"One such as that boy," Brand went on, "has the heart of an army all by himself."

Shorty sighed. "But not the swords."

"No, not the swords. But they will come too."

Sighern came out of the homestead. One moment he turned back and looked at it, then his gaze swept over the farm. And then he was jogging toward them, his sword dangling at his side and a hessian sack in his hands. No doubt it contained a few treasured items, a change of clothes and some food.

Brand and the others mounted. "Stash your things in the saddle bag, and then you can get up behind me," Brand said when the boy reached them.

Sighern did as asked and then climbed up awkwardly behind Brand. "You'll not regret this. I promise."

"Perhaps not. But you might yet. I wasn't lying about the dangers we face."

"I know. But better them than staying here."

Brand nudged the roan forward and his two friends did likewise. They were on the road again, and soon they followed it up slope and toward the crest of the next hill. When they reached it, Brand felt the boy turn for one last look at his home. And then they slipped down the other side and the farm was out of sight.

They moved through the countryside, and it felt strange to Brand. There were more farms, but there was no sign of people. Sighern seemed to be the only survivor of the outlaw raids. But there must have been others too, if not many.

Passing another homestead, Brand turned his head to speak to the boy. "Did Unferth truly do nothing?"

"Nothing at all," Sighern said. "And the raids were carried out over a few weeks. There was time for him to act, had he chosen. The rumor was that he sent the raiders himself. It's said that he's short of coin, and certainly taxes have been going up."

Brand let it go. There was nothing he could do now to help the people of this district. All he could do was work to ensure others did not suffer the same fate.

They crested yet another hill, and the farming lands were behind them once more. Ahead, the countryside was ungrazed by livestock. It was uncleared also, and the track continued through a patchwork of woods and scrubby hillsides. The sun was lowering, and midafternoon lay dozily upon the land. But a sound rose far behind them that sent chills up their spines and destroyed any thought of rest. Wolves. Howling wolves.

Brand drew his mount to a stop and looked behind him, but there was nothing to see.

"Some have our fresh scent," Taingern said calmly. "And they gather the pack to them."

Brand thought he was right. He looked back at Sighern. "I'm not familiar with this part of the Duthgar. How far is it to the nearest lord's hall?"

"Not far," the boy said. "A day's ride from here."

Brand refrained from cursing. "That's going to be further than you think, with the wolves behind us. This may be your last chance, Sighern. You can leave now if you want. The wolves are after me and will follow where I ride."

The boy shook his head. "No. I'm coming with you."

Brand grinned at him. "Then it will be a ride such as you won't ever forget. And let us hope there are good men at the hall."

"There are," Sighern answered. "It's Galdring's hall, but it's small with few men."

Brand thought he recognized the name. "Is he the son of Baldring?"

"That's him."

"Then let us hope the son is as loyal as the father was."

Brand waited for no answer. He nudged his mount into a canter with the others and they began to ride. It was not as swift as he would like, but they had to preserve the horses. They would be riding through the whole night.

Behind them, once more, the howling pierced the quiet afternoon. This time it appeared to be split up, with the chase fanning out to left and right behind them. No sound came from ahead, but that did not mean there were not wolves there also. Wolves were known to herd their prey into a trap, and these wolves were smarter than most. Brand was sure of that.

"Can the horses run all night?" Sighern called out from behind him.

"They're fine animals, but they'll need to be rested at times too. We shall see."

9. A Long Night

Brand led the way as the small group of riders cantered through the night. It was difficult going, for the dark created dangers. A horse could kill itself, and its rider, by placing a hoof in an unseen hollow. Yet the track remained clear and free of obstacles, so far as Brand could tell, and the risk was necessary.

The wolves continued their hunt. Fanned out behind the riders they gave vent to their eerie howls from time to time, and each time it seemed a little closer.

"They grow more eager!" Taingern called as they rode.

Brand sensed it also. The wolves had their scent, and knew their quarry was on the run. This caused them to chase harder, and excitement was in their howls that bordered on frenzy. Something other than hunger drove them, and Brand knew what it was. Sorcery. It explained something else too. Wolves on the hunt did not howl. These wolves were different. They were sure of bringing their quarry to bay, and the purpose of the howling was to instill fear.

The track took them into higher ground. Behind, the land was wrapped in the shadows of night, and the patches of woodland were darker still. And those patches grew increasingly thick. It was a long way from civilization, from help of any kind.

Despite the gathering pursuit, Brand took good care of the horses. Every hour he signaled the riders to dismount and lead the animals by foot. Then they were rested briefly. He knew the wolves took no such rest, yet the horses might need speed at the end. A horse could outrun a wolf, but not for long. But at the end of the pursuit that could mean the difference between life and death.

They rode in this fashion until the middle of the night had come and gone. Ever the wolves gained on them, until at last the howling seemed just behind and grew in such frenzy that Brand feared the wolves might have even sighted them.

"Ride!" he called, and finally he led the others into a gallop. The horses needed little urging. Fear was on them now, and this lent them strength and speed even after their many hours of cantering. But it could not last.

They rushed through the night. The sound of the hooves of the horses was as thunder in Brand's ears and the wind of their passage whipped at him. On they went, and the wolves came after them.

It was a race, and the prize was life. The muscle, bones and will of the horses was pitted against that of the wolves. The horses strained, sweat foaming at their sides, and the wolves fell away. But already the horses began to tire, and Brand's most of all for two riders weighed it down.

"How far away is the hall?" Brand asked.

Sighern thought for a moment. "It's hard to tell in the dark, and I've been this way only twice. But it's at least an hour away, probably more."

Brand looked around. There was no lightening of the sky in the east yet. Dawn was still some way off, and he did not think that light would hinder the wolves. It would make them easier to fight, though.

"We'll not get to the hall in time," Brand called to the others. "Look for a good place to make a stand."

They rode on, the flanks of the horses white with sweat and their pace slowing. All about them was forest. It was dark and grim and filled with fear. The wolves had not given up the chase. They would never give up, for sorcery drove them. He sensed frustration in their occasional howls, and though they had fallen back it was not by far. Even now they were gaining ground as the horses slowed.

"There!" cried Shorty.

Brand saw straightaway the spot his friend had meant. He had been looking to the left where the forest had grown thick, but to the right there was a steep bank, almost a cliff. The ground before it was clear of trees, and the wall of dirt and rock rose at least fifteen feet high. The wolves could not come at them from that side. It was the best defense they would find.

They drew the straining horses in and dismounted. Swiftly they drove in their picket stakes and tied the horses up. If the men were killed, the horses would die also, there would be no escape from the wolves. But Brand did not intend to die. Not if he could help it.

"Keep watch," Brand told the boy. "Yell if you see anything."

He did not wait for an answer but signaled Shorty and Taingern to him. "We need wood for a fire."

They ran across the track and into the forest on the other side. There they quickly gathered some fallen branches and old pine cones lying on the ground. The wolves were close now, the howling filling the night all around them.

They ran back. Sighern had realized what they were doing and drawn a flint from his few possessions. Even as they dropped the branches and cones into a pile on the ground he was kneeling and striking sparks. His hands trembled, and he tried again and again but at last one of the cones caught fire and a curl of smoke rose in the air, fueled by a tiny flame that grew and then, slowly, began to spread.

The cone began to blaze, and they each grabbed other cones and held them to the first. When they caught, they

86

spread them through the pile of branches. The fire took, growing rapidly.

In its flickering light they drew their blades. It was none too soon.

"There!" yelled Taingern. The others looked where he pointed. Along the track they had just ridden themselves, some gray shadows loped toward them. The wolves drew up and stopped before they came into the light of the fire.

"Over there too!" Sighern said. There were wolves now in the timber across the path where they had gathered their firewood.

"Well, Sighern," Brand said. "Do you regret coming with us now?"

Before the boy could answer some of the wolves on the track leaped forward. They crossed the ground swiftly, all bristling fur, snarling lips and white fangs. The men stood in front of the shying horses, and Brand stepped before Sighern. They faced the left, toward the wolves, but these wheeled away as the ones in the forest leaped in to attack instead. It had been a distraction, and Brand realized these wolves were intelligent. Unnaturally so.

Yet the men were not caught by surprise. Shorty guarded their left flank, Taingern the right. And Brand held the middle. The main attack came against him.

The blade of his forefathers swept in shining arcs through the night. Blood spurted. Wolves yelped in pain. Animals fell dead. To either side Shorty and Taingern fended off attacks. But again and again the wolves came for Brand. They crawled and bit and scrambled over each other to reach him. And died.

Yet one slipped through, leaping high for his neck while his blade swept low. The creature smashed into him, knocking him back. Even as he fell he twisted so that his neck avoided snapping jaws. Then he crashed into the ground.

87

The wolves swarmed over him, but even as they snarled in fury, Sighern loosed a battle cry. "For the Duthgar!" he yelled, and his sword cut and chopped.

The boy now stood before Brand, protecting him from death. Yet he was not skilled with the sword and the wolves gathered to him. One clamped its jaws to his left leg, and another, though its neck streamed blood from a previous blow, bit down at his sword arm.

But Brand was up again, his glittering sword in his right hand and a burning branch in his left. This he thrust into the face of the wolf that hung on Sighern's arm. Taingern impaled the animal attacking the boy's leg.

Swift as the attack began, it ended. The wolves loped back into the rim of firelight, and there they padded in agitation. Some whined with pain. Others barked and yelped. And one, blue-eyed and calm, stood motionless in their midst.

"They will come again," Shorty warned.

Brand summoned his magic. It came to life within him, woke from the dormancy of his everyday life. He sent out faint tendrils toward the wolves.

He sensed some of the dark sorcery that went into their making. He became connected to them, and merged his mind into the magic that gave them purpose. It was a strange feeling to him, for this was a power beyond his experience. It did not have the feel of anything that he knew.

And then he sensed another presence. His enemy was connected to the wolves also. He who had made them of dark sorcery and horror was within their minds, was looking out through their eyes.

Brand softly withdrew. It would be best, if they were able, to fight these creatures with swords alone. He did not want to reveal his own power just yet. It would give his enemy a measure of him. Better to keep that a surprise for when it was needed later.

The wolves rushed in to attack once more. Snarling filled the night and gray shapes hurtled through the dark. Swift steel met them.

With the wolves came a wave of hatred, for the magic that made them drove them on against blades, against the certainty of death. The creatures knew what swords could do, knew the skill of the men who wielded them, and they came on anyway, unable to stop themselves. Brand felt sorry for them even as his sword rose and fell.

The bodies of the dead animals piled up. Ever the blue-eyed wolf was in the thick of the attack, but ever it evaded the fate of its packmates. Yet like a wave that spent itself against a rocky shore, the attack lost force and dwindled.

But this only drove the remaining wolves into a greater frenzy. One leaped high and crashed into Brand. He staggered back, then surged forward flinging the snarling animal back into the pack. He felt blood wet his shoulder and a slow throb began.

Sighern now fought to his right, unwilling to be protected, and though unskilled his sword swept among the pack with speed and strength. But one of the wolves slipped through his defenses and tore at his hip with wicked fangs. The boy fell, but Brand turned and his sword flashed, the Halathrin steel hewing the head from the beast in a single cut.

The boy struggled up. Taingern killed another that leaped for him while Sighern did not have his blade up. He swayed where he stood, blood coloring the right side of his trousers.

But even as the men stood, their swords weaving through the air ready to defend, they realized all the wolves were dead. All, bar one. Before them crouched the blue-eyed leader, snarling and growling, the lips of its muzzle pulled back horribly and blood welling from a sword slash to its chest.

Brand faced it. "Die, shadow spawn," he muttered. Then he stepped forward to attack.

But the wolf growled back at him, and there were words in its snarling voice.

"Die yourself!" And it rushed at him.

Brand was so taken by surprise that the wolf was able to crowd him, ducking under a weak sword blow and fixing its jaws to his leg. The leg gave way beneath him and he fell, exposing his throat. The wolf released the grip on his leg and pounced in for a killing snap of its jaws.

But Brand was swifter. His sword came up, tearing through fur and skin, and driven by the leaping weight of the creature, it slid through its belly, disemboweling it. Still it struggled to reach his neck, but Sighern kicked it away and Brand's sword flashed again, this time severing an artery in its neck.

The creature lay there, panting. Blood bubbled from its throat, and the pale eyes fixed on him until life faded out of them.

"Well done, lad," Brand said to Sighern.

The boy flashed him a grin, but Brand saw the blood on his trousers and knew he was wounded. They all were.

Brand set Taingern to watch in case there were more wolves, and while he did so the other two tended to each other's wounds, washing them first with water and then applying a salve and bandages. Then Shorty watched while Brand looked after a wound on Taingern's sword arm.

"A nasty fight," the freckled man said, indifferent to the pain the salve caused as Brand applied it to the jagged rent in his skin.

Brand worked quickly, one eye watching the shadows beyond the reach of the fire's light.

"They all are. But I fear there are worse fights to come."

After that they watched the dark for a little while, and Sighern moved back to pat the horses and calm them.

"The boy surely has guts," Shorty said quietly.

Brand nodded. Twice Sighern had helped him, and he may have died without that aid. It was a debt that he owed, but it puzzled him too. Few boys not yet full grown would willingly place themselves in such danger. Brand would not forget it. But where did such courage come from?

The forest was now silent about them. Nothing stirred. But Brand did not trust it. Perhaps all the wolves were dead, but what else may yet be sent against them?

The fire was dying down, but they dared not risk leaving the light nor the cover of the cliff face to gather more wood. Brand glanced at it, careful not to look directly into the flames and destroy his night vision. It would last until dawn. Just.

And dawn was not far off. They sat down and waited for it, but they did not sheathe their swords. No one was willing to risk sleep, even if they could so soon after an attack such as they had endured.

They spoke no more than a few hushed words now and then, and no one mentioned the blue-eyed wolf. But Brand thought about it. Sorcery had been invoked of the darkest kind, and he wondered what power his enemy had. Whoever it was must be someone of enormous skill. And also someone willing to do whatever it took to obtain their goals. It was a dangerous combination.

The forest lightened. Dawn came, and with it a growing sense of unease. The long night might be over, but a new day with new dangers was beginning.

They ate a cold breakfast of stale bread and cheese, unwilling to waste time cooking anything. All they wished was to leave their camp, where the bodies of the dead wolves lay nearby and the memory of a bad night was strong. And all the while Brand's sense of unease grew.

They removed the picket stakes and mounted. At last they were leaving, and they nudged the horses out onto the track. The sun was well up now, but even as they began to ride they stopped. A little way ahead of them a strange figure walked the dusty path directly toward them.

10. The Noblest of Tasks

Horta stirred from his trance, the shadow of death upon him.

He had broken the link with the last wolf, knowing even as it leaped that it must die. He had no wish to experience what that felt like. Not again. One of his master's had made him do so, repeatedly. It was supposed to inure him against the fear of dying. Perhaps it did, although that master certainly had fear in his eyes when at last Horta had learned all he could teach, and killed him.

The fire in the hearth popped, and a plume of smoke swirled upward. Horta felt the warmth of the flames, and eased back a little in his chair. He was alone in the small cottage set aside for him by the king. It was away from the village, surrounded by pastureland and sheep. The Arnhaten dwelt close to the king's hall, working in the village to support their keep. He did not miss them. The peacefulness of this place was near to the quiet of the desert wastes of his youth. Only the constant bleating of the sheep marred it.

Brand had surprised him. He had lived. So too his companions. It was worrisome, for the magic had been potent, and the wolves, though not powerful, were smart. Most of all, they were driven by the touch of the god. They attacked relentlessly, and that should have seen them overpower the men, no matter that all the pack died to accomplish it.

But the men were skilled. They fled when that was the best course of action, and fought when they had to. They did neither with fear, or anger or uncertainty. Each step they took was measured and spoke of confidence. They were men who had endured great dangers in the past, and learned from it. But this much he had known already.

He must learn more. He knew also that Brand possessed magic himself, though he had not been forced to summon it. What was it like? What powers did he have? This must be discovered. Brand intrigued him, and he must learn more of him. In that way he would ensure the next attack was successful.

He made a decision. Knowledge was the root of effective action, and he must discover more of his enemy. He withdrew a norhanu leaf from one of his pouches and reluctantly placed it under his tongue. The taste was bitter, but the effect was swift. Within minutes the color of the fire in the hearth changed, becoming red, and the air about him swirled and shimmered with shadowy shapes. This, he knew, was illusion. Yet it was but the first step to what he must do.

The air grew cold. He was unsure if this were the hated climate of the Duthgar or the effect of the leaf. Each time he took it the effects were different. He stoked the fire anyway, and then sat back again to wait.

The trance state crept upon him, yet a part of his mind remained lucid. This part he brought to the fore. Others would succumb to the drug, but long years of hard training gave him some control. He began to chant, no more than a mutter let loose in the smoke-hazed room, but it would be enough to invoke aid again.

He called upon the gods once more, yet this time he specifically spoke the name of one that would best suit his need: the falcon god of the flat deserts.

"O mighty Har-falach, hear me. I have need of thy aid. Hear me, and answer my humble call."

The room grew colder. The red flame in the hearth dimmed, and the bleating of the sheep faded from his mind.

A second time he called, but now he withdrew a tiny statuette from a pouch. It was made of a dull stone, highly polished and smooth to touch. It was an ancient thing, fashioned to resemble a man with angled wings and the head of a hawk.

"Hear me, O mighty one. Hear me, winged messenger of the gods. I call upon thee for aid."

The fire snuffed out. The room grew black as the tomb. Fear stabbed Horta's heart, for he felt a presence with him and thought he sensed the movement of air above.

"I beseech thee, Ruler of the Skies. Take my mind where I wish. Let me sit here, yet also walk in another place. Show me my enemies that I may know them. Lend my thought wings."

The room began to spin. Nausea gripped Horta, and a rushing filled his ears. Then it seemed to him that he fell from a great height. Blinding light stabbed like a thousand knives into his watering eyes. For some moments he was blinded, and then he began to see.

He stood upon an old track, dusty and surrounded by trees and hills. The sun was up, just barely, and its light lit the road but night lingered in the shadowy stands of trees to either side.

He knew where he was. He had seen this track through the eyes of the wolves, but of his enemy there was no sign. He walked forward to find them. They would not be far.

Ahead was the sound of hooves and the jingle of harness. Horta smiled. The enemy was coming to him. He came to a stop and waited with patience.

The riders saw him, hesitated and then walked forward toward him. Horta assessed them all in turn. The unknown boy with them was irrelevant. He was less than nothing and posed no threat. And yet Brand had allowed him to come. That must have some import. Brand saw something that he did not, and for that reason the boy must be assumed to be dangerous. He had a role to play in all this, if he lived to fulfil it.

Next, Horta's gaze fell on the short one. Here was a great warrior, and one swift to fight and slow to ask questions. Yet he was far more cunning than he looked, and inside him beat a heart that would drive him to deeds of loyalty beyond other men. He was dangerous.

Horta flicked his gaze to the tall one, pale skinned and freckled. He carried himself like a lord, yet somehow humility also exuded from him. He was a deadly warrior, yet would sooner study philosophy than ever draw a blade. He was at least as dangerous as the short one.

Finally, Horta turned his attention to his true enemy. Brand sat easily in the saddle. He was a man sure of himself, confident in his skills. His eyes were a pale blue, and though there was no sign of alarm in them, yet they gazed out at the world with an acuity that missed nothing, underestimated nothing, nor was daunted by anything. He was a man with no give to him. Had he a shovel and a reason to do so, he would move a mountain.

Horta shivered. This was a man of destiny, someone who worked the threads of fate himself rather than waited for them to be woven. There were few such as he, but it changed nothing. He must die, and that was an end to it.

Something else occurred to him then, some further insight. Brand was much like himself. He did what he did for duty, and nothing would stop him. Yet his heart was elsewhere. He did not wish to be who he was. Perhaps that could be used against him.

The riders drew up before him, and he sensed a little of Brand's magic. But not enough to determine its exact nature.

Horta gravely inclined his head. The riders did likewise, never taking their eyes off him.

"Greetings, friend," Brand said. "It's a lonely road, and a long one."

It was the customary greeting among the Duthenor for strangers meeting on the road. Horta nodded again, adjusted the portion of bearskin that he wore over his shoulders, and then sat cross-legged upon the dusty track.

"Greetings, and may your travels be swift and your night's rest long." It was the ritual response. The exchange was intended to declare that no hostility existed between strangers on the road.

"We have just eaten," the Short one said. "But we have a little food if you're hungry. Traveling by foot is hard going."

Brand gave a slight shake of his head. "This man came here by other means than his legs, and an image of a man needs no food."

Horta felt a cold stab of fear. Never before had anyone detected the difference between him and an image of the gods. It shocked him, but he would not show it.

"It is even as you say," he answered. "An image of light and air, no matter how real seeming, needs no sustenance."

A slight smile played over Brand's face, and Horta cursed himself for a fool. The man had not *known* he was an image, merely surmised it.

"What do you wish?" Brand asked. The man's blue eyes gazed at him casually, but Horta sensed that for all his seeming ease he could unleash turmoil with steel or magic in the blink of an eye. Here at least was a worthy adversary, and an intriguing one.

"What do I want? From you? Nothing but your death."

Brand's expression did not change There was no anger, or fear, or bluster. He merely answered.

"That is a gift I will not give."

"So I see," Horta replied. "The wolves were not enough. Yet the hawk plucks the rabbit from the field, and makes the gift his own."

"I am no rabbit."

Horta allowed himself a laugh. He *liked* this man. Nothing disturbed him. Nothing put him off balance. But there was no reason to show his admiration. It served no purpose.

"You mean nothing to me. Nor does this land. But I have a task, nearly achieved now, and your presence threatens it. Leave the Duthgar, and live. Stay, and die. The choice is yours."

Brand regarded him silently a moment, and then shook his head.

"No. It's my duty to return. It's my duty to free my people."

"Then you will die."

"Perhaps. Or maybe you will discover that this rabbit has claws."

Horta regarded Brand in turn. Then he stood, gracefully rising without the accustomed pain he would have normally felt in his left knee.

"So be it." He turned his gaze to the short one. "Thank you for your hospitality, even if not needed."

Brand's horse grew agitated, and he bent down to stroke its withers and whisper in its ear.

"What exactly is the task you mentioned?"

"Ah, I cannot say much. But it is the noblest of tasks, and it is a duty even as is yours. I shall not fail in it. The stars sing of it, and the earth calls for it. It is ordained."

Horta awaited no answer. He had learned little, but he would learn no more even if he talked for an hour. He willed it, and his image faded and his mind flew back to his body.

It was dark again, dark as the void, and his mind spun. Then he heard the distant bleating of sheep and felt the warmth of the fire in the hearth before him. He was back in the cottage.

He felt weak and nauseous. His glance fell to the small pallet bed within the room, and he wanted to rest. But he could not. His task was too important, Brand too great a threat. The wolves had not been enough, and he must act again and swiftly. More would be needed, and he knew now which god it would be best to call upon. From him, and that which he would send to kill, there would be no escape.

It was all a pity, for Horta truly liked Brand. But fate could not be turned aside. He sighed, then got up out of the chair, his limbs stiff from long sitting. He must gather the Arnhaten again. At once.

11. The Helm of the Duthenor

Brand led the small group of riders on through the morning. He rode silently, for he had met his true enemy at last and had much to consider. What occupied most of his attention was whether or not the man *was* his true enemy. He had a great duty to fulfil, which suggested that he served someone else. Perhaps.

It did not take long before they left the rugged hills and forests behind. Soon the track sloped downward, the forest thinned to isolated stands of trees and the land became cultivated.

They passed many farms now, and even several villages. Smoke rose from chimneys, sheep bleated on the hillsides and cattle roamed the lower slopes. There were people too. Shepherds, farmers in fields and tradesmen in the villages.

Brand felt at last like he had returned home. It was one thing to stand on the soil of the Duthgar, another to be among its people. And though they were wary of strangers, as was proper, they still gave a friendly greeting or wave. Not few of them looked long and hard at the horses too. They were fine mounts of a quality rarely seen in a land known for foot warriors rather than cavalry.

The Helm of the Duthenor was safely hidden away within a sack attached to Brand's saddlebag. It was in easy reach should a battle break out, though that was unlikely for the moment. More importantly he was not identified yet. Nothing would mark him more for who he was, except his ring and sword. The first was hard to see, and the blade of the second was sheathed. He was not ready to declare himself just yet, though he would do so when he reached the lord's hall, and that would be soon. But what reaction would he get when he did so?

The hall came into sight. It was small, for this was one of the most remote and thinly populated districts of the Duthgar. It showed signs of poor maintenance also, and the doorward when they came to the entrance was slovenly. Brand had heard that many of the true lords had been overthrown by the usurper, but this hall was not one of them if Galdring ruled it.

Despite his appearance, the doorward was polite enough, and he helped them hitch the horses. As they did so, Brand gave the hessian sack carrying the Helm of the Duthenor to Sighern, asking him to carry it for him.

When they were done with the horses, the doorward bid them state their names and business at the hall.

This was a moment Brand had long imagined, returning to the Duthgar and declaring himself. But it was anticlimactic when he did so.

"I'm Brand, and once I knew the father of the lord who rules here. The son should still recognize the name."

The doorward shrugged. "If you say so, but it's best not to displease him. He doesn't take kindly to being bothered for no purpose."

Brand raised an eyebrow. His name had not even been recognized, despite it only being used in the lineage of the chieftains of the Duthgar. No matter. The lord would know him, though what his reaction would be was hard to say. That he still ruled indicated he had not overtly opposed the usurper.

The doorward opened the building's great door and led them up the hall. Men seated at the mead benches to each side eyed the strangers carefully. It would be rare to see so many strangers, and neither Shorty nor Taingern had the look of Duthenor warriors about them. They were obviously foreigners, yet that they were warriors nonetheless would have been noted instantly.

They passed the firepit in the middle of the hall and walked up toward where the lord sat at a small table with some courtiers and guards. They were drinking and playing a game of stones.

The doorward came to a halt. Slowly he turned around, and Brand saw his eyes narrow and then widen. He had finally recognized the name.

"*What* did you say your name was?"

Brand gazed serenely back at him. "You heard it right the first time."

The man grew suddenly nervous. He looked surprised, scared and happy all at the same time. Then he masked his face so that it was expressionless and addressed Galdring.

"Hail, lord. I bring visitors to the hall who have business with you."

Galdring looked up with a bored expression on his face.

"What are their names?"

"Their leader is Brand."

The doorward said no more. Silence gradually fell over the hall, for if the doorward had not instantly recognized the name then many others did.

Galdring stood. He was not much older than Brand. His blond hair was long and tied back with a gold band, the sword strapped to his belt bejeweled at the hilt. And his eyes were piercing bright with authority. Once he would have impressed Brand, but he did not do so now. While he lived in luxury, outlaws plundered his district.

"That is a dangerous name to bear," Galdring said at last. "The more so if it is true."

"It's true, Galdring. But you overestimate the danger. What should the rightful heir to the chieftainship of the

Duthenor have to fear just for revealing his name in the Duthgar?"

Galdring was about to speak, but a black-haired man beside him placed a hand on his shoulder and silenced him. Brand understood at once where the true power in this hall lay.

The black-haired man took a step forward. "If you're who you say you are, you're a dead man. Perhaps you're a dead man anyway, just for claiming it. Either way, you're a fool."

Brand held his gaze. "I'm Brand, as I said. And I've returned to the Duthgar to bring justice. Unferth shall pay for his crimes. But I was talking to the lord of this hall, and not you. Not to the usurper's lackey, not to one who serves a traitorous cur."

They were hard words, and words that would lead to a fight. But Brand knew such a fight was inevitable. He knew also that the story of his coming to the hall, and the words spoken would spread like a raging grassfire throughout the Duthgar. He must appear strong and in control. Otherwise he would not gather an army.

The black-haired man drew his sword. "Kill him!" he ordered.

But Brand was expecting that, and a throwing knife came quick to hand from within a sheath at his belt. The black-haired man was the leader, and the first to die. With lightning speed Brand flung the knife. It arced through the air in a silver flash to strike the man's neck. Red blood spurted, but Brand was moving again before it hit.

He drew his sword, and even as its blade flashed he heard gasps. There was no other like it in the stories the Duthenor told, and the Halathrin-wrought blade confirmed his identity better than words. Two men moved at him from beside the now dead leader. The doorward drew his own blade, but he did not turn on

Brand. Rather he slew one of the two men. Brand leaped at the other, deflected a clumsy stab and hewed the man's head from his neck.

There was no further threat from in front of him. Brand spun and saw that Taingern and Shorty had killed a man each that had acted on the black-haired leader's instructions.

No one else moved. No doubt Unferth had more supporters in the hall, yet the unleashing of sudden death had shocked them to stillness. And their leader was taken from them.

Into the silence Galdring spoke. "You fool. You think you have won something here? You are already marked for death, but now all of us shall also pay that price. Unferth will kill every one of us."

Brand bent down and cleaned his bloodied blade on the trousers of the dead man before him. Then he sheathed it.

"You are wrong, Galdring. I can hear your heart quake from here with fear, and it speaks rather than your mind. I am Brand, and I have returned. Unferth shall die, and the Duthgar shall be free. This I swear, as the rightful chieftain of the Duthenor."

Brand spoke to the lord of the hall, but he knew all others would hear his words. They would be carried to Unferth and all over the Duthgar. It would unsettle the usurper and instill hope all over the land.

Galdring slumped back in his chair. For the first time, Brand noticed that a young woman was beside him, so like in appearance that she must be his sister. She was a shield-maiden, dressed in chainmail armor and with a sword at her side. But the blade would not have been as sharp as the glare she gave him.

The lord of the hall laughed bitterly. Then he turned to Brand once more. "All this, and yet there is no proof that you are even who you say you are."

"Of a time," Brand replied, "the word of a Duthenor warrior was taken as a matter of honor. This land has fallen, in more ways than one. Yet these tokens I will give. The first you have seen, which is the sword, and you know how I acquired it, even as a child from Unferth who stole it from my father. The second is this ring." He thrust up his hand so that the ring handed down through his line was visible. Galdring looked at it carefully, but said nothing. "And last, and greatest is this." He gestured to Sighern and the boy came forward bearing the hessian sack.

Brand took it, and let slip the cloth to reveal the shining Helm of the Duthenor. Then he placed it upon his head. It was battle accoutrement, yet to the Duthenor it was a crown.

Then he spoke, and his voice rang through the hall. "This is the helm of my ancestors, the Helm of the Duthenor. A thousand years ago it was stolen from us by Shurilgar, betrayer of nations. But I reclaimed it, at no small risk. I wear it now, and by these three tokens I proclaim myself, and I send warning to Unferth. His reign draws to a close. His past deeds will catch up with him. Justice, long delayed, is coming."

Brand stopped speaking. The hall was deathly silent. A long while Galdring gazed at him, and then slowly nodded.

"I believe you. And how you came to possess the Helm of the Duthenor, I cannot guess. Long it has been lost to us, but however you regained it must be a story of courage, I do not doubt. But even with sword, and ring and helm, even if you had the heart of your fathers of old, how do

105

you expect to win back this land? Unferth has an army of thousands. How many swords do you bring?"

Brand grinned at him. "I have only my own sword, and the courage to wield it. That, and a handful of friends. But it is not I who shall win back this realm. It is the people, and they will gather to me. Have hope! The history of the Duthenor will be shaped anew, and the pride of old will return. Do not doubt it. Wait, watch and see. I shall set a fire before me that will overrun our enemies."

Brand took command. He turned to the others in the hall. "Go forth," he said. "And spread word of my return throughout the district. Let warriors, let those farmers with swords or spears or bows gather tomorrow morning. For tomorrow I march, and the first steps against Unferth will be taken, but not the last."

There was a cheer from the doorward, and many others took it up. The hall resounded with it, though not all cheered.

Brand turned to the doorward. "Where is the best place to meet?"

The man thought for a moment. "Things like this have always been done at the Green Howe."

Brand liked the idea. An ancient hero would be buried in the howe, and that would help fire the men's spirits.

"The Green Howe!" he called out to the hall. "I will leave from there on the second hour after dawn."

The cheering subsided and many men rushed from the hall. Some would be supporters of Unferth, and that was good. Brand *wanted* word to spread.

He took a chair at the table where Galdring sat, and did not ask permission. It was the other man's hall, but Brand did not like him and events had carried beyond the simple lordship of a district. Brand had proclaimed himself, and now the kingship was at stake.

Galdring gave orders to a few men that had stayed with him. They began to remove the bodies of the slain, and then the lord looked grimly at Brand.

"You have doomed us all. There are few warriors in this district. And against Unferth, they will fall as wheat before the scythe. And he will come against you, hard and fast."

Brand removed his helm and placed it on the table. "So I would expect."

The shield-maiden looked at him, and there was a cold fire in her eyes. "You're sure of yourself, aren't you? But I see no reason for it. Titles and tokens don't win battles."

"This is my sister, Haldring," the lord said. "She usually gets straight to the point."

"So I see. I like that."

The fire in her eyes grew colder. "What you *like* means nothing to me. It's what you can *do* that I'm interested in."

Shorty sat down at the table with Taingern. "Making friends again, Brand?"

"I try." Brand turned his attention back to Haldring. "You will see what I can do, if you come with me. Shorty and Taingern here are my generals." He gestured at his two friends. "I want you for my third."

She looked at him as though he were mad. "You know nothing of me, nor my abilities. I don't even like you. Why would you offer me such a role?"

"Because I know more than you think. You don't like me, you say? And yet moments ago when the fight broke out you had a knife to hand and you were ready to fling it. You could have killed me, but you stayed your hand. Not only that, I will have no man or woman about me who tells me what they think I want to hear for the sake of advancement. I want advisors who think of the land first and give counsel based on reality, not dreaming. In short, I want you."

She looked at him, stunned. "You saw the knife, even while other men were trying to kill you?"

"Of course. I see much, but not all. That's why I want your help. You know this land, while I only know what it once was and what it yet could be."

Haldring looked at him in silence a long while. "For someone with no army and little hope, you can be convincing. Very well, I'll come with you. Unferth had our father killed, so I would risk nearly anything to see him overthrown. I just hope you know what you're doing as much as you *sound* like you know what you're doing."

It was a good point, and Brand knew it. If he failed, life would be worse for the Duthenor. And if it were just Unferth that he had to worry about, he would not have doubts. But there was the magician to worry about too. Who was he? What did he want? What threat did Brand pose to him? About all this, Brand knew too little, and it was dangerous not to know. What he did know was this, though. The magician had great power. He was driven to fulfil his duty, whatever it was. And he was of a race of people that Brand had never met before. That made it even harder to guess his purposes.

Brand glanced at the Helm of the Duthenor. He had won it back from Shurilgar at great risk. But then the only stakes were his life and death. Now, the future of a nation rested on his skills. That helm was as heavy as any crown, and not by its weight in metal.

He made a choice, and it was driven by past experience. In politics and war, deception could gain much. But in matters of loyalty, honesty was the strongest bond.

He looked at Haldring. "This also I should tell you. I want you to come with me for all the reasons I said, but this is also part of my reasoning. You'll not like it, but you will appreciate the benefit of it."

She held his gaze, her blue eyes cold and remote, but this he was beginning to feel was a mask. She was a woman of passions, even if they were held tightly in check. And it was yet another marker that his choice of her as a general was good. A general, a warrior, must feel and believe in things. This drove them to fight. But they must also be able to distance themselves from everything when in battle. In battle, only the winning or losing mattered. Consequences were for afterwards.

"A shield-maiden will lend my army a certain mystique. It will give prominence to it in men's minds, give storytellers something to talk of and spark interest all over the land. I don't seek to *use* you for this purpose, otherwise I wouldn't admit this. But it is the truth of the matter nevertheless, and you should know it."

She looked by turns angry, surprised and finally thoughtful. "You're correct in what you say. So be it. But I *will* speak my mind when situations arise and not just be a figurehead."

Brand knew she meant it, and it was perhaps something he needed. Shorty and Taingern never hesitated to tell him if they thought he was doing something wrong, but they did not know this land as did she.

He looked at Galdring. Anger and frustration showed in his eyes, and Brand understood that. The lord had lost command of his own men, and now war was coming. He seemed beaten before it began. For all that he and his sister looked so similar, the one thing that was different was the fire in her eyes.

"I cannot command you to have hope," Brand said. "But have it anyway. Watch! And over the coming days you will see."

Galdring sighed. "Perhaps I've been under Unferth's yoke too long. It hasn't been easy. But I still think you've doomed us all." He paused, then spoke again. "You know, I met your parents once, when I was a child. You are your father's son. But you have your mother's gift of speech. So even I shall try to have some hope, but I expect to die because of all this, and many others with me."

12. There Must be Blood

All day the Arnhaten prepared. They had to be gathered from the village first, then they had to collect dry timber for the bonfire. Finally, they ritually cleansed themselves by performing the sacred chants. And all the while Horta ran through in his mind what must be done. There could be no mistake in what was to come, for to err was to die.

What he attempted now was one of the grand rituals. It summoned not just a god, but one of the greater gods. He had done so before, at need. He did so now, because of necessity. To accomplish his task, there was no risk he would not take. Yet still, he felt his heart pound in his chest and the sweat on his brow was as ice against his skin. Only the slow sucking of a norhanu leaf eased the strain.

For this ceremony, he had need of a special assistant. Olbata aided him, running through with him the words of the ritual, helping him direct the others in what they did once more in the sacred grove of the Duthenor. Yet Olbata was unaware of one vital step in the ceremony, one part of the procedure that had vital significance. Had he known, he would have refused. Horta would not have blamed him, so that information he held back.

Dusk crept over the land. Shadows filled the already dark woods and a deep silence descended. Horta made a gesture, and Olbata lit the gathered timber. Some while it took to catch, but then swifter and swifter the bonfire caught until it roared to life and sent a plume of fiery sparks high into the night. But for all the flame, the darkness of the woods only pressed in closer.

111

Horta placed a fresh norhanu leaf under his tongue. It was dangerous, but necessary. And he had been sucking on the first for hours. Its potency had diminished.

He signaled Obata to join him, and he drew from one of his pouches a statuette of obsidian, black as the night around them. It was one of his great talismans, and it was in the shape of a man with a bat's head, teeth bared. This he gave to his disciple, telling him to hold it in his left hand and not to let go, no matter what occurred.

Horta moved to the southern end of the bonfire. His positioning influenced which gods may be called. So too the direction of circling, or whether there was circling or not. In this case, ancient tradition prescribed no circling, and he followed what had been handed down from the magicians of old.

The Arnhaten drew near him, and then they also stood still, gathering to each side of him. From one of his many pouches he took some powder, and this he cast in a single throw into the flames.

The fire roared and leaped. Red sparks plumed into the smoke-laden air, followed by trails of white and black. A sweet smell drifted to him, and he was careful not to breathe much of the scent in.

And then he commenced chanting, his words rising up into the darkness with the smoke and heat-shimmer of the fire, up into the fathomless night and toward the hidden stars. The Arnhaten chanted also, intoning the ancient words that he had taught them.

Upon a god he called, one of the old gods that ruled air, sky and earth. In this case, the god was of the earth. His voice rang with power, beseeching aid and asking for audience.

"I summon thee, O Shemfal, god of the underworld."

At the speaking of the god's name, the flickering flames of the bonfire parted as though they were a curtain. And even as a man looked through a window, Horta saw into another world. It was not clear, yet he discerned through the writhing smoke, not all of which rose from the bonfire, a great cave.

He did not wish to see, but he must, and his gaze was drawn despite his abhorrence. Within the cave towered a mighty throne of obsidian, polished to a sheen and glimmering with dark lights and myriad reflections. Upon it Shemfal sat, a vast figure of shadows and hidden power. His body was that of a mighty man, and the head was a bat's, and the sharp eyes within that animal head looked up through the window between worlds and pierced Horta's soul.

"Come to me, O Shemfal, Master of Death, and hear my plea," Horta whispered, his voice thickened by fear or the numbing of the norhanu leaf.

And Shemfal came. The shadows that were about him unfolded to become giant wings, leathery but supple. He swept into the air, leaving his throne and rising above his court. Other creatures there were beneath him. Some serpent-like, coiling, sliding, creeping within the shadows. Others walked as men, but were scaled and tusked. Horta saw beings from nightmare and myth, monsters of massive size and small creatures of fang, and sting and poison.

The air moved in waves, beaten by the vast wings of Shemfal. Sickly light from braziers of dull red flame flickered and died. And the god rose higher, higher, higher, his eyes unwaveringly fixed on Horta.

The god drew closer. The throne room and all within it were blocked by the vast wings. The bonfire roared to life, sparks streaming and scattering into the air. The Arnhaten fell to the ground like trees blown down by a storm, but Horta stood on quaking legs, sucking desperately at the norhanu leaf.

Into the world of men the god ascended, summoned from the underworld, and Horta felt the blast of those great wings beat upon him, heard the roar of wind flow through the sacred wood of the Duthenor. He glanced at where Obata lay sprawled on the ground, and relief washed over him when he saw the man still clutched the statuette in his hand.

Horta kneeled and closed his eyes. Like a man in prayer he spoke.

"O mighty Shemfal, Lord of the Grave, will you hear the pleading of your humble servant?"

Shemfal answered, and the voice of the god smote Horta's ears. He felt the words enter his brain, and make it thrum inside the casing of his skull.

"I hear you, mortal. Speak, and I shall pass judgement."

Horta told the god of his great task, of how he served the gods and of what manner of man Brand was. He told of how Brand threatened his plans.

And the god weighed his words, deciding on the worthy and the unworthy, contemplating life or death.

"You serve me well, Horta. I am not displeased. I shall send one of my own to destroy Brand. He shall be fit for the task, yet what you ask requires blood. That is the age-old pact."

"Mighty Shemfal, I offer Brand himself as the sacrifice. His blood is of an ancient line, and magic sings within it also."

"This I know, Horta. Even here echoes of Brand's deeds are muttered in the dark. He will attend me well, once in my realm and broken into servitude beneath my throne. And great is the one I shall send against him to ensure it comes to pass. Yet the chances of the world are ever uncertain. Should fate go awry, are you willing to pay the price and honor your debt?"

Horta bowed. He knew what the god meant. There must be blood one way or the other. But the blood would not be his own. He glanced at Olbata to ensure the man still held the statuette. Through this, the presence of the god in this world was invoked. If Brand were not killed, Olbata would serve as sacrifice in his stead.

"I accept the price, O lord."

The great wings of Shemfal beat once more, and the trees in the sacred wood bent against the blast. The god descended into the underworld whence he came, but a light glimmered as something rose in his place.

The force of the wind thrashed Horta's face onto the ground, but when it dissipated he lifted his head once more. Standing before him was the creature Shemfal had sent to kill Brand. Straightaway Horta sensed its power, greater than that of the wolves, and held in check by intelligence and an iron-like will. All this he read in the keen glance of its eyes, for it stood before him as a man.

Horta studied the assassin. Though he indeed looked like a man, there were differences. The skin, where it showed at face and hand, was pale as snow. And the eyes were a piercing blue, glittering like none he had seen before. The cheek bones were high, the ears delicate and slightly pointed. Trousers and tunic were of close-fitting leather, gleaming black. But over this he wore a chainmail shirt that glinted as though it were made of silver. On his back were strapped twin swords, the hilts of pale ivory and the little that showed of the blades black as obsidian.

The assassin was a warrior, yet Horta sensed magic also, but of a kind he did not understand. The warrior-assassin looked Horta up and down, and the magician felt the contempt of that deathly gaze. There was an arrogance about him that was immensely dislikeable, but Horta sensed it was born of experience. The man, if man it was, had defeated all his enemies in the past. And they would have been great, for he was a creature of the underworld where the one rule was survival.

Without speaking, the man turned on the balls of his feet and strode from the clearing. He moved with grace and purpose, his every motion that of a sublime warrior. Horta was glad to see him go. He had no wish to talk to him and potentially incur his wrath. Here was an enemy that even he would fear to have, and for the first time in a very long while he wondered if he had gone too far. But the man hunted Brand, and relief washed through him.

13. A Hero of Old

They spent the night in the hall, and for all that Brand loved sleeping beneath the stars, it was good to have a roof over his head for a change.

But they were up before dawn. Galdring did not join them, and for this Brand was glad. It did no good to have a lord in an army who at best only half believed in the cause. He knew it would be like that throughout the district too. Not all who were able to come would do so.

Haldring was there though, and for this he was glad. She would give him trouble at every step, but perhaps it would be of the kind he needed. He tended to reach too high, to expect too much. She would temper that, probably at every opportunity. She liked what had been done to her brother no less than Galdring himself.

It was Haldring who led them from the hall. A dozen men came with them. As many as that stayed behind. They readied their horses, but they did not ride. The Green Howe was not that far away she advised, and Brand had no wish to meet the beginnings of his army from atop a mount as though he were a king. Instead, he must be a general: in charge, but still one of them.

They walked south-west, continuing along the same trail they had yesterday. The sun was up now, roosters crowing from farms they passed and sheep and cattle watching them with mild curiosity.

There were trees here, and copses and woods mostly on the hilltops, but for the most part it was clear ground and farmed. It was a fertile land, the grass growing green and the animals healthy. It was still cool of a morning, for summer had not yet come, but it was approaching.

The track led slightly downward now, and they moved into a valley. It was less farmed here, and there were more trees. A creek ran through it, and it was mostly about this that farms had been established. But in the middle stood a large wood.

Haldring pointed. "In those trees is where the Green Howe stands."

Not long after, the trees were about them and the sound of men's voices, hushed by the morning and the nature of the event in which they were a part, drifted to them.

The trunks of the trees formed a wall, but one moment the track wound tightly between trunk and root and overhanging branch, and the next they were in a large glade. The grass was green and short. The murmur of the creek came from somewhere close, but hidden.

Within the center of the glade stood the Green Howe. It was a barrow, a burial mound for the final resting place of a lord of old. It stood some forty feet long and was at least half as wide. Its rounded slopes, smooth with green turf, rose to a domed summit as tall as two men.

And there were men around it, and they gathered now as they saw the newcomers arrive. These were Duthenor warriors. Most were pale haired, some brown haired as was Brand, yet others dark-eyed with raven-black hair. All wore chainmail. Some had helms. Here and there were spears and bows and long-handled axes, but most carried swords in the plain scabbards hanging from their belts.

"There aren't as many as I had thought," Sighern said quietly from beside Brand. He had been given his own horse at Brand's request.

His observation was correct. There were some three hundred of them, and many had the look of untested youths. But Brand smiled anyway. He had worried that there would be none.

"It is perhaps half of what the district could muster," Haldring said. She offered no comment on why that was so.

"Yesterday we were four," Brand said. "Now we are hundreds. It's all a matter of perspective."

"If we waited, more might yet join us," Haldring suggested.

"No. There is no time to wait. We must be swift and gather momentum." Brand handed his reins to Sighern and stepped a little way ahead of the others to meet the warriors.

They eyed him warily, as well they might. Many glances fell upon sword, ring and helm. They had *heard* the rightful chieftain had returned, but they wanted to see it for themselves.

"Warriors of the Duthenor!" he called. "You will have heard much. Most of it will have been rubbish. This I say to you now, as the truth. I am Brand. I have returned. When I went into exile, I was little more than a child, though one that had learned the ways of the world. But I return now as a man, tested in battle as a warrior. And also tested in battle as a leader of armies and a nation. I was victorious. I will be victorious again."

He fell silent. The Duthenor studied him. One man, perhaps in his fifties but still hale, stepped forward.

"We hear you, Brand. We recognize you. You are the rightful heir, and tales of your deeds in faraway Cardoroth are told even in this land. We are brave men, and true. Too long have we endured Unferth, and we shall follow you. But we worry also for our families. We are too few to challenge the enemy. We are hundreds, but he has thousands at his command. We fear, though this army may grow, that we will *always* be too few. And when

119

Unferth comes, he may not kill just us but ravage the land as well."

Brand studied him. "What's your name, warrior?"

The man spoke proudly. "I'm called Garamund. In my youth, I served your father."

"Then hear me, Garamund. I know you speak for all these warriors." He swept his arm out, gesturing at the gathered men. "Everything you say is true. I will not lie to you, even as my father did not lie to you. So this I say truly. Our first task is *not* to fight Unferth. That way lies disaster. That fight is for a later time. Now, our task is to bear a torch. We will hold it aloft, and it will be a beacon of hope. We shall sting Unferth, and then disappear. We shall sting him again, and vanish once more. All the while word of our deeds will spread. Our army will grow. When we are ready, then we shall strike him down."

As always, when people saw a plan they felt inclined to follow it. And in the plan, sketchy as it was, they saw hope because it acknowledged the difficulties and provided a solution. Brand knew by their expressions he had won them over. But with that winning came responsibility. Now he felt the weight of trying to make reality conform to the words he had spoken. It would not be easy.

"Where is the closest supporter of Unferth?" Brand asked. Now that he had them, he must get them moving before they had a chance to change their mind.

"That would be lord Gingrel," Garamund said. There were murmurs of agreement from the men, and Haldring gave a slight nod when he looked at her.

"And how far away is he?" Brand asked.

"He has a large hall," Garamund answered, "only half a day away."

"He's one of the usurper's own men, belonging to the Callenor, and he has many of that tribe with him," Haldring added.

"Aye, those pigs like to lord it over us." Garamund leaned forward and spat, accurately but not eloquently giving his opinion of Unferth's tribe that now occupied the Duthgar.

"Then it is to there that we shall march."

Brand had them now. He had given them a purpose, and through Garamund's actions emotion had been invoked; they hated the Callenor. Purpose and emotion served as the basis for any military effort. The two went hand in hand, and one without the other soon dwindled into failure. It was probably so for any human endeavor.

He drew his sword slowly, allowing men to see the Halathrin-wrought blade. Then he pointed it at the Green Howe.

"In there sleeps a hero of old. I know not his name, nor his battles, but they are finished now. I know this, though. He was Duthenor. The dark will take us all, in the end, even as it took him. But our battles are not yet finished. For a while we stand, as warriors, in the light. Our deeds yet need doing."

There was a roar from the men. They had been compared to a hero of old, and at the same time challenged to live up to his standards. Brand felt the surge of pride ripple through them, and for a moment he wondered if he were doing the right thing. Was he manipulating them for his own purposes, or speaking as he felt himself? Or perhaps both?

He lifted his sword straight up into the air, the pattern-welded blade shimmering. "We are few!" he called. "But we are like the point of the blade – the most dangerous part!"

There was another roar of approval, greater than the first.

"The edge of the blade is yet to come, but it will as our army grows. Then we shall swell until there is point, blade and hilt – until the sword is complete!"

The crowd yelled and cheered, but Brand was not done. "And when we are a complete sword, we will strike Unferth down!"

He swept the blade in a killing stroke, flourished it in the air a moment, and then sheathed it swiftly all in one smooth motion.

The men drew their own blades, yelling and cheering and lifting their weapons high. "Brand!" they began to chant. "Brand of the Duthenor!"

Brand pointed behind him. "These are my generals. I trust them with my life. Shorty, Taingern and Haldring. They will not fail me, and I shall not fail you!"

There was a deafening roar, and many eyes glanced at the generals. Not least of all at Haldring. She stood tall, her blonde hair spilling free as she removed her helm so that the men could see her.

"The time of words is done," Brand said more quietly. "Now is the time to march. Follow us, and believe that the journey we now take will be chanted by storytellers in times to come."

He led his horse forward, his generals with him, and the three hundred warriors fell into a tight group, marching behind.

They had not gone far when Taingern leaned in and spoke to him quietly.

"So, what's the plan?"

"It's simple," Brand answered. "Very simple."

Shorty, who was walking his horse on the other side, drew closer as well.

"Simple is always the best."

"So it is," Brand agreed. "In a nutshell, this is it. We need a win. It doesn't have to be a big one. It *can't* be a big one, yet. But that doesn't matter. A win is a win, and that will encourage others to join us. Momentum is everything."

Taingern seemed to expect this. "So far so good, but this lord we march on will have heard news of your coming by now. He'll be expecting us. Maybe even had time to summon warriors."

"Ah, that could be. But probably not. No doubt, he'll have begun to take steps. But he won't know for sure that I'm marching on him. There are other places I could go. And he'll not think that I'll march so soon. As was pointed out before, if I waited another day or two more people would join us. Most leaders would wait for those extra numbers."

"I see," Taingern replied. "Now all the better do I understand your reasoning for marching swiftly. Perhaps we will catch them by surprise."

They moved ahead at a good pace. Brand allowed little time for rests, stopping only once every hour for a short while. Surprise would be needed, and speed was the foundation on which that depended.

The track led out of the valley and toward a forest. By the afternoon they had moved within the trees and the track had become a road. Some little while later they ceased their march, and looked down through the cover of trees at the hall situated many hundreds of feet away. It lay below them, on a slight slope of green grass. There was a village too, but this had grown up near a stream further down slope. The hall itself stood in the open, and a path of the road branched off and headed to it.

Brand and his generals slipped through the trees that formed the eaves of the wood for a closer look. They saw signs of activity. Even as they watched two riders hastened toward the wall. They had come across country rather

123

than by road. Otherwise, Brand's force would have detained them.

There were half a dozen guards at the hall entrance also. They looked alert.

"They've heard of our coming," Haldring said. "What do we do now?"

14. Will You Surrender?

Brand considered the situation. What to do was no easy question.

"They've heard of my return, but they're not ready yet. There are more warriors to come in, perhaps a lot more, I think."

"Probably," Haldring said. "So, will you attack then?"

Brand hesitated. "Some of the men down there will be Duthenor though, will they not?"

"Of course, but they'll be in the minority. They might even turn to our side."

"They'll need time for that. Just taken unawares by warriors attacking, they'll fight first."

"Maybe. But I see no way around it."

Brand knew he should attack. And he should do it swiftly. But it was not so easy as that.

"Duthenor killing Duthenor is no way to build an army. I must think not only of the battle at hand, but of what's to follow."

"But you *do* need a victory," Shorty said.

"I need a victory, but I must do it without killing Duthenor. I'll not do that unless I must. And here, just at the moment, I think we have the greater force. I'll give the Duthenor a chance to see what's happening and come to our side."

They seemed uncertain of this course, but he had made up his mind. He gave signals. The warriors formed a tight group, and then swiftly they walked from the forest and toward the hall. They blew no horns, nor did they draw any blades. Brand would not provoke the enemy into a fight, but rather he would give them an opportunity to surrender.

The opposition would hold tight in the hall, being outnumbered. And should other forces arrive, they would likely come from outlying areas in small groups and be outnumbered too. But it was not a situation that could last. The longer it went on, the worse it would be for Brand. But he was glad he had resisted the temptation to attack. There was that side to him that was violent, and could justify the violence as necessary. It was a side to all men, but it must be resisted. All the more so because he had authority over others. As he acted, so would they be influenced.

His warrior band strode forward. Ahead, the opposition saw them, hesitated and then moved inside the hall. There was yelling and shouting, and Brand had no doubt he would find the door to the hall closed and barred from the inside when he reached it.

So it proved. He set men to guard all sides of the hall so that they could not be taken by surprise nor anyone escape. And he set lookouts also, with an eye to any attack that might be launched from outside. The enemy would build out there somewhere in the surrounding countryside, but he guessed they would bide their time. It would take some while to find each other and join together. Only when there were enough of them, if their number reached that high at all, would they attack.

Brand himself hammered at the door three times. "Open!" he commanded. "I am Brand, rightful chieftain of the Duthgar. I would speak with the lord of this hall."

There was muffled talk from inside, and a few moments later a voice answered, calm and aloof.

"Unferth reigns as king in the Duthgar, and I do not know you or recognize any authority. But if you wish, you may come inside. You alone."

Brand smiled. He wondered how many steps he would take into that hall before a sword found his heart.

"I think not, Gingrel. But you will have men in there that know me. Duthenor men. Let some of them out so that they may see me."

"No." came the answer.

Brand expected that. "If you do not, then I will hold it against you when I come into my own and judge you. And I *will* come into my own, and when I judge you it will be harshly."

That would give him something to think about. He would not surrender, for then he would fear having to answer to Unferth. But he could not be certain that Unferth would prevail, so he would also be wary of what would happen if Brand gained control of the Duthgar.

The silence grew. There was muttering on the other side of the door, and then at length Gingrel gave an answer.

"Very well. Stand back, well back."

Brand gestured to those with him, and they walked well back from the door. Whatever conversation took place, he wanted to keep it private. But they drew their swords also, for Brand was not trusting. They could be attacked, but he did not think Gingrel had the nerve for that. If he attacked, he had nowhere to go but back in the hall. And that could be set to fire if he angered his opponents.

The door opened, and two men came out. They wore swords, but the blades remained sheathed. Men crowded behind the entrance they had come through, but there was no indication of bowmen.

Brand did not know the two men. They approached, slowly and cautiously, their gaze alert but not alarmed. They did not seem to distrust the warriors they faced, or Brand, and that indicated to him that they were Duthenor.

127

Very slowly, Brand drew his sword. "I am Brand. Rightful ruler of the Duthgar." He spoke softly, and he did not think those in the hall could hear what was said.

Their gaze had gone first to the Helm of the Duthenor that he wore. Then the naked steel of his Halathrin-wrought blade. When they had studied it a moment, he sheathed the weapon and showed them the chieftain's ring he wore.

They glanced at each other first, and then one spoke. "We know you, Brand. The tokens you bear are enough, but we know you also. We were young when we met, and it was but briefly. Our lord took us with him when he visited your father."

"Then you will tell Gingrel, and all else inside, that I am who I say?"

"We will. There is no doubt."

Brand spoke carefully. This was a delicate situation. "My return changes much. And I know a great deal has happened in my absence, but why do men of the Duthenor serve a foreign lord?"

The men looked uncomfortable. "Gingrel has supplied food for us, and our families. He need not have done so. Without that, we would have been reduced to poverty."

"I see. And I understand. I assume also that you, and the other Duthenor in the hall, have sworn oaths of loyalty to the new lord?"

"Yes," they answered simply.

Brand had learned something valuable. There were more Duthenor in the hall. Now was come the time to play on that, and open old wounds.

"And what happened to the old Duthenor lord?"

"He was murdered."

"By whom?"

"By the lord who now sits in the high chair," the first man answered. There was no emotion in his voice, which served to show to Brand that great emotion existed, otherwise it would not need to be so severely restrained.

"How many of you are there?"

There was hesitation here, for the men saw where this must lead. The second answered eventually, though.

"We are thirty, but they are seventy."

Brand hesitated himself, though it was deliberate. He would give them time to think on what had been said, for long suppressed emotions to bubble to the surface.

"Bring them out, and join me," he said at last.

The first man slowly shook his head. "We have sworn oaths to Gingrel."

"I see." Brand knew this would have been the case. "I guessed you had, and I would not ask you to break an oath. But that does not mean you are not needed, you and men like you throughout the Duthgar. Unferth's time of reckoning has come. And there is this too. What of the older oaths you would have sworn to your dead, and murdered lord? Which oath shall you keep, and which shall you not?"

The men did not look happy. "You put us in a hard place," the first said.

Brand had sympathy for them, and all like them across the land. There had been no exile for them. It had been a case of serve, or suffer.

"I know I do. I do not wish to, but fate has so decreed it. This is all I ask – think on what we have said."

The men returned inside after that. Brand waited until they were gone from view, and then he spoke to those who held the door.

"I have proven now that I am as I claim. Let Gingrel stand forth."

There was movement inside the shadows of the hall, and a voice answered him, though he could not see clearly who spoke.

129

"I can hear you from here, Brand."

"You know who I am, and this choice I give you. Surrender to my justice, or die."

Gingrel answered him. "I have done no wrong. Let me send a swift rider to Unferth, and I will ask him to come here. I am but a lord, not the ruler of the Duthgar. These matters are above me, and I must await his instructions."

Brand knew he would get nowhere here, not this way. Shorty also whispered in his ear. "The man is merely playing for time."

"There shall be no riders, no messages and no delays," Brand said loudly. "I give you until one hour after dawn tomorrow to surrender."

There was movement again, and the hall door was slammed shut. There would be no more talk.

Night came soon after, and Brand's men became restless. They knew as well as he that enemies could come upon them while they were in the open. It was a danger, but Brand did not think Gingrel's supporters would be here yet. His coming and march here had been swift, too swift for the enemy to properly mobilize. But that would change tomorrow. After that, they were increasingly likely to be attacked.

"What now?" Haldring asked.

"Now we wait," he replied.

"Have you considered attacking the hall?"

"I have, but we would lose men that way. The doors are narrow, and even if we broke them down one man could hold us off."

Haldring hesitated, and then spoke again. "We could burn them out."

Brand knew this suggestion would come up. It was a terrible thing to do, even to an enemy. But there was a history of it, though usually it was considered a crime in the Duthgar, no matter what prompted it.

"I'll not burn them out."

Haldring looked at him a long moment. "Do you have the guts to lead men into war? Not all decisions are easy."

He could not complain, because he had told her he wanted the truth from her. And it was a valid question. She knew as much as did he that he needed a victory, and that time was running out in which to obtain it.

"I have the guts," he said. "But I'll not kill Duthenor as well as the enemy. And besides, the night has only just begun. It will be long for us out here, but it will be long in there also. And the oaths the Duthenor swore to their old lord will grow restless."

She studied him a while longer, but said no more. She had suggested the burning, and it was her job to do so. But she pressed it no further for her heart was not in it either. He was glad of that.

Night fell. Fires were lit, scouts sent out and a perimeter of guards established. It was a dangerous situation. Nor could Brand rule out a sudden attack from within the hall either. It was not likely, but it must be guarded against.

The Duthenor he commanded were of good cheer. Finally, after years, action was being taken against the invaders. That good cheer would not last though. The long night would wear it down, and failure to secure a surrender tomorrow would erode it further.

Brand thought on what he would do if that occurred. He would not burn the hall, but he could attack it. The doors could be destroyed, yet both the one at front and the one at the rear were narrow. This was on purpose, and it ensured that even one man at each door could long hold off an attacking enemy. And all the while the threat increased that other hostile forces would arrive, group together, and attack.

He had another course of action. He could withdraw, and pursue one of the hostile forces that would soon gather. If he destroyed that, he would have his victory. But Gingrel would then be free, and able to attack.

Yet another option was to divide his forces. He could leave a large enough band here to hold Gingrel within the hall, and lead the rest to find and destroy what forces he could find in the district that supported Unferth. That was a dangerous tactic also, for he did not know how large those forces were and his own was not so large as to make dividing it an easy decision.

He had problems, and he knew it. But it would not help to worry over them all pointlessly. He would decide in the morning as he must, and the night would be long and could bring news or events to change his plans anyway.

They slept, but it was a restless sleep. Always there was the movement of sentries as they patrolled or changed shifts. At some point, the sky clouded and rain threatened. But it held off and remained dry. After a few hours, the clouds dissipated.

Brand woke, slumbered again and woke once more. All was hushed, and yet he sensed that something was happening. Had he heard a noise? He looked to the sentries, but from what he could see of their dim forms nothing had disturbed them.

It was some while yet until the dawn, but not that long. The eastern sky seemed a little paler, perhaps. And then there was a sudden noise from within the hall. Brand heard banging and raised voices.

Swiftly he rose and drew his sword. He had slept in his boots, as had the others. They were up quickly also, and Brand woke other warriors nearby.

There was more noise from within the hall, loud now and urgent, and the clash of steel on steel was a part of it. Suddenly, the door flew open and men struggled within it.

132

One fell, dead. Out staggered a Duthenor warrior, but there were others behind him. They held the door open against a force from within that sought to kill them.

"Attack!" Brand cried, and he led the way. The Duthenor inside had done what he hoped, but he knew also that they were outnumbered and would be killed swiftly unless help arrived.

Brand was the first in. There was light inside, and it showed turmoil within the hall. There was desperate fighting, mostly near the doors. There were several bodies on the floor, and the air was full of battle-cries and the clamor of sword against sword.

With a flick of his wrist Brand deflected a stabbing blow at his head and slew the man who had tried to kill him. He pressed forward into the fray, his sword flashing and his helm glittering. Men fell back before him and space opened to allow more Duthenor into the hall.

Somehow Sighern had found his way in, and his sword cut and slashed close to Brand's. He should have stayed without, and Brand knew he would not forgive himself if he were killed. But he could do nothing about it now.

A huge man with a red beard came at him, and Brand leaped forward killing him with a swift jab the other had never even seen coming. The clash of steel was deafening, and he saw Shorty and Taingern close by. Haldring was with them, her blonde hair spilling out behind her helm and her sword darting like a serpent's tongue, dealing out death wherever she strode.

The hall was become a charnel house, full of spilled entrails and the smell of blood and urine and smoke. More Duthenor entered the hall and pressed forward.

"Halt!" Brand cried. "Halt!"

He stood among them, Duthenor and Callenor alike. He was taller, and marked by a kingly sword and helm, but there was an authority in his voice that allies and enemies both heard.

"Halt!" he called yet again, and opponents who had been fighting stilled, eyeing each other warily. A hush descended with the stillness. Brand knew that at any moment turmoil could break forth again. It hovered in the air and a man just blinking at the wrong time could unleash it once more.

"There is no need for more death!" Brand called. "Stand back a pace. Everyone. Do it!"

Warriors all over the room shuffled. Some moved back more than others.

"There has been enough killing," Brand said more quietly. "Let it end now. Duthenor and Callenor alike are but following their leaders. Let Gingrel stand forth!"

A tall man approached from the back of the hall. He was thin, and dressed in princely clothes. His hair was red, grown long and tied back behind his head with a gold band. Rings glittered on his fingers. A prince he seemed in truth, living in wealth and luxury in his hall. Yet he had the look of eagles about him, and there was a cold light in his eyes, cold as the steel of the naked blade he held loosely in one hand.

"I am lord Gingrel," the man said.

Brand studied him momentarily. "Will you surrender?" he asked.

"No. I will not. You may be in my hall, and death may come, but we shall kill many of you before it does."

Brand was silent a long while. "Duthenor blood is precious to me," he said at length. "I will not spill it unless I must. And Callenor blood is precious also. We fight here as enemies, but of old did we not belong to one far greater tribe? Do we not sing the same songs and share many of the same heroes?"

134

No one answered him. He did not think they would. Gingrel continued to study him with those same cold eyes.

"Let there be an end to this," Brand said. "Let Gingrel and I alone fight. One of us will die, and that will be an end to it."

Gingrel seemed surprised. "You would duel with me?"

Even as Gingrel spoke Brand heard a hiss from Haldring and saw her give a slight shake of her head. It seemed that Gingrel had a reputation as a fighter. He certainly looked the part.

"This I swear," Brand said. "If I am killed, I command those who follow me to leave and return to their homes."

Gingrel grinned at him, and for the first time there was a light in his eyes. He was a man who loved to fight, and he saw a chance for victory in this.

"Will you tell your men to surrender, if you are killed, Gingrel?"

Gingrel moved slowly toward him. "I will not be killed, but yes. They will surrender."

"Then stand back, everyone. Sheathe your swords, and clear room for Gingrel and I to face each other."

The two men drew close. The fire pit in the middle of the hall was to Brand's left. Embers shimmered there, and he felt the heat off them even where he stood.

Gingrel moved like a viper, all smooth and effortless. He was a natural-born warrior, but so too was Brand. And Brand saw opportunity in this. What happened now would spread from district to district and cross and re-cross the Duthgar. If he won, and he intended to, it would help establish his credibility. Moreover, if he won in spectacular fashion…

Gingrel leaped forward, his blade cutting a shadowy arc in a backhanded strike. It streaked through the air, faster than thought. Time slowed. Brand watched the blade, allowed it to whisper death close to his head as he ducked just barely enough to avoid it. Before it had even passed over him he had begun to move forward himself, the blade of his forefathers sweeping out.

There was a sickening noise. Red blood spurted from severed arteries. Brand's blade took Gingrel in the neck between helm and chainmail coat. His body remained still, but the lord's head toppled away. It fell into the fire pit. Smoke rose as the long hair of the head caught fire. Skin sizzled. The body, still pumping blood, slowly fell backward.

It was over before it had begun. Brand lowered his sword, resting its point on the floor and leaning on it casually.

"Thus is justice done," he said solemnly. "As Gingrel fell, so too will Unferth."

The Callenor men looked at him, uncertainty and shock in their eyes. They knew their lord for a great warrior, but he was now defeated, and easily. And they were in a hall full of their enemies.

Brand spoke before they had a chance to decide what to do. "Callenor!" he called. "I am true to my word. I accept your surrender. Moreover, I promise you shall be allowed to keep your swords and walk freely from this hall. What say you?"

There was movement among them. One man stepped forward after a while, older and grizzled, his face showing a scar from a long-ago battle. His gaze fell momentarily down into the firepit, but he looked back up at Brand quickly.

"Truly? You will let us go free?"

Brand answered without hesitation. "I will let you go, with your swords. I will not ask oaths of loyalty from you. You may not give them, and if you did you may not keep them, for your alliance is to your old lord. It was *his* mistake to think an oath of convenience would bind forever. This only I ask of you. Swear that you shall leave the Duthgar, and never return here armed for war."

The old man looked at him hard. "And if we do not?"

Brand answered once more without hesitation. "Then you will die. And you will die for nothing. Think carefully."

The old man gazed at Brand, his expression unreadable. "We shall so swear it."

Each man then came before Brand, and he swore the oath as Brand had asked. And then they followed the old man out the door of the hall and disappeared into the new day that was beginning.

The Duthenor held the hall, and Brand had given the men the victory they needed. And the story of his growing army and quest to unseat Unferth had been enhanced. But Shorty was not so certain.

"Can the men you just let go be trusted? I fear, despite their oaths, that we might end up fighting them anyway. Only next time they'll be with Unferth."

He did not say it in front of the Duthenor, but spoke quietly to Brand while the men were clearing the hall of dead bodies.

"It could be," Brand agreed. "But I don't think so. They seemed good men to me, it was the lord they followed who was bad. And besides, the story will spread among the Callenor. Better to face men in battle who know they can surrender than those who know they must fight to the death. Because then they will, with everything they have."

Brand gave orders then. He had the treasury of the hall brought to him. This was in a locked box, and it was no great treasure. But there were gold coins and rings and precious stones. It would help him keep the men on side, and it would pay for supplies also.

He also ordered whatever food could be found to be gathered up as well. Haldring raised an eyebrow at this. She understood what it meant, but did not say anything.

A little while later they left the hall and closed the door behind them. The Duthenor were gathered there now, and an extra twenty men they did not have before.

"See!" Brand said, addressing them all. "Our army grows and word spreads. It is a slow start, but sure. The usurper will come to fear us! This I promise, but for now we march again."

The men cheered and got ready to move. Sighern, standing near Brand seemed confused.

"Aren't we going to rest here first?"

"No, lad. We could all do with some, but we must move fast instead. We must *never* be where we are expected to be. Not while our force is small."

"The men are ready," Taingern said. "Where do we go next?"

"A good question," Brand answered. "But I don't know."

Shorty laughed. "A simple plan is good. No plan … not so much!"

Brand gathered the reins to his horse. "I'll have one when I need one," he said with a wink. "For now, the only plan is to get away from here. We've done what we came to do, but there could be other hostile forces anywhere. It's time to disappear."

15. A Man of Secrets

Unferth sat on the high chair, oblivious to the goings on in the hall around him. Brooding they called him, often. But they were fools. He was thoughtful, as a great leader of men must be. Few understood that. Of them all, perhaps only Horta.

The magician sat nearby, his disciple Olbata beside him. Strange names for a strange people, but they were useful, which was all that really mattered. And yet Horta always seemed to give him bad news. He had done so just now, and yet he always had a solution to any problem.

But why were there so many problems? Unferth shifted in his chair. Even the high seat seemed uncomfortable of late. He should be enjoying all his successes now, instead of worrying. It was the way of the wolf to fight toward leadership of the pack. This he had done, and he had succeeded. He ruled two lands now, side by side. The Callenor were his own, the Duthenor subjugated. He had become now a king instead of chieftain. And he could do more, yet. Surely things should be getting easier and not harder?

Horta would be a help with that. He *knew* things, not least of all the hearts of men. That he looked strange did not matter. That he dressed strange was irrelevant. He was a man who wore a skirt and a bearskin rug over his shoulder. But no one ever dared laugh at him.

Unferth cast his mind back to their first meeting. The foreigner had been dressed the same way on that very first day. He had felt the urge to laugh, but the cool, steady gaze of the other forestalled it. Here was a man of power, a man who could kill and who had used that skill often. And when he had proclaimed himself a magician, causing thunder to boom in the hall and mead in cups to turn to ice as proof, Unferth had believed him. More, he knew that together they could achieve much. And all the little man asked in return was permission to explore the Duthgar.

What the magician searched for, Unferth did not care. Treasure probably, for men had dwelt here long, long before the Duthenor came. But whatever treasures there were would long since have been found. But none of that was of import now. Now, that Brand had come back.

Of course, he only had Horta's word for that. Somehow, Brand had entered the realm despite the precautions set against him, and begun to build an army. Horta would not say how he knew, only that he had spies through the land and that the king's own messengers would confirm it very soon. Magic of some kind, Unferth guessed.

"*How* did Brand get across the river?" Unferth asked. "It was guarded!"

The magician gave an elegant shrug. All his movements were elegant, as though he were born of nobility. But looking at how he dressed, that was not possible.

"It doesn't matter. He's a man of skill and determination. He found a way, and he is here now, moving against you. That's what's important."

Unferth tried to restrain his irritation. "The man is a nuisance," he said. Quietly, he seethed, but it would not do to let his advisors see the effect Brand had on him. Horta looked at him silently though, as if he knew exactly what was going on. Unferth did not like it. The man knew too much, but kept too many secrets of his own.

"Brand has three hundred men," Unferth said. "He's hardly a threat, and yet I must take steps. For his effrontery, I will send a thousand against him."

Horta did not look happy, but he smoothed his face when he spoke.

"He has some three hundred and twenty now—"

"Another twenty men makes no difference!" Unferth stormed. He did not like being corrected.

Unferth bowed, unruffled. "The twenty men are nothing," he said. "Their only relevance is that Brand is gathering more followers. What will his band number in a day, or a week?"

"Who is to say it will not diminish? That's just as likely."

"Perhaps." Unferth somehow made the word sound as though it were a denial. "Whatever the size of his band, it will take four or five days for him to reach us. Much could happen in that time. His army could multiply. Or he could die. The latter is preferable."

He said the last words drily, and Unferth caught a hint that he had already taken steps. A strange look passed over his face too, before it was smoothed over once more. Always, he was a man of secrets.

But Brand must be stopped now, before he gained momentum. He turned to his advisors. "Muster two thousand warriors. Choose our best general, and send them against Brand. He'll not survive that."

His advisors stood to leave, but Unferth was not finished. A new thought occurred to him, and he liked it.

"And make sure the word spreads to each of those two thousand men. There shall be a reward. I will give five gold pieces – no, I will give *fifty* gold pieces to the man who hacks Brand's head from his body and brings me the Helm of the Duthenor."

They looked surprised, but there were various murmurs of "Yes, my lord."

Unferth sat back, and he felt good. Two thousand men and fifty gold pieces were extravagant. But to see Band killed? For that, he would do anything.

16. Least Expected

Brand led his band of men back up to the path. Then he turned southward once more. The path was now a road, and better known to residents of the Duthgar as the High Way. And high it was, for it wound its way over the plateau of a range that divided the Duthgar in two.

They marched swiftly. Ahead of them, scouts were sent out to determine if the enemy were ahead. Likewise, men ranged behind them to see if they were followed. So far, the men had found nothing. It was a stroke of luck, but it was founded on Brand's speed, and he knew it.

Haldring led her horse a little behind him, and he knew she did not like walking. But she also recognized his thinking: the men followed leaders better who walked when they walked and endured what they endured. He beckoned her forward.

"What lies ahead," he asked.

"More halls, just as the last one that we left. All the way to where the king sits in his own."

"Yes, I know that. I've traveled this road before. But my memory is better of what's further south. I mean, what halls are close by?"

"There is a hall coming up on the left, and not long after another on the right."

"And whom do they favor?"

"They are both ruled by Callenor lords."

"And the next hall after them?"

"That is ruled by a Duthenor. Though there will be Callenor there also."

143

Brand considered that. What should he do next? He now had a force probably as great as any lord of a single hall could muster. At least in this part of the Duthgar. Further south they were more prosperous and larger. But he need not worry about that yet.

"Are these halls close to the road?"

"Aye, both of them."

"Good. Spread the word back among the men. We're approaching enemies, and they should be ready for battle. But we intend to pass by the next two halls unless accosted. We go to the third instead."

Haldring hesitated. "But are we going by the road? If so, the enemy will see us."

"Good," Brand said. "I want them to."

She fell back then to pass on the decision.

"I see you have a plan now," Shorty said.

"The beginnings of one," Brand answered.

It was not much of a plan, and he did not like calling it such. It was really no more than they had been doing. The unexpected. But that was perhaps the greatest military strategy of all.

They passed the halls. No one was visible, the fields around them being empty. It was a slightly eerie feeling, but there was no sense of danger. Word had reached the enemy of their coming. That was to be expected traveling along the main road. The scouts had seen no one, but the purpose of scouting was to identify if the enemy laid in wait somewhere, not to find one or two men in the wilderness that may be watching them.

At regular intervals along the road were chest-high cairns that served as markers. Each one measured five miles progress. Brand counted them off, knowing they marched swift and hard. Twenty-five miles in a day was a fine effort, and they had achieved that.

He stopped as daylight faded, allowing the men a rest, campfires to be lit and a meal. But he told them the day was not over yet.

Night fell. The fires blazed and then died down. But Brand let them burn on as embers as he gathered the men and led them off the road and down into a valley. The hall he sought was not far away, and he decamped in a grove of trees and lit no further fires. With luck, any enemy following would stop well before they reached the fires on the road for fear of scouts. They would not attack themselves, for it was foolish to attack at the end of such a long march except in extremity or with superior numbers. And that he was sure they did not have. Not yet, but Unferth would send warriors when he learned what was happening.

By dawn, Brand had marched to the third hall. But there he found a pleasant surprise. Word of his coming had spread this far already, and the lord of the hall, an old man, slight and frail yet with fire in his eyes, had expelled the Callenor who lived there. He had done this in the expectation that Brand would raise an army, though he knew nothing specific of events yet.

It was pleasing, and Brand thanked him. The lord surprised him again then by bowing deep. "My hall is your hall," he said. "More importantly, my men are your men. And you will need them, for the task you face is great."

"But the more I meet like you," Brand replied, "the easier it becomes."

The warriors camped outside and the lord took Brand and his generals into the hall to break their fast. It was not a large hall, but when they left they had a hundred new warriors with them. It would have been more, but at Brand's insistence the lord retained a large enough force to protect himself.

A cheer went through the army as the new men joined it.

"So far so good," Shorty said to Brand as they surveyed the growing force. "Now what?"

"Now, we backtrack."

"I thought as much. The enemy behind is more dangerous than the enemy ahead."

Brand grinned at him, but never answered. One of the new warriors approached, a younger man, tall and blue-eyed, with a red tinge to his blond hair.

Brand recognized him. "Caraval?"

The younger man bowed. "Yes, sire."

"There need be no sire or the like for me, Caraval. Not from you or your family."

The young man grinned. "Then you remember me?"

"Remember you? Of course! How could I forget that time we stole apples from farmer Thurgil's only tree? And he set his dogs after us even though you said his son had the dogs with him at a neighbors?"

Caraval grinned. "I lied, just so you would do it with me. But the apples were sweet, as I remember."

"Ah, that they were. The sweetest apples for miles all around."

"It's still there, you know."

"Really? It was an old tree even then."

"The apples are even sweeter."

Brand narrowed his eyes. "Are you trying to get me into trouble again? I bet the dogs are still there too."

The younger man laughed. "The tree and the dogs are still there. Thurgil too, but he'd set no dogs on you now."

"I'm not so sure of that! But I tell you what, when this is all over we'll go and see."

"Really?"

"Truly. But we'll call at the farmhouse first and ask permission this time."

The younger man grinned, and then his face grew serious.

"Are we going to win, Brand?"

"I got us away from the dogs that time, didn't I? And I'll outsmart Unferth now. Just watch me!"

Caraval grinned again. "You always did have a trick or two up your sleeves. Unferth better watch out."

A horn blew and the band was ready to march. Fresh supplies had been given to the men of food and equipment. Brand shook the younger man's hand and he went back to his place among the warriors. Brand gave a gesture, and the force began to march behind him.

"An old friend?" Taingern asked.

"An old friend, and a good one without a doubt. After Unferth … killed my parents I was hidden in house after house, district after district. Sometimes I only spent a night or a week in one place. Other times, months. I must have been with Caraval's family for near on six months, and I liked it there. But ever I had to move before the assassins learned of my presence. It protected me, but it protected the families also. So yes, he was a good friend during that time, and I know others like him all through the land. They were all good, strong country folk. And loyal."

Brand led them into the woods, and not back onto the road. He knew better now where he was, for these lands were familiar. But still he sent out scouts ahead and had them watch the backtrail behind.

They traveled swiftly, for though their number was growing they were still a small force. And though they moved through the woods there was a forest trail to follow, and Brand led them at a grueling pace along its length.

Toward nightfall, they had approached the last hall that they had earlier bypassed. There was no sign of a special watch, and it was a small hall anyway. Though the men were tired, this was a time where surprise counted above all.

Brand attacked. His men swarmed from the woods and converged on the hall. They took the doors swiftly, and crowded the occupants of the hall into the building's center.

Three of the enemy had been slain, Callenor warriors who drew their swords and tried to hold the door. Everyone else fell back in confusion, including the lord. They had not expected Brand to come back once he had gone past them, nor had they anticipated the speed at which he had done so or the direction from which he came.

Swords were drawn. Battle was near to breaking out. Only Brand standing there, slowly sheathing his blade gave the two sides pause.

"Let the lord come forth!" Brand commanded.

The lord came. He was an older man, gray haired and with a white beard streaked with darker hairs. He bowed, slightly, and kept his hands away from the hilt of the sword he wore. But he was not as old as he had at first looked. The beard gave him that appearance, yet no doubt he was still able to fight as a warrior, and Brand noted the way he stood, at ease but ready to act.

"I am your humble servant," the man said. "There need be no further killings."

Brand did not trust him. "You will swear allegiance?"

"I swear it, my lord. I am loyal."

Brand still did not trust him. He was not the true lord of this hall, at least according to the traditions of the Duthenor. The previous lord had died without children, and Unferth had given this man the lordship. But the chieftain of the Duthenor had never had that power. In

148

such cases, the people of the district met and chose their own lord.

"Very well. This is what you will do then. First, you will expel any Callenor warriors from the hall. Let them go freely, if they will, with their blades but under an oath to do no harm in the Duthgar. And then your men will move on the next hall back down the road. This is ruled by a Callenor lord. You will take the hall, and expel the Callenor there, including the lord. You will have this done in my name, but the hall must not be fired."

The man bowed. "It shall be even as you say."

Brand still did not trust him. "And as a sign of your goodwill and loyalty, you shall order all this done, and your warriors to march tonight, but you yourself will come with my army."

The man hesitated at that point. He looked as though he were about to argue, but when he spoke he showed no sign of it.

"It shall be as you say, my lord."

Brand watched and listened as the man gave the orders to his most senior advisors. They did not seem pleased, but Brand detected no attempt to circumvent his instructions.

He had been using the stick so far, now it was time for a sweetener.

"If all is carried out as desired," Brand promised, "then you shall retain the lordship of this hall, and your heirs after you."

The lord nodded grimly. He had been forced to take sides when he would have preferred to have remained neutral and then claimed loyalty all along to him, or to Unferth, whichever one triumphed in the battles ahead. Brand did not like that, nor did he see it as a crime. But now the lord understood well enough that his future was linked to Brand. Unferth would not forgive him for

149

supporting the enemy, even if he had done so under duress.

The warriors of the lord left, unhappy and yet also under the same compulsion as their lord. Even as his success was now tied to Brand's, so too was theirs to their lord's. If they did not carry out their orders, and their lord was deposed, a *new* lord, coming to power under either Unferth or Brand, would have little use for them. He would pick his own advisors and battle leaders.

Brand and his army watched the band of warriors depart into the night. It was good to see others march while they rested for once.

"Nicely done," Haldring said. "You rounded them all up and herded them like sheep."

"But?" Brand said. He could see by her expression that there was more.

"But you now have a sheep in your herd, one at least, that will turn into a wolf and bite you if he can."

Brand glanced over at the lord, standing by himself and watching the dark where his men had vanished.

"You're right. Keep an eye on him, but at least while we're winning I think he'll be true to his word." Brand looked at his own men, tired but happy. They were due not just a rest but a celebration of their successes. He grinned. "And since that lord will never be my friend, we may as well stretch things further. Leave his treasury intact, but crack open his larders and distribute his mead to the men. It's time they enjoyed things a little. But tell them we march at dawn tomorrow."

Haldring seemed amused as she went to carry out those instructions. And why not? So far, things were going well. Brand felt confidence creep up and over him, but he pushed it down. So far, things had gone well enough. But there was a lot yet to do, and there was the magician to worry about as well as military strategies.

Shorty broke his line of thought. "What now?" he asked. "The army is growing and morale is good. Back to the road and our next victory?"

"No," Brand said quietly. He did not wish anyone to hear. "Tomorrow will be a forced march. We go to a place that we must, but not one the men will like. It'll be unexpected to them, and therefore to Unferth."

17. The Pale Swordsman

It was a bright morning with a clear sky. A soft breeze blew, and it was neither cold nor hot. It was perfect weather to walk the farm and check the hazel-branch fencing. It was a job Dernthrad enjoyed. But not today.

He had come to a section where an ancient hedgerow served as a fence between his and a neighbor's land. He liked the hedgerow, though of late his sheep always seemed to find a way through to his neighbor's property. And his neighbor was never in a hurry to herd them back or try to fix his side of the hedge. There were signs today that sheep had got through again, and he had forced his own way through until he was peering out onto the field beyond.

His neighbor's cottage was not that far away. Smoke rose lazily from the chimney, but of the neighbor himself there was no sign. Dernthrad felt his temper rise. The man was lazy, never working his land properly and always complaining about how hard it was to earn a living. But curiosity drove Dernthrad's temper away.

A man was walking across the field, and toward his neighbor's barn. He was a man such as Dernthrad had never seen before. He moved with grace, as though each step were part of a dance, but he also moved with a sense of unhurried speed. He crossed the land like a fox, or a wolf, intent on his own business. And there was something of the predator about him.

The man was dressed in black, but silver chainmail glinted against it. And over his back was strapped two swords, the hilts sticking up and within easy reach. He was no farmer, that was for sure. But nor was he a warrior, at least not a Duthenor warrior. They dressed differently from that, and never had he seen one with two swords. Nor had he seen one with skin like this either – pale as new-fallen snow.

The warrior went into the barn. Dernthrad watched, uneasy. He should do something, but what? This man was up to no good, but he *was* a warrior.

He still had not made up his mind by the time the man emerged from the barn. He sat atop young Starfire, a mare that showed promise in the district for racing. With a kick, the warrior sent the horse into a gallop and they raced across the paddock toward where Dernthrad watched.

The path of the rider would take him close, and the farmer knew at last what he must do. He thought little of his neighbor, but he could not allow horse theft to go unchallenged. He forced himself through the rest of the hedge, tumbled into the grass on the other side and then rolled swiftly to his feet.

Thunder sounded in his ears as the black mare, the white star on her head blazing, raced toward him. He could see the rider clearly now. Fear stabbed at him. This was no man. The eyes burned like blue fire, the ears were pointed, and he moved in the saddle as though he were a part of the horse. This was an elf out of legend, though the tales did not describe them as so pale-skinned.

The eyes of the elf caught and held him. There was death there, cold and unmerciful. With a nudge, the rider angled the horse straight at him. In one swift motion he drew also one of his swords. Dernthrad caught the sheen of black steel. The blade swept at him.

Like a fool he had been standing there, like a fool caught by elf magic, but with a wild curse he dived to the side. The wind of the dark blade passed by his head. The thunder of the horse's gallop rolled by.

Dernthrad came to his feet, expecting now to die. But the rider did not even look back at him. Deftly, the black sword was sheathed, the rider bent low in the saddle once more, and the horse leaped a hazel-branch fence and raced away into a wood.

Starfire was gone. The rider was gone, but the fear of death remained. The cold eyes of the elf haunted him. All the more so for tales told that the elves were good people. But that had been a creature from the pit.

It had not been a good night. The hunters, empty handed, tired from a long night and irritable, made their way back home along the High Way. The sound of hooves came to them, louder and louder of a galloping horse.

They moved to the side petulantly. Around a bend came the rider, his black mount sheened by sweat that foamed its flanks, its great lungs straining for breath. If ever a rider was going to kill a horse, it was this man.

But the yells forming in their throats died. It was no man. It was a creature of nightmare, an elf out of story, a fiend from the pit. The elf looked at them, if elf it was, and the flash of his eyes burned with hatred and contempt. And then he was gone, vanishing around another bend and the thunder of his passage dwindling away like a storm that did not strike. But if a storm missed one village, it hit another.

"That thing, whatever it was," said one of the men, "had murder on its mind."

"It was an elf," said another of the hunters.

"No, not an elf. They're good folk."

"But it's ears. Did you not see them? It was an elf."

"No," said yet another. "It was a devil, and I pity the poor soul that it's chasing. Devils are summoned to kill men."

"How do you know it was chasing someone?"

154

"Why else would it ride like that?"

The men hurried on. The cooking pot might be light tonight, but at least they would sit around it. Alive. They knew that they had never come so close to death as just then.

The boy had climbed the old oak tree, as he often did. It was quiet in the branches, and he had a view of the land around, and especially of the road that ran past below. It was a good view, and a comfortable branch on which he sat, if a branch could be called such a thing. But it was better than his chores which he had finished. Now he had some time to think, some time to himself away from his brothers and sisters.

He thought of Brand, and the stories he had heard. He thought of the coming of a new king, and what it would mean for the land. Brand was of the old blood, descended from heroes of legend. And it seemed that the old stories were coming true. Rumor spread from farm to farm. Tales were told, hopes voiced. He was only a boy, and no one paid him any mind. So he listened and learned.

Luck had been with him too. He had been here in the tree when Brand and his men had come through. He had seen the great man, the silver helm of kings gleaming on his head, the way the men he led looked at him. He had seen it, and he would remember it all his life.

But now he saw something else from his high vantage. And suddenly he wanted to climb down the tree and run, but he would never be fast enough. A rider was coming through, but not like one he had ever seen before. It was a black rider, but his armor glittered silver like Brand's helm. The horse was black, and yet silver also, for the foam of sweat all over it glistened.

He felt sorry for the horse. It staggered and lurched, yet still the rider urged it ahead. Two swords were

155

strapped to the warrior's back, and he drew one and used it as a whip to spur the horse on. There was blood on its flank where this had been done before.

The boy *hated* the rider. If he were old enough, he would stop him. The thunder of hooves and the harsh breathing of the horse came up to him. The rider passed beneath, all black and silver and pale skin. It was no man, but some kind of monster.

It too was from the old stories, whatever it was. Legends now roamed the Duthgar, and the boy realized something else. He did not know how he knew, but the certainty of it fixed itself in his mind. It was no coincidence. That monster, that creature of evil, was after Brand.

The rider passed. All noise died away. But the boy stayed in the tree. He was scared.

18. Sleeping Magic

Brand led the army forward. He knew this part of the Duthgar, but not as well as he liked, or needed. As they marched, he sent Haldring back among the warriors to find one who knew it well. That would be needed if he was going to do what he had in mind.

He led them through the low ways that he knew, following old trails into dark woods and avoiding farms and villages. Most of all, he avoided the High Way. He had been seen there, had traveled it, and could expect forces that supported Unferth to be looking for him along its length.

The march was quick, but they could not match the pace they had set previously. The terrain did not allow for it, and the men needed more rest. Some were still paying for last night's celebrations, but for most a rest was needed anyway. He stopped regularly, and he allowed a longer break than he had previously.

It was at one such break that Haldring returned to the front with a man.

"This is Hruidgar," she said. "He's a hunter."

Brand shook the man's hand. "I'm looking for a guide," he said. "How well do you know these parts?"

The man had a strong grip, a farmer's grip. But farmers made the best hunters. They knew the land like few others ever did, and they had patience.

"I've hunted, fished and herded cattle and sheep all over this part of the Duthgar. Ain't no one knows it all, but I know it better than most."

"And do you know where we'll end up if we keep heading as we are?"

"I was wondering about that. There's nothing in these parts but wild lands and trees. Good for hunting, but there are few folks about. I figured you wanted to lay low for a while, but you'll need to turn west and climb up to the High Way if you're looking to get far from here."

Brand kept his voice down, not wanting others to hear yet.

"But if we don't? If we keep heading south as we are?"

Hruidgar gave him a long look, as if seeing him for the first time.

"Aye, well, I guess from the question you know the answer as well as me. That way lies the swamp."

"The swamp indeed. And have you been there, Hruidgar?"

The hunter looked at him, his brown eyes darker than his tanned skin, and Brand guessed he had hunted in many places including some that he should not have. Some lords liked to set aside forests for their own use alone, but Hruidgar struck him as a man who would take such a thing as a personal challenge. Brand began to like him.

"I heard the stories as a youngster. It's a bad, bad place. But I took that as a dare. So yes, I've been there. I had to see if the stories were true."

Brand had heard the stories too. A beast-man was said to roam there, strong as ten men and evil as a cold-hearted snake. Men had seen his dark shape at dusk, haunting black-watered tarns and climbing the fells that rose above the swamp. Grinder, he was called. According to legend, he liked to lay hidden in water and lurch up to catch unwary men. He carried no weapon and killed them with his bare hands, and then ate them. So legend said.

The hunter studied him. "Aye. You've heard the stories. I see it in your eyes."

"I've heard them. And other things beside. The swamp is a bad place, of that I don't doubt."

"You don't know the half of it. I saw him once. *Him*. You know who I mean. He right proper put the wind up me, and I ain't been back since. What do you think of that?"

Brand did not answer straightaway. A hunter this man might be, but he was testing him. And Brand did not blame him. He did not like to follow a stupid man either.

"The old stories became a story for a reason in the first place," he answered at length. "I have no wish to go into the swamp, but necessity compels me." He gestured with his hand to take in the men resting all around. "I have an army here, of sorts. But in truth it's only the beginning of one. If Unferth catches us at the wrong place at the wrong time, he'll crush us. My job is to see that doesn't happen. The swamp will help me do that, because I'll disappear and then reappear, at a time and place of my choosing. Unferth will be looking for me in all the wrong places."

The hunter grinned. "Unferth is one that needs setting to rights. He's low as a snake's belly that one. Alright, I'll lead you through, if I can. It's a strange place, and I may not rightly know the way out again. We'll see. But even with an army it could be dangerous. You might disappear from folks out here looking for you, but there's lots of things in the swamp, and there's no hiding from *them*."

Brand took his hand and shook it. "You're the man I need. What I do is a risk, but so is staying out here."

Brand called an end to the rest after that. They went on, and now Hruidgar led them. The man took his time, studying the trail ahead and casting his gaze from ground to trees and back again. He even seemed to sniff the air at times, but Brand let him do as he would. There was no point in seeking expertise if you did not pay attention to it when you got it. And though Brand was no great hunter or tracker, he recognized that this man was. He just hoped he was good enough.

Grinder was one danger in the swamp, but he had heard of others. And as if that was not enough, he knew that generals had led armies into swamps in other lands than the Duthgar and never been seen again. Shifting waters, pathless mazes, land that was not land and sickness were only some of the problems a general faced in such a place.

The track they followed dropped down steeply into a valley. Thick scrub grew about them, and the path had dwindled and nearly died. This strung the warriors out in a long line, which was something Brand did not like. It made them vulnerable to attack, but less and less he feared Unferth's men. More and more he worried about the swamp. Already the smell of it was in the air.

He sent Haldring back along the line to tell the men where they were headed. He used her to deal with the Duthenor more than Taingern and Shorty. She was one of them while the others were not. He must grow the trust between the army and those two slowly. But they knew that as well as he, and he often saw them at breaks mingling with the Duthenor and talking, establishing a bond and getting to know one another.

There was a creek nearby. Brand heard it, but he could not see it. It would no doubt run at the bottom of the valley, which meant they were close to that themselves.

Their progress slowed. Some of this was the narrow track, but some was the reluctance of the men. Many would have heard of the swamp ahead, and those who had not would soon hear tales from others. He had given Haldring specific things to say. It would not be pleasant … have courage … walk warily … and think of the enemies we are leaving behind. He hoped that would be enough, and he knew the Duthenor were doughty men.

But if they balked at this he would be in serious trouble. His enemies would be gathering behind him. And if he had to turn back his leadership would suffer irreparable harm.

On the other hand, if they followed him through the swamp and came out the other side, they would be bonded to him and to each other all the more strongly.

Haldring returned. "How did they take it?" Brand asked.

"Not well."

"But they are coming?"

She looked at him coolly. "Have you been gone from the Duthgar so long that you forget what the Duthenor are like? You lead, and they will follow. Loyalty drives them, and pride. Wherever you walk, whatever danger you face, they will too."

They continued on. Brand would have felt relief, except for the fact they were going to the swamp. But he knew he was right to do so. It would give him an advantage over his enemies, and he needed that given they far outnumbered him. And it would help build the reputation of his growing army too. One of their generals was a shield-maiden. They came, stung their enemies and vanished into thin air. They had walked through the legendary swamp ... all things to build their aura so that allies were more likely to join them, and their enemies to fear them. It was not swords, nor spears nor the clash of arms that won battles. It was the hearts of the warriors who fought them.

The army trod on. Hruidgar led them, slower and slower. The hunter seemed to have eyes everywhere, for he saw each bird that flew in the dim light of the tree canopy, watched every step he took to find a trail where the path they followed had disappeared. Only it had not. It might have been years since a man had walked this way, but the hunter found the path they took. Brand would not have seen it, yet once he strayed a little to the side of where the hunter led and noticed that branches scratched his face and the ground was uneven and grown over by tufted grass and twisted tree roots.

He had long since decided the hunter knew what he was doing, and there was no point in having scouts ahead. They would probably get lost, or killed. He had sent them to the rear where there was a far greater need for them. They were to discover if the army were being followed, and to kill any of the enemy that did so.

The noise of running water grew louder. It was more of a roar now, and Brand realized it was not the river. More aptly, it was still the river but it had become a waterfall.

The ground dropped suddenly. They clambered down, and to their right the trees thinned. There was a rocky outcrop there, and slightly above them but to the side the river disgorged into the air, flashing, turning and twisting in threads of silver. Foam flew from the rushing streams. The roar was louder, and the spray of water misted the air with swirling vapor. Through this, rainbows arced to the ground far below.

The hunter had no eyes for the waterfall. He kept his gaze mostly on the trail now, for it was rocky and slick with water. Carefully, he descended. Brand followed, leading his horse. The army came after.

It seemed an eerie place to Brand. It was like no other land that he had journeyed through, within or without the Duthgar. The trees changed, turning from the oak woods that they had been passing through into stands of black alder, old and weary looking with arched crowns and crooked branches. The trunks were dark gray and fissured, and here and there catkins still hung.

Down they went, deeper into the swamp, and the trail eventually leveled out. There was water everywhere, but land too. The rocks had given way to spongy soil. Mosquitoes swarmed around them, insects chirped and frogs croaked. Yet there were no birds that Brand could see, and for all the noise the land itself seemed quiet and brooding.

And well might it be. For in a place such as this the old magic was strong. Brand sensed it, a dormant thing, slumbering away through the eons. But there was power here, and he had no wish to wake it. Yet even as he thought that, he sensed that not all the powers of this land were asleep.

He realized with astonishment that the stretch of land that they now walked over was not land at all. It was a pathway of corrugated logs, like a bridge over water. Only they were set in mud, covered by slime and slowly decaying like everything else around them. Someone had laid this track. But who? And when? He looked up and saw Hruidgar looking back at him, a gleam in his dark eyes. It was almost like a question, or a challenge. *Did he still want to come this way?*

Brand stepped forward. One hand held the reins of his roan mare, the other was close to his sword hilt. But he went forward, and the hunter turned and stepped carefully ahead also. His hand was near his sword hilt too. If he knew who had built the path, he was not saying.

The hunter led them deeper into the swamp. The army trailed behind, each warrior following in the footsteps of the one before, the whole mass of them, one after another, stepping where Hruidgar had trod.

About them, the alders grew thickly, then thinned, and then grew thickly once more. Sheets of water lay to left and right, sometimes with clumps of swamp grass and weeds and lilies growing through. At other times the water seemed deep as though it were a lake. At yet other times there was ground, seemingly dry and above water level. The hunter led them over this at whiles, but not always. If some land was safe while other land was not, Hruidgar did not explain.

They were deep in the swamp. Brand felt like an intruder into a world in which he did not belong. There was a plop in the water beside him, and then a ripple over the hitherto still surface. Something large, very large indeed, had moved. He saw a glimpse of a creature, shadowy and vast as it turned and twisted in the depths, and then it was gone. Or at least he hoped so.

They climbed a little now. The land became rocky, but lined with moss and slime. Footing was treacherous. The swamp had become small ponds, covered in green algae. Through this maze they walked. But Hruidgar rarely seemed to hesitate. He seemed relieved though to be away from the deeper expanses of water. Or what dwelled within them.

The ground changed. It was dryer, and there was grass here. Brand knew, however, they had not begun to leave the swamp yet. It was too soon. The ponds were fewer. They had in fact become tarns, stone rimmed and dark watered. The hunter kept as far from them as was possible, but ever he found a way forward.

It was hard to tell time in the swamp, for the growth of trees was mostly thick and the sky was obscured. But it was clearer here on the rocky ground, and Brand realized the day was nearly over. Soon, they must find a place to gather together and camp. He whispered as much to the hunter, and the man nodded.

"I know a place," he said. "A good place, if such exists around here." He trod on, and Brand wondered if the army would find its way out of the swamp if something happened to the hunter. But so far, for all the eeriness of the place, he had sensed no great danger. But that meant only that for the most part the creatures that could bring it slept, not that they did not exist.

The hunter led the army to a rocky slope. It was not quite a hill, for there was no such thing within this swamp, but it was as close as they would get.

"Do not drink any water." Hruidgar warned.

It seemed good advice to Brand. They had supplies enough of food and water to last them until out of the swamp, and that would do. There would not be any fires either. There was no such thing as dry wood here.

Brand supervised the establishment of a camp. He was glad at least that all the warriors could be brought together in one place, and at a distance from any water. The rocky slope offered little concealment for anything to stalk them too. Another benefit. Yet he set a watch of roving guards as an outer ring to the camp as well as a closer ring of stationary sentries. This was no place to take any chances. Who knew what was out there? But if anything was drawn to them in the night, the many watchful eyes of the guards should give it pause.

It was a cold dinner. And the men spoke only in hushed tones. Brand walked among them, sharing a word here and a joke there. He was getting to know them. Shorty, Taingern and Haldring did likewise.

The dark grew deep. The night became old, and everyone settled down to sleep as best they could on the hard surface. They slept with their boots on, because it was the sort of place a warrior always wanted to be ready to stand and fight. But the boots also kept the mosquitoes at bay. Against this nuisance the men also wrapped a spare cloak, tunic or cloth of some sort around their faces.

Between the hard surface and the insects, sleep did not come easy. And when it did, they were woken often enough by strange grunts and moans and shrill cries that came from all around. The swamp at night was alive with animals, with hunters and prey and prey that could defend itself. Screams tore the air at whiles, the last breath of some creature that defended itself less well than it needed to. Death was all about them, and the old magic stirred. It was stronger in the dark.

19. The Mists of Prophecy

Brand spent most of the night dozing but never quite asleep. Nearby, other men snored softly. Haldring tossed and turned. And the hunter lay still. He was awake though, and at times Brand thought he saw his dark eyes gleam as they gazed out toward whatever cry had last signaled the final misfortune of some animal.

Dawn finally came, and the army trudged on. The men were scared. A night in this swamp was more than they had bargained for, and in some ways it was worse than a battle. They were trained for that, but they had no idea how to deal with a place where the land itself seemed an enemy.

The rocky ground gave swiftly away to wetlands once more. Again, there was a patch of felled logs that formed a corrugated bridge over stretches of black mud. They were slippery, but they felt secure beneath Brand's boots. He wondered how old the timber was. In places such as this, submerged in water or covered by mud, wood did not rot for decades. Even centuries. He had heard once that timber and even human bodies could be preserved for thousands of years. That was a possibility too. Whatever the case, he did not believe the Duthenor had ever laid this trail. But someone had, and he guessed it was long, long ago.

The hunter raised his arm and pointed. Away in the distance, steam rising from it in a slow-drifting cloud, lay a tarn.

"That," whispered the hunter, "is the home of old Grinder." He smiled then, his sun-browned face a flash of

167

teeth and a glint of dark eyes, and then he led them on once more.

They avoided the place. There was no sign of the legendary creature though, but Brand sensed a presence, alert, brooding and watchful. Even a monster was wary of an army, and as Brand sensed him the thing probably sensed Brand. Sleeping dogs were happy to let other sleeping dogs lie. There was nothing to fight over, no need to stir up trouble.

The hunter came to an alder tree. It was an ancient thing, leaning over and its trunk heavily fissured. Its bark had been scored in places by an axe. Or claws.

"This is as far as I have ever been," Hruidgar told Brand. "But I learned from the old man who showed me the ways of this place that when he was young he found a way out not far ahead. He went that way only once though, and never dared return."

They pressed on. Brand was no longer sure if there was a trail, but the hunter seemed confident of where he walked. Soon, a wailing noise drifted to them, a sound full of the woe of the world. The hunter nodded to himself as though he expected that, and he walked on, his hand gripped tight to his sword hilt.

The alder trees grew thickly here, as though they formed a fence, even, perhaps, had been planted as a barrier. And from the branches hung human heads. Some were mere skulls, but others were fresh and the smell of rotting flesh hung in the air.

Brand moved ahead of the hunter and investigated. He walked slowly, his gaze taking in the scene but also searching out any sign of a trap or ambush.

A slight breeze picked up. All there ever was in the swamp. One of the heads moved, and it moaned. The sound was horrifying, and behind him Brand heard swords being drawn and also the sound of retching. He stayed still, his gaze fixed on the head.

The lips did not move, yet the moaning continued. The head swayed in the breeze, and then its movement lessened as the breeze died down. The air became still again, and the moaning faded to silence.

Brand reached out. Gently he touched the head, sought its mouth with his fingers and withdrew a length of pipe. It was made of a reed, and there were holes in it. The back end was narrowed, perhaps bent by steam to catch the wind and whistle. Tooled leather, with holes in it, slid back and forth over the holes as the head swung in the air. It was a flute and the source of the noise.

He examined the head now, dismantling it. The hair was woven of animal hair, probably from a goat. It was glued to a skull constructed of various animals. Skin and nose and ears were made from thin leather, now rotting.

Brand turned to the men. "These are not real. They are fake, and the noise of the moaning is caused by this."

He threw the flute to Shorty. The little man caught it deftly, shrugged, put his lips carefully to its end and blew. The flute moaned, and he danced a little jig. The men nearby laughed nervously.

"Pass it back through the army," Brand said. "Let everyone see the fakery. While we march."

He gestured for the hunter to lead them forward again. Hruidgar muttered to himself. Had he known what they would find here?

They pressed ahead, finding a gap between the trees. What Shorty had done was no surprise to Brand. He had thrown it to him for a reason. Shorty always had a sense of humor, and that was precisely what the army had needed just then. Laughter banished fear.

But the question hovered in Brand's mind; why had he thrown the flute to Shorty? Had he just known it was the thing to do? Was it his instinct as a leader of men, especially warriors? Or was it what Aranloth had called riding the dragon's breath? How much of his life, of moments just like that, had been blind luck or the operation of some hidden force, some sort of destiny or fate?

The feel of the land subtly changed. Brand sensed the creature known as Grinder out there somewhere, perhaps close enough to watch them. But there was something else too, something older and stronger.

To their right the land dipped into a series of murky lakes, one at the back very large. A gray heron flew overhead, gracefully lumbering, its head turning to the side in midflight as though it were deciding where to land and then thinking better of it. The bird disappeared behind a stand of trees ahead.

To their left the land rose higher into some craggy slopes, strewn with tumbled rock and overgrown with moss and tufted grasses. Ahead, through the stand of trees, was a kind of meadow. There seemed to be good, solid ground there. Green grass grew upon it, and a cottage stood in its center. Smoke rose in a lazy column from a rickety chimney that looked as though it were about to fall into a pile of bricks on the ground.

"The witch!" hissed Hruidgar.

Brand had not seen her at first, but as she stepped out of the cottage and walked toward them he studied her. His magic flared to life, ready. She had power, and she looked as though she had the confidence to use it. An old woman she seemed, an ancient crone. Her hair was lank and bedraggled. Teeth were missing. Warts tufted the skin of her face, and her eyes were rheumy. But they fixed him with a stare that belied her outward appearance. Old she was, but strong.

She came up to him, and Brand bowed, not taking his gaze off her.

"Good morning, lady," he said.

She closed one eye and studied him. "A lòhren is it? Yes and no I'd say. You have the look about you. But not quite."

"A leader of men, at the moment. My name is Brand, and I seek out Unferth."

Sometimes it was best to be direct. She would know who he was and what he intended. And she would know he intended no harm to her. He had made that clear by declaring Unferth his enemy.

She peered at him through her other eye. "Yes, well. I know that. What do you take me for? A stupid old hag?"

"No, lady. You choose to look like one just now, but you could look any way you want."

She looked at him for the first time with both eyes, her bushy eyebrows raised. "Yes indeed. And don't forget it." She laughed then, a cackle suited to her appearance. "In truth," she said, "I *am* old. Very old. But I like you anyway, despite your youth. Doesn't mean I won't kill you though, if it suits my purposes. I'm a bad, bad person."

Brand grinned at her. "I like you too. And likewise."

She regarded him then a moment, and she seemed amused. "You have style, boy. I like it. Because of that I'll tell you something." She dropped her voice to a hoarse whisper that half the army could hear. "You're being followed."

Brand nodded slowly. "I have sensed something. Perhaps it is the ... creature that lives in the swamp?"

The old woman grinned at him, her blackened teeth showing.

"No. Not him. Someone else. *Something* else, summoned from the pit. Something new, and that intrigues me."

She reached out quickly and took his right hand between her own two. Her touch was cold, the feel of her skin like tattered leather. Brand did not flinch. He had a feeling what would come next.

The witch closed her eyes and muttered incomprehensibly to herself. Then her eyes flashed open and they fixed him with a milky stare. Her irises had changed color, and he knew she saw nothing of this world but the world of the future.

"I shall prophesy for you, boy. I have the talent, if you have the courage."

"A man makes his own fate, so tell me the future if you will. If I don't like it, I shall change it to suit me better."

She cackled. "The confidence of youth! Well then, let me see." There was a pause, and then she spoke again. Her voice was different now, less breathy, younger, sure of purpose.

"Ah, yes, the mists pass and I see. You shall succeed in your quest. But you shall fail also. Yes, yes. That is the way of it. And what you want … you shall never have. Oh, but I have seen that so often before. And … this one is new. Who you are is not who you were meant to be."

"Are you done, lady?"

She gave him an irritated look. "Hush, child. There is more. I see a darkness, old as the hills. It sleeps, but it wakens. Your sword shall be broken, but the land will make it new again. I see … I see. Nay, the mists return and obscure it all."

She dropped his hand, and Brand felt for the first time that it was cold as ice. When she had withdrawn her touch, she had withdrawn her magic.

"Aye boy, the mists are cold."

"So it would seem. Thank you for your foretelling."

She looked up at him, her gaze suddenly fierce. "Don't patronize me, child. I'm older and stronger than I look.

And I have the true talent. You think my prophesy is vague and uncertain? You think it made up charlatanry? Well, you will see!"

Her mood shifted again, and she cackled. Brand wondered how sane she was, but looking into her eyes he also wondered how much of all this was an act. Perhaps she really did have the talent. Perhaps she had learned more than she said.

"This has been interesting, lady. But we must march on now. Yet there are dangers in this swamp. Are you safe from the creature who lives here? Will you be safe from that which follows me?"

She pursed her lips, the skin of her mouth wrinkled and fissured. "Ha! I'm safe from the first, safer than all others. As for the second. Well, aye, I am safe from him too. We are much alike. We will walk warily around each other. *You* are what he hunts."

Brand hesitated. "I don't think you're quite as bad as you pretend. Will you help us?"

She grinned at him. "Oh, you overestimate me. I'm a bad, bad person. I've done things that would shrivel your soul. Oh yes, yes I have. You're safe from me, today. But I'll not help you. Nor will I help that which hunts you. I care for nothing outside of this swamp, and you will both be gone soon enough to leave me in peace once more. I offer no help, nor will you ever see me again. I have given of my gift, and that is enough. From time to time I feel the need to do so. If a bird has wings, does it not wish to fly?"

"Then, lady, we shall be on our way. Fare you well."

She did not answer, but she cackled as she turned and walked back toward her cottage. Brand signaled the army forward, and they crossed the meadow in silence. On the far side was another wall of alder trees, and they pressed through it.

They were back in the wetlands, and most were happy for it. Better the swamp than the abode of a witch, yet she had offered them no harm.

The day drew on. At whiles they glimpsed higher ground through gaps in the trees. Again, there was a path of sorts, but probably only one the hunter could find. And though he said he had never been this far before, he seemed to lead them true enough.

By dusk, they reached a strange land of tree ferns and rocky soil. They were higher now, and Brand sensed the swamp stir to life below. He felt also the presence of that which followed him. It was vague, and he could detect little of it. The witch's senses were keener than his own, and he was grateful for the warning.

They came out of the stand of tree ferns, and there was solid ground all around them. It was neither rock nor swampland, but the earthy smell of soil made rich by eons of leaf fall. It was a forest, mostly of oaks, and they had passed through the swamp without harm. It was one danger survived, but Brand felt there were other obstacles ahead, drawing close swiftly, and deadlier yet. He would not sleep soundly again until his task was accomplished.

20. Promises to Keep

The army moved through the growing dark, happy to put distance behind them and the swamp. They were tired, weary to the bone as few of them had ever been before, but they plodded on regardless.

Brand led them now, the hunter moving back into the ranks after a handshake and quiet word of thanks for his work. They climbed gradually uphill, and this meant toward the High Way. But Brand had no intention of traveling that way yet. When they had gone far enough from the swamp, he veered left. There, amid a stand of oaks with a small stream nearby, he finally set a camp.

The men nearly collapsed, but he had walked every step they had, and he knew exactly how tired they were. It was nothing that a warm meal and a good night's rest would not fix, but they had gained much in return. Unferth did not know where he was, and he could move with relative ease. His force was small and quick, and could strike unexpectedly.

It occurred to him that he could attack Unferth himself. His force was not great, but he could pass over the land in secret. He knew the ways. If so, he could strike at Unferth with total surprise. He could possibly kill him, for he would not have all his warriors to hand. But what then? He would be exposed, and he would not have sufficient numbers to hold the hall of his ancestors, the same hall that Unferth now ruled from, should Unferth's captains choose to move against him after their leader's death. And that, they might well do. No, something more was needed yet before he moved directly against the usurper.

The deeper into the Duthgar that he traveled, the better he remembered it. He knew these lands, for he had spent much time here. The districts around this area were the most loyal to his parents. He had hidden here in many farms, and the people who had concealed him had risked their lives to do so. Here, with luck, he could swell his force with warriors and not lift a blade to do so.

With such thoughts, Brand drifted slowly into a restless sleep. The fires burned low, and the army was still. But there were sentries moving about, double the normal amount, for he took the witch at her word: he was a hunted man. And the magician was no doubt behind it.

The next morning they decamped and moved out over a flattish land. This was rare for the Duthgar, which was mostly dominated by the rolling uplands through which the High Way ran, or the long slopes that flanked it.

All the Duthgar was farming country, but this was perhaps the best of it. And though some was pasture for sheep and cattle, most was cultivated fields. They trod a land where wheat and oats and barley were grown, where orchards stood in the sun and vegetables flourished in the deep soil watered by shallow wells.

The farms were smaller here, but more profitable. This showed in the farm houses, some of which were cottages but most double story houses. Some had barns as large as halls in other districts, while others made use of the lower story of the house as a barn in which to winter cattle. This helped provide warmth in the long, cold winters.

This was not country in which an army could easily hide. There were fewer trees and woods, and the farm houses were plentiful, which meant there were the eyes of many owners and farmhands to see them. So Brand made little attempt to hide here. Instead, he marched in the open, and the warriors sang as they marched. Old songs and good songs, stories of the Duthgar of long ago that made them proud of who they were.

There was a road, and Brand took it. Haldring had told him the Callenor did not like it here, and this matched his own experience growing up. The people hated them, and the Callenor in turn hated the flat land coming themselves from an even steeper and hillier country than the Duthgar. Instead of settling warriors here, Unferth taxed it heavily. It was a mistake, but one that Brand was glad of. It supplied the district with more reason to hate the usurper, and more freedom for its youth to join Brand's army.

He saw movement as he marched. Men raced away on horseback, people came out of the houses and watched. Farmhands in fields stopped what they were doing and peered at them. When the road took the army close to people, they clapped and cheered. Rumor flew on falcon wings in the Duthgar. They knew whose army this was, and what it was going to attempt. And they liked it. Not least did they like it when he drew his sword and raised it high. This brought the loudest cheers. Farmers they might be, but they came from a long line of warriors and there were swords and spears and shields in every house, and the youth of the district practiced with them. They were not seasoned fighters, but they were doughty men with passable skill.

Thus the morning passed. "It's a different land here," Taingern observed.

"It is," Brand agreed. "But also, my grandmother on my mother's side came from this district. There's a bond of blood between them and me. And it sings to them."

Taingern gave him a curious look, but Brand did not mind. He was in a curious mood. Almost fey, and he liked it. Danger was behind him as well as ahead. The future was uncertain. But this moment, this feeling he had right

177

now, it was what it was to be alive. Or perhaps that was what Aranloth had called riding the dragon's breath. At any rate, the deeper he traveled into the Duthgar the more at home he felt.

Yet, suddenly cool of thought once more, he knew that in truth he could never come home. His feet might tread the same paths of his youth, his eyes see the same sights, but *he* was different.

The next few hours passed by, and it seemed like weeks. As the road came into settlements Brand greeted people, shook their hand and showed them his sword. At times, he wore the Helm of the Duthenor, but at others he lifted it free of his head and showed his face. The warriors he led continued to sing, and the countryfolk around often took up the song themselves. And wherever he passed, and to whomever he spoke, it always ended the same way. Brand told them he was here to overthrow the usurper, and he needed stout men, men willing to fight and risk their lives for freedom. If there were such men here, let them come with him.

And they came. At first in groups of two or three. Then in troops of twenty or thirty. And finally in their hundreds as word spread. They came now from before the army as well as behind it. There were older men, men who remembered Brand's father and grandfather when they sat in the high chair of the Duthenor. And there were younger men. Men who had no memory of Brand himself, but they knew who he was and what he stood for. And they trusted in him to rid them of Unferth.

Brand's mood changed. It was fey no longer, but cool and rational. These people depended on him. If he erred, they would die. That was responsibility enough to topple a mountain, for the weight of other people's hopes was heavier than the weight of stone.

But he went on. There was no turning back now. And the chances of the world were as great for fortune as misfortune. And he had skill besides. He had led armies to victory. He had outwitted enemies. He had command of magic. Neither he nor his army would be easy prey.

They camped that night outside a great village. Here, the army acquired food and supplies. Brand paid for it, for he brought gold with him, some his own and some from Lord Gingrel's treasury. This endeared him to the district all the more as many armies would simply requisition supplies without payment. And all through the night new recruits arrived.

The next morning saw them marching again, this time to not only cheers and song but the blowing of horns and the throwing of flowers. It was like a celebration, but Brand better understood the truth. Beyond doubt, some of the men with him would be slain in battle. Perhaps even himself. It was nothing to celebrate, and yet a man, nor a whole people, could go through life fearing death. Because if you did not go out to meet the great dark, it would creep into your house and sweep you into oblivion anyway. Celebration was as good a way to deal with truth as denial and fear. Perhaps even better.

While in view of the village, Brand rode his horse. The roan strutted proudly, and it was fitting that the people should see the rightful heir to the kingship with pomp and ceremony. But when he had passed beyond sight Brand dismounted and walked just as the soldiers did.

All the while he could see Haldring grow agitated. Finally she spoke.

"You might as well have written Unferth a letter and told him where you are. What use disappearing in the swamp only to announce your presence to the whole world soon after?"

179

Brand was not upset. This was why he had made her a general – to offer her opinions freely. And there was truth to what she said.

"I don't disagree with you. But Unferth has supporters everywhere. We've vanished from sight of those behind us. They may suspect we went into the swamp, but even so they'll not know where we're headed afterwards. And they'll not try to follow, I think."

She was not mollified. "And what of Unferth's supporters ahead of us?"

"A good question. In truth, I don't know the answer. I suspect Unferth will have already taken steps. And likely he'll have sent a force against me. But that force will be sent to my last known whereabouts. With luck, they'll have gone past us on the High Way. If not, then at least I have gathered a much greater force myself. Either way, I'm now in a position to force a battle if circumstances favor me, or to maneuver away if I so choose."

The army proceeded. They were coming now to a part of the district that Brand knew very well. He had lived here, and it was a strange feeling to be returning, stranger still that he had an army with him.

The flat land was giving way. It rose to hills in the east, thickly forested. He had hunted in those hills, and he had learned to fight there too. Many had been his teachers in the ways of the warrior, but one of the finest had been an old man who lived a secluded life as a hunter trading furs once a year. He had little money, and in truth was no great hunter. But he was a sword master of the highest skill and loved to pass on his knowledge.

There would be no chance to go visit him or see if he were even still alive. The road turned south west, and Brand followed it. But here also was a reminder of his past. These were farms that he knew. It was the fringe of the district, and the land was not as fertile as it had been, but it was still good land and there were good people here. The best. And these at least he might have a chance to see.

They came after a short while to the very farm that he had lived on. The cultivation at the front was now showing the new green shoots of a cereal crop. The soil was good there, and he remembered ploughing it, the smell of the fresh-broken earth filling his nostrils. He had cut hay there also, drying, turning and stacking it. A creek ran down the side boundary, and there he had caught his first fish. Near the cottage stood an orchard of pear trees. These he had pruned in winter and harvested later in the year. They were juicy and sweet.

But it was the cottage that drew his gaze. He had lived under that roof, eaten and laughed there, been protected from his enemies. For a while, it had been home. And the two people who had given him this stood there now before it, watching the army.

Brand signaled a stop. He told Haldring it was time for a break, and to Shorty and Taingern he suggested they have a drink at the farmer's well and see if they had any news. He had to be careful here, for he was hidden from farm to farm in his youth. The people who sheltered him had risked much, and he could do nothing here to reveal the identity of such a family. There could be spies in his army that would eventually report to Unferth.

When they were out of earshot, he told his two friends what was going on. They nodded, understanding.

They came to the well and drew water. From the cottage the two people walked out to meet them. They were older now, in their seventies at least. Harad had silver hair, and his beard was silver-white. Hromling was thin as a whip, her hair gray and her back slightly bent. They came over, hand in hand.

Brand felt a wave of emotion roll over him. These people had been parents to him, at risk of their own lives.

181

Yet he must be careful to give no sign of how he felt for fear they may be targeted by Unferth, and that hurt him.

There were tears in their eyes as they approached. "It's good to see you lad," Harad said.

"And you also. Both of you," Brand answered. "I wish I could hug you, but we must be careful. The army thinks I'm just having a drink."

"We understand," Hromling said. "Unferth has eyes everywhere. But welcome home anyway."

Harad glanced at Shorty and Taingern, and Brand knew what he was thinking.

"These are two friends of mine. I trust them with my life. They'll not say anything."

The old man seemed relieved. "You've done well, Brand. Most folks are lucky if they find one such friend all their lives."

"I've been lucky," Brand agreed. "All my life I've been lucky with the friends I've known."

Hromling wiped tears away from her eyes. Harad reached out and held her hand again, but he kept his gaze on Brand.

"Can you win?" he asked.

"I can win. I *will* win, for you and others like you through the Duthgar."

He saw belief in their eyes. They knew he would not have returned unless he could overthrow Unferth, but hearing it made that belief real. And saying it made it real to Brand as well. He *must* win, and he would. But it would come at a price.

For a while they talked. The two of them had heard rumors from time to time of his exploits. They were proud of him. They missed him. But talk returned to the battle ahead.

"When I had to leave here," Brand said, "I fled in a hurry. I left something behind. By chance, do you still have it?"

They knew what he meant. "We kept it," Hromling said. "We kept it hidden all these years."

"Fetch it for him," Harad said. "He'll need it now. And throw some bread in the bag as well. It will give him a reason to walk away from here with something in his hand."

Hromling hurried away. "Thank you for keeping it," Brand said. "Thank you for everything."

"It was our pleasure, lad. Don't worry about that. You just give Unferth what he deserves, and the world will be a better place."

Brand sensed the curiosity of his two friends, but there was no time to explain to them what Hromling carried as she returned. In her hands was a plain hessian sack. It seemed light in her grip, as though there was no more in it than a few loaves of bread. She gave it to him.

He thanked her, not with the hug that he wished to give, but with a handshake. But he had slipped a gold coin into his palm. He shook Harad's hand as well, and did the same with him.

They surreptitiously pocketed the coins. Two gold coins, as much as the farm would earn in a year, but he wished he could do more for them.

"When this is over, I'll return," he said.

They grinned at him. "We'll look forward to it. Then we can talk properly," Harad said.

"And I'll cook you roast mutton," Hromling offered. "It was always your favorite."

He left then, steeling himself so that his face showed no emotion as he went back to the army. To them it would seem he had passed the time of day with an old farming couple as he drank at their well.

183

The army moved off. Brand led them, his gaze to the front instead of his old home and people he loved. He hated it, but it was for a purpose and there was no sacrifice he would not make for the safety of people who had risked so much for him.

On they went, and Brand set a hard pace. His army was much bigger now, but secrecy and surprise were two of the greatest factors for military success. He may have lost it, but he did not think so.

By nightfall, he had veered back toward the High Way and established a camp. After the army had eaten, and he had carried out his customary walks, talking to sentries and soldiers, he returned to his usual place near the center of the camp. Sighern was there, tired and sleepy, sitting down near a dying fire.

Brand gestured to him to stand up and come over to where the horses were tethered.

"We haven't spoken much, lately," Brand said. "How are things with you?"

"I'm fine. I've been keeping my mouth closed and my ears open. And I've been watching how you lead the army."

"Really? And what have you learned?"

"Keep morale high. Keep your enemies guessing. Strike where you can win, and shun fights you might lose. All the while, gather your strength."

Brand was not sure what to say. The boy *had* been watching. He understood warfare, and politics for that matter, better than most men twice his age. He had a talent for it.

"Good! Keep watching. You just never know when such knowledge will come in handy. But in the meantime, I have a task for you. If you're willing."

"Anything," Sighern answered.

"You shouldn't be so quick to accept," Brand said with a smile. "It could be dangerous."

"Even so," Sighern said solemnly, "I'll do it."

Brand drew out the hessian sack from his saddlebag that Harad and Hromling had given him. He handed it to the boy.

"Don't be fooled by appearances. What's inside this simple sack could get you killed. Men have followed it and died. Unferth would murder you to destroy it. Do you still wish to carry out my task? If not, I'll understand. Just give me the bag back, and we'll speak no more of it."

The boy held the bag close to his chest. "I'm game, whatever it is."

Brand nodded slowly. Shorty was right – the boy had guts.

"Then you should know what it is that you carry. It's the banner of the chieftains of the Duthenor. My father, and his father before him owned it. It has seen war. Men have died beneath its shadow, died for what it represented. Say nothing to anyone, nothing at all. But cut yourself a staff when next we camp."

Sighern took it all in slowly. "And then what?"

"Then, if you wish it, you will be my banner bearer. Do you want to do that?"

"Yes!"

"Good!" Brand said. "Wait though to reveal it. Tell no one, show no one, until I give you the word."

"It shall be as you say," Sighern said. "Thank you, for I know this is an honor normally given to some trusted warrior who has proven his worth."

Brand clapped him on the shoulder. "And so it is. You've proven your worth to me when swords were flashing and death in the air. And in other ways too."

The boy stood taller. "Now what? Where does the army march?"

"We march to war, for I have promises to keep. And though you and I have fought together, the army speeds now to its first proper battle, but if we win, not our last."

Sighern seemed to think about that. He had a quick mind.

"It was safer when our army was smaller, was it not? Now, we'll have to fight and win just to keep the men fed?"

"Indeed so. It was safer when it was just you, me, Shorty and Taingern facing the wolves. What comes next will be worse."

21. It Comes

Harlach sat in the reed chair by her hearth. It felt cold, as it never did in the swamp, and she carelessly tossed another chunk of alder into the fire. It hissed and smoked as the flame took it, for there was more moisture in it than there should have been. It had not been properly cured yet.

She paid no heed to the smoke, ignored that it made her cough. She was always coughing. It was a symptom of living in the swamp. Once, she had lived elsewhere, but that was long ago.

She shifted uncomfortably in the chair. No use thinking about that now. Keep your mind on the present, woman, or the present will kill you.

Had she said that aloud, or only thought it? She was not sure. She spoke to herself often these days. Another symptom of living in the swamp, mostly by herself. And age, of course.

With age came a diminishment of power. Once she would have killed the creature that trod her swamp without pause. Now it came to kill her, and fear gnawed at her empty stomach. She had thought herself a match for it, even now, but the closer it came the more of its power she sensed. It might kill her, but then again, why should it? She would give the thing freely of the information she had. Brand was nothing to her, the fate of the Duthgar even less.

Think, woman. What does it want? The answer came to her quickly. It did not want information, as such. It knew as well as she that Brand had come through, and when. It was following him, and it was gaining on him. It did not need her for that. So, then, it wanted of her power. She had the gift of foresight. It wanted to know *who* Brand was, what he was capable of, what he would do. It did not take him lightly as an enemy, and it wanted to understand him before it struck. In that way, it would guarantee its success. As if the creature needed more advantage than it already had.

The swamp was silent, even though night had fallen. It was here, just outside. She sensed it, sensed its anticipation, and she cursed herself for a fool. It was going to kill her.

She stood, her back paining her as she did so. A knife lay on the table next to her, but that was useless. Her eyes scanned the room. For the first time she noticed what a hovel it was. It was no place for such as she to die.

Anger ran through her. She straightened. She had better weapons than steel with which to defend herself. Whatever devil this was, she would make it scream if she could.

At that moment, the door opened. The creature passed through the threshold, and she knew it for what it was. And fear quelled the rush of pride that moments before had enlivened her.

Tall he was, his every movement one of sublime grace. Black leather clad him, gleaming like polished coal. Armor he wore, chainmail brighter than silver. A helm was on his head, and he removed it, showing eyes that burned like blue fire and white hair, long but tied back with an obsidian ring. His cheekbones were high, his ears pointed and delicate. He was what the Duthenor called an elf, what many others called a Halathrin. But he was of a kind older and deadlier than others in Alithoras. He did not come from Alithoras at all, but from the pit itself.

188

"Speak, witch. And your death will be swift. Defy me, and you will endure torment beyond your imagination."

Harlach laughed. She was scared, but threats had no effect on her.

"Listen, boy. I was steeped in evil before you were spawned under a rock. Time was when you would be on your knees before me, begging to serve. Do not think to frighten me."

The elf looked at her, no sign of what he felt on his face.

"That time is gone, if ever it existed. Tell me what I want to know. Tell me of the warrior called Brand."

"Go to hell!" Harlach cried. She raised her hand. Fire spurted from it, a rush of crimson tongues.

But the elf was swifter. It ducked and rolled and came again to its feet. Its left hand knocked her arm aside, its right gripped her throat and squeezed. And its eyes bored into her own, probing her mind.

She felt its magic then. Her own rose in defense, but the elf swept it away. His eyes filled her vision, and she sensed her mind drawn into them, sensed him sifting through her thoughts and memories.

She resisted. He forced his will upon her. Pain tore at her brain, and she felt blood dribble from nose and ears. She could not stop him. His was the greater power, but hatred gave her strength, and the certain knowledge of her death added to it. If she could not prevail, then she would do something for Brand, some small thing that perhaps would give him a chance at life. Through him, she might yet have vengeance.

While the creature read her mind, she read his and saw how he would attack Brand, saw like pieces on a gameboard the greater strategy that was afoot, and who the true players were. She shuddered at the enormity of it.

189

She went limp, and though pain ripped through her, she allowed the elf to find all that he sought. All, save for one thing alone. This she concealed in her mind within a wall of flame. And when the creature probed it, seeking out what she hid, she turned that flame upon herself, burning out her mind and ending her life.

The last thing she sensed was the chagrin of the elf. He had failed to dig out that final secret, and he did not like it. He was one that could not abide being thwarted. Disappointment rushed through him also. He had been looking forward to tormenting her.

With a bloody smile on her lips, her spirit fled into the great dark.

22. The God-king

Horta did not like to ride. Riding was for peasants. Of old, when he had the need to travel from his estate he did so by sedan chair, the four litter-bearers mindful, for fear of death, to make the experience smooth.

Not so the horse. It jumbled him around like a sack of vegetables on its way to market. It was unfitting, as all of this land, its people and its ways were.

But despite his discomfort, the mount helped spare his arthritic knee and allowed him to cover a great deal of ground, and all the while his gaze never faltered. He looked around him wherever he went, studying the countryside, scrutinizing the ridges and cliff faces and the sides of hills. Always he looked for signs of digging or tunneling, or at least places where such things could be concealed.

And his heart quickened now, for the side of the hill that he approached was a little too steep, and recent rains had eroded soil that exposed rock beneath. The rock was smooth, unnaturally so.

He drew closer. Had his years of searching become fruitful at last? Too long he had wandered around, almost aimlessly, until he had come to an old storyteller west of the Duthgar who told him a tale of an ancient battle. Much was myth, much was a mixture of other stories and other battles far too recent, but some of the details, just enough, rang true. They told of a battle between that ancient race of tyrants called the Letharn, and their great enemies, the Star People. Could that be a twisted name for his own race, the Kar-ahn-hetep, the Children of the Thousand Stars?

He had thought so, and so it had proven. But the site of battle was in the place called the Duthgar, and there he must seek permission of its king to explore. The Duthenor did not let foreigners roam freely. So he had met Unferth, convinced him to allow him to wander the lands in return for his services. Unferth, fool that he was, did not know what a magician was capable of. But Horta had proved it to him, and worked his way into his confidences quickly.

It had not taken long to find the remnants of the battlefield after that. And he knew he was close then, knew his time was coming.

He studied the surface of the newly-exposed rock before him. It was smooth. Almost too smooth and too flat to be natural. His breath caught in his throat. Were there not faint chisel marks in the stone?

Quickly, he retrieved a shovel that was strapped to his saddlebag, and his hands trembled as he began to dig away more dirt.

Long he had looked, and long were the years since the great battle had been fought. More than ten thousand. Up from the south-west his people had come, warlike, their swords glittering in the sun, their armies marching as ranks of gods. Against the Letharn they struck, two mighty empires clashing in a war that spanned a continent. Blood had flowed. Rivers of it. Men fought men, sword clashed against sword, the spells of the magicians contended with the magic of the wizard-priests of the Letharn.

Sweat dripped from Horta's brow, but he felt a cold chill pass through him. He almost thought he had been called to this place, such was the certainty in his mind that he had discovered what he had long sought. And then there was a mark upon the stone. It was a rectangle, nothing within it and nothing without: but it was certainly carved by man and not nature.

His heart leapt. Reaching into dim memory, he drew forth long-forgotten words. It was a simple spell, primitive even. But it was known only to him and his kind. He uttered the words and passed his hand over the stone. And waited.

Of old, the kings of his people built mighty tombs. They were massive things, fortresses of stone, guarded by men, magic and traps. The dead kings rested in eternal peace, their bodies preserved so that they might keep their form in the afterlife. But the great king, the greatest to have ever lived, and the last of the Kar-ahn-hetep, he had no such tomb prepared for him. He was yet young when he set out in war against the Letharn. He was yet young though he led his warriors for ten years of war, surging against the enemy. And the enemy had fallen back. A thousand miles they withdrew, ceding land after land, country after country.

But what fate gave fortune stole back. The Letharn strengthened their positions, and held them. Then they began to creep forward, retaking lands they had lost. The great king could not abide this. West he went with one of his armies, and then north. He tried to catch his enemies by surprise, but was surprised in turn.

Battle followed, mighty and terrible. He who should have ruled the world was slain. But his loyal magicians saved his body from the enemy, and the army fought a fighting retreat. So the secret lore told.

Horta held his breath. The stone grew slowly darker under his impatient gaze, and then paled. The rectangle turned into a cartouche, what the ancients termed a *shenna*. Within it, the sign of the great king sparked as though the sun shone through the stone itself. Three stars, one

193

ascendant over the other two, glittered momentarily and then blinked out.

He had found what he was looking for. No more was needed. He felt the weight of destiny on his shoulders, felt the call of his blood. It was for *this* that he was born. It was his life's work, nearly come to fulfillment, but not quite yet.

This was a tomb. Not the great tomb that should have existed for such a king, but a hiding place, a place to preserve his body from the enemy and from time itself.

The army had fled, pursued by the Letharn. The magicians took the body of the king, and by their arts of magic and the science of their lore, they preserved it. But death was upon them, for the enemy pursued relentlessly.

In the night, the magicians led a hundred men from the army. They excavated a tomb and hid it; a place safe from the enemy. There they laid the king to rest with what rites they could, and preserved a memory of their deed. So Horta had learned, for he was descended from one of those magicians.

Yet nearly all of the hundred men were killed. None could know the secret of the king's last resting place and live, for treasures were buried with him, and he himself was a treasure greater than them all. But even kings had enemies, *especially* kings, and these would seek to destroy him if they could, to deprive him of his enjoyment of the afterlife by maiming his earthly remains. But the secret story came down, even to Horta and others like him. They *all* searched, but *he* was the finder.

The magicians of ancient days were mighty. After the great battle, their empire crumbled around them and their arts fell into decline. Yet, in the peak of their powers, the magicians were supreme, and they could preserve the dead in a state very close to living. And the years would not have destroyed this.

Upon that knowledge, a prophecy was born. The king would be resurrected. The king would live again. The god-king, for such he was called, would return when the Kar-ahn-hetep were at their lowest ebb, and he would lead them to glory and conquest again. And now, the Letharn were no more. Who would oppose them as they swept across land after land, their swords red with blood and victory lighting their eyes?

Horta shuddered. What glory would be his if he made this come to pass? What rewards would the god-king bestow upon him? What power would he not command as the first lieutenant of a god, returned from death to rule the world?

And Horta knew he *could* bring this to pass. He knew the spells. He knew forbidden rites that even the ancients had shunned and feared. For he was mighty also, perhaps the greatest to have lived since those far off days of old. And he was of the house of the god-king, and blood called to blood. It mattered not that the laws of magic forbade what he intended. Prophecy was stronger than law.

But this he could not accomplish all at once. The god-king would be vulnerable after so long a sleep of death. He would need aid and succor until his strength grew. He would need an army to protect him, and to fulfill his will. It would not be fitting to wake him without servants.

Horta frantically worked with his shovel, piling dirt back over the stone. The time was not yet right to wake the god-king. First, he must summon an army loyal to his own house so that they might destroy any opposition. They must clear the way before the god-king came.

And Brand was a threat, and even Unferth. But the first would die soon, and the second would fall to unexpected war. The Duthgar would be ruled by the Children of the Thousand Stars. It would form the cradle for an ancient civilization to be born anew.

Horta hastily retied his shovel to the saddlebag and leaped upon his horse. He must send word back to his people, at least to his own sept. They would flock to his call. The Duthgar would fall, and the god-king would rise and have an army at his command. Small it would be at first, but it would grow. And the world would tremble.

23. I do a Man's Work

The time of skulking was over.

Brand veered west toward the High Way. The army followed, greater by far than it was before. Battle drew near, and lives would be lost. It was all on him, and that was pressure that made for poor decision making. So he did not think about it. At least, he distanced himself from it as best he could. Yet he must also keep it in his thoughts to some extent. Otherwise, he would forget that his choices had become life and death for other people.

It was a tight balance, the kind that a person needed in order to walk a narrow mountain trail with a vast drop into oblivion on the left, and a steep hill of snow to the right that could gather into a deadly avalanche. And all the while the trail beneath their boots was treacherous with ice.

The army passed through an empty land, and there seemed no sign of people, no indication of habitation. But the Duthgar was like that. It was a settled land, kept and cultivated, but still many parts were not. These were wild and remote areas, notwithstanding that at any time a farming district could begin nearby.

But he knew this land, remembered it well. Here there were rolling fields of grass and clusters of trees. Soon, when they neared the road, the farms would begin again.

He called a halt a mile or so short of where they started. The men settled for a rest, and Haldring approached him.

"It's soon, is it not, to stop for a break?"

"It is, but I need news. What's been happening? What has Unferth done and where is his force? He'll have sent one to defeat me, of that I'm sure."

"Really?" she countered. "How do you know that he hasn't drawn his forces to him and decided to wait for you to attack. That way his men would be better rested and closer to their supplies of food."

Brand did not think so at all, but he could not fault her argument. She might even be right.

"Taingern? Shorty? What do you think?"

Shorty gave a shrug. "What does it matter either way? Thinking about it won't change anything."

"What do you say, Taingern?"

"I think he'll try to hunt you down. He'll have sent an army, but where will it have gone? It's probably bypassed us already and traveled along the High Way further north, back where we came from."

"I hope so," Brand said. "But we know nothing for sure, and though knowing may not change anything, I'd rather know than not. So we're back where we began. It's time to get news. The army can wait here until I have it."

Brand looked around him, ready to pick someone to move forward into the farms and gather news. But Sighern had heard the conversation and stepped forward quickly.

"I'll go," he said.

Brand hesitated, uncertain.

Shorty clapped the boy on the shoulder. "You're game lad, but I think you're too young for this."

"I may be young, but I do a man's work. You can't deny that."

Shorty nodded slowly. "No, I'll not deny that. You do a man's work. You fight like one anyway. Better than many."

Brand felt everyone's gaze on him, the boy's most of all. Responsibility was heavy on him, and deaths would be on him soon as well when battle was joined. And he could not send a boy into danger, no matter how great his courage. The answer would have to be no, but what he said instead was yes, and it surprised him more than anyone else.

Sighern looked proud, and Brand did not have the heart to take it back, no matter that he did not understand what had just happened. Twice now this had occurred, and it worried him. Was this what it was to ride the dragon's breath? To have some sort of fate or destiny guide him, even force him, down a path that he did not understand? Or was it his own instinct surfacing and taking control?

But the decision was made now, and Brand accepted it. Quickly he explained to Sighern what was required, and then the boy was gone, walking off into the countryside with the gaze of the whole army upon him.

Haldring looked grim. "You've sent him into danger," she said. "He's too young for the task and many others would have been better suited."

Brand did not know what to say, so he just voiced his thoughts. "I think you're right. But there's *something* about him. He's everything a Duthenor should be, and more. He is, perhaps, even made for greatness. There's a destiny upon him."

Haldring did not look happy, but she said no more. Nor did Taingern and Shorty, but he felt their gazes upon him, burning with curiosity. Those two had seen this before, but he had no answers to give them.

Sighern walked at a fast pace. He was young, and this was an adventure of a type he had not believed possible just a short while ago. It gave him strength. That Brand believed in him was everything. He was a hero, and a man worthy to follow. And Sighern knew he would follow him anywhere, undertake any task asked of him.

He had a sword belted at his side. He knew how to use it. He had the trust of Brand, and the responsibility to do the right thing for the army. News was needed, and he would gather it. Who better than someone his age? He would not be taken for a warrior, and people would speak freely to him. An older man asking questions would draw suspicion, and the supporters of Unferth were everywhere. But a boy? They would not think him a scout for an army. He grinned to himself and pushed on. All was right with the world.

He soon passed a few farms, but they seemed small and there was no one in sight. It would be better to move up to the High Way where he could find out what was needed from those who would have heard or seen things first hand.

It did not take him that long to reach it. Straightaway he noticed that the grass of the road was trampled by the passage of many feet. It would take an army to cause so much damage. But how many men were there and which way had they gone?

He had no answer to the first question. He would have to talk to someone for that. But studying the tracks he soon realized they headed north, back were Brand had come from.

Sighern set off on the road following them. It might be that he had already discovered all that Brand needed. But he would be questioned when he returned and it would be better to be able to give numbers. How big was the army sent against them? Brand would want to know that. And also how long ago it had come through here. The tracks looked quite fresh to him, but again it would be better to get confirmation.

Ahead, a village came into view. It was quite small, little more than a gathering of huts. As Sighern approached, he thought of how best to go about his task. He could just ask anyone what he wanted to know, but the best people for him to speak to would be boys of his own age.

Just before the village, he saw a small creek running south-eastward. It was more a gulley than a creek, but it grew bigger as it went and other gulleys joined it. Further along, tall trees overshadowed its banks. If he lived here, that's where he would go to fish and hunt and while away the time. And if he were sheepherding, he would find a paddock close by. He bet the boys of this village would think the same way, and he turned his feet off the road and toward it.

He walked downhill, now following the little creek. There was a well-beaten path here. He came across women washing clothes, and he stayed clear of them. Further along, he heard the bleating of sheep. This was more promising, and sure enough there was a lad there his own age who stood up from where he had been sitting with his back to a boulder, his shepherd's crook in one hand and a curious look in his eyes.

"Who are you?" the boy asked, his tone neither hostile nor friendly. It was what Sighern expected.

"I'm not from around here." His own reply was neutral also. And he left the other wanting more. Obviously, he was not from around here, but he left the explanation hanging.

The other boy looked at him, and Sighern knew what he saw. A boy like himself, but one who carried a sword and traveled the Duthgar. Not old enough to be a warrior, and yet old enough for the other things.

The boy made up his mind, and stuck out his hand. "I'm Durnloth."

"Sighern."

"Ah, that's one of the old names."

Sighern let go his hand. "I was named after my grandfather. And he after his. It's a long tradition."

Durnloth heaved himself up to sit on the boulder. Sighern followed his lead. Sheep grazed placidly in a small paddock to their left and Durnloth eyed them momentarily before he spoke again.

"So, you don't look quite old enough to be a warrior. What are you doing here?"

"Maybe not quite yet. But soon. Mum and dad were killed by raiders. Since then, I've been wandering. I hear an army came through here. Maybe I'll join them."

Durnloth looked at him with sympathetic eyes, but he only spoke of the army. "I'd stay away from them. That was the king's army. He who should not be king, anyways. They went through fast, and cleaned out most of our food, without paying. Besides, they'll be fighting soon. You can bet on that."

Sighern answered cautiously. "I may not like them, but if they kept me around, even to run errands and messages it would be good for me. Three meals a day in the army, they say."

"If it's work you're after, some of the farmers around here might take you on. But you'd earn more in the army. And if you can use that," he indicated Sighern's sword, "they just might let you fight and pay you a full wage. Maybe."

"I can use it. When did the army come through?"

"Yesterday morning it was. Quite early, but they'd been marching a good while already. They sure were in a hurry, trying to catch Brand by surprise, we reckon."

"Do you think they will?"

"Hard to say," the boy answered. "All we hear are rumors, and one has barely spread before the next overruns it. No one knows where Brand is, or what he's doing. Only that his army is growing and he's coming for Unferth."

"Maybe I should join *his* army."

202

"Better him than Unferth. But Unferth pays better, I hear. Then again, a dead king pays no wages."

"Do you think Brand will win?"

"He's the true king. A hero in foreign lands, they say. He'll win, or he'll die. One or the other."

"How big was Unferth's army?"

"Two thousand men. So my dad tells me. They took his finest horse, and he was in a right temper about that. But he wasn't saying anything. Not until after they left. Then he swore the roof down, mum says."

Sighern was shocked. Two thousand men was more, much more than he expected. Brand would want to know that. Suddenly, he felt anxious. It was time to be gone from here, time to get back to the army.

He jumped off the boulder, and the other boy did likewise.

"I'd better hurry," Sighern said, "if I'm going to have any chance of finding either army."

They shook hands again. "Good luck," Durnloth offered. He seemed as though he meant it, but Sighern knew that Brand needed it more than him. He hurried away.

Brand sat with a small group of men, playing dice and getting to know them. His life would depend on them soon enough, and theirs on him. But he excused himself when he saw Sighern hurry out of the woods.

The boy emerged, walking quickly but with a telltale swagger to Brand's eye. Moreover, he held in his hand a fresh-cut pole for the banner he would carry.

Brand met him before he reached the camp. He was eager for news, and despite the boy's surprise information that an army of two thousand men had been sent to defeat them, Brand was pleased. The enemy had traveled past them, and that gave Brand several advantages despite being outnumbered. Above all, the enemy would now have to react to *him*. That was vital, if he could find ways to turn it to his advantage. And he would.

"You've done well," Brand told him after Sighern had finished his report. "Very well indeed."

News spread after that. Brand was happy for the size of the enemy to be discussed, for he did not believe in lying to his troops. With the news also went his confidence that they would win.

Dusk settled soon after. Brand told Sighern to keep the banner close. It would be unfolded soon, possibly even tomorrow. "Hold it proudly when the moment arrives lad, for the Duthgar is coming to a time of change. You, and those who follow the banner, will be a part of history."

"And against whom will we march?" Sighern asked. "The army that tries to find us, or Unferth himself?"

It was a good question. "I'll think on it overnight."

24. Fortune Favors the Bold

The next morning was an early start. And it would be both a long and hard day.

Brand took the army up toward the High Way. The men seemed eager. They were outnumbered, but they were confident nonetheless. They had outwitted the enemy repeatedly. But Brand himself was reserved. His tactics were successful so far, but when armies clashed people died and hopes burned away like smoke on the wind.

His three generals came to him. They all knew what approached was a pivotal decision.

"What's it to be, Brand?" Taingern asked gently. He understood better than the others what emotions would be running through someone's mind at a time like this. Brand knew his capacity for empathy was enormous.

"My heart yearns to turn south when we reach the road and strike at Unferth. He would be unprepared, believing the army he sent would have found and engaged me. And he is the real enemy, the one that must be defeated."

"But?" Shorty said.

"But Unferth has a magician in his service, one of great power. I'm wary of him. Therefore wisdom dictates that I turn north, defeat the army of two thousand sent against me with one of one thousand two hundred. This I believe I can do, and in the doing send a chill of fear through Unferth and his remaining forces. What would be disaster for him would be a resounding call to arms for others. The Duthenor would flock to me then by the thousands. And

I could confront Unferth, and his magician, with a much larger army."

"There's yet a third choice," Haldring said.

Brand sighed. "Yes, I could continue as I have been, and move by stealth, fight skirmishes and grow my army slowly. But though that seems the safest course of action, I believe it to be the most dangerous. At some point my enemies would pin me down, and I would have to react. But by attacking myself, either north or south, I have the initiative and an element of surprise. They are unprepared, and must react to *me*."

They approached the High Way, and the decision was upon him.

"What's it to be then?" Shorty asked.

Brand's mare trod the first steps onto the High Way. "It grates my heart, but Unferth will have to wait." He led the roan to the right. "North it is. And speed is important. I want to take the enemy by surprise. Spread the word that this shall be a quick march."

Down the High Way they moved. He saw the marks of passage of their enemy, and allowed himself a slight smile. By now they would have realized that he was not where they had thought. They would have heard rumor and gossip. They would imagine him lying in wait in every wood, hiding behind every ridge. They would fear that he had slipped away to wreak havoc elsewhere in the Duthgar. They would feel foolish, and frightened and angry. None of these things were good for morale.

The army moved quickly. Here and there men from tiny villages joined them. Should they win the upcoming battle, that trickle would turn to a flood as they moved back toward the richer and more populated lands closer to Unferth and the seat of power in the Duthgar.

Brand led the way, though there were scouts ahead and to the sides. He had the advantage of surprise, and he was not going to lose it. Speed was essential now, for already supporters of Unferth may have seen them and ridden ahead to take word to the enemy.

On the army hastened, and the road helped them. It was smooth, wide and well turfed. It was ancient too. According to legend, older by far than the Duthgar. He believed it. He had traveled the roads of the Letharn before. They built things well and built them to last. Few of the Duthenor would have heard of them, but he had traveled more widely than they. But why they had built it and to where had it led? Its other name, the older name from the Duthenor legends though not nearly as old as the road itself, was Pennling Path. That sounded like a Duthenor name, but he did not think it was.

Shorty leaned in toward him, keeping his voice low. "Are we still followed by … by whatever it is that follows us?"

"I can still feel it. Like an itch in my back. I don't know if it's any closer though. I can't tell much at all. The old woman had a better sense for it than I."

"Well, we'll be ready for it if it comes." Taingern, close on his other side, nodded grimly.

"Actually," Brand said. "I'm going to send you two ahead. I'll deal with whatever that thing is if it shows itself. We still have few horses, and none of the quality of yours."

He could see that they did not like that, but he had an army with him. He thought he would be safe. "I need you to talk to the scouts, to get ahead of them and scout yourselves. The enemy is out there, likely returning toward us by now. I want word of them as swiftly as may be."

They were reluctant, but they understood the need. They trotted off, wary now for what they did was dangerous. They worried for him, but he worried for them.

It turned out to be a good decision. Hours later they returned, the flanks of their horses frothed with sweat. They had ridden hard.

They drew their horses to a halt before Brand. "The enemy is ahead," Shorty said.

"How far?" Brand asked.

"Five miles at least," Taingern said. "And the lad's information was correct. We estimate their number at two thousand."

Brand remained dispassionate. A commander must be so at all times, and men were watching him. He must show neither excitement, surprise, anger or anything other than quiet confidence. He set the tone for the army, and he knew it.

Almost casually, he gave orders. The army encamped where it was, on the middle of the road. It was as good a place as any to force a battle, for the land was flattish in this spot with a slight advantage of slope. Any more advantage than that, and the enemy might not attack, and this Brand wanted them to do. The enemy was marching and caught by surprise. They would be tired and worried. His army would have the benefit of rest and a feeling of superiority despite their smaller numbers. They had outsmarted and outmaneuvered their opponents.

Brand studied the land, thinking. Well to the right, it dropped down a steep slope. The enemy would not veer out that way and come at him up the hill. Nor was there cover for any sort of strike force to secretly come up that way to try to create chaos while the main army approached from the front.

To the left, the ground dropped down into a tangled wood. This was some distance away. Again, he did not think the enemy would venture that way, but he sent scouts there to watch. Should the enemy come, they would be observed and have to attack uphill.

Haldring seemed to read his thoughts. "They'll come straight at us," she said. "With their greater numbers they'll try to push us back, disrupt our formation and then overrun us."

"Like a bull through a gate," Shorty added.

Brand thought they were right. He ordered his best troops forward, those with battle experience and those who were strongest. He would stand in their ranks, offering a target to the enemy and a rallying point to those less experienced in his own army. If they held against the first charge, the ranks of less experienced men behind them would gain in confidence.

And there was one more thing to do, and this he knew would raise morale. Timing was everything in war, and he had saved it for a moment such as this.

He glanced at Sighern. "It is time."

The boy knew what he meant. He retrieved the bag that held the banner. Slowly, reverently, he drew the cloth out and tied it by loops on its edge to the pole. Then he unfurled it and held it high above his head.

The cloth rolled back and a gust of wind stiffened it. Brand cried in a loud, clear voice so that all in the army could hear him.

"Behold! The banner of the chieftains of the Duthenor is with us. It is our banner of old. The same under which our fathers fought and their fathers before them. It has never seen defeat in battle!"

The wind gusted again, rippling the white cloth of the banner so that it shone bright in the afternoon light. Upon it, all in vivid red, was a dragon. Its four muscled legs, clawed and poised, seemingly walked as the cloth ruffled. It's long body and barbed tail undulated. Its head, held high and proud as it seemingly looked to the side, was royal as a king's and the eyes set in that head surveyed the field, two ovals of white gleaming to match the background.

"The Dragon of the Duthgar!" called some of the men, astonished, for it had not been seen since Brand's father was killed.

"The dragon! The dragon! The dragon!" men began to chant. They beat the sides of their swords against their shields also, raising a tumult that carried far. It was the music of war, the building up of fervor, the raising of the battle spirit of warriors. Brand felt it stir in him also, felt it fire his blood. But he knew also that it meant death for some, perhaps all. Whoever fell today would fall in his name. And he did not like it.

The men kept chanting. Sighern looked serious as he shifted the pole about so that the breeze best caught the banner. Haldring was looking at Brand, her gaze unreadable, but the fair skin of her cheeks was flushed and her eyes bright with emotion. Shorty and Taingern appeared normal. They had seen this type of thing before, and it was to them he spoke.

"Quickly," he said. "There are perhaps fifty warriors with horses here. Take them down into the forest. There will be paths there. Travel wide, and circle around the enemy. Come at them from their rear when they are engaged with us."

Shorty seemed surprised. "This is a … dangerous battle. Are you sure you want Taingern and me away from your side?"

By *dangerous* Brand knew he meant that they might well all die. "I'd always rather have you by my side, but there's need for this. Fifty is only a small force, but the skill each of you have with a blade is worth several men each, and your experience will be needed to judge when to intervene. Too early will achieve nothing, as will too late. Go swiftly, and go with good luck!"

210

He was sorry to see them go. They would be needed here too, but they could not be in two places at once.

"Was that wise?" Haldring asked. "We're already outnumbered, and if the enemy breaks through on the first attack, we're finished.

Brand did not disagree. "Fortune favors the bold, Haldring. And we'll need boldness to win here. Should we survive the first charge, they'll still come against us again and again and try to wear us down. We have the advantage of rest and morale. They have the advantage of numbers. I want one more thing on my side, and a well-timed attack to their rear will give it. The enemy will not have scouts behind them, so Shorty and Taingern will be able to loop around and approach from the rear unseen."

"You may be right," she said. "But fifty men here might make the difference between holding the line and defeat."

It was true, and he knew it. But he could not do both. Anyway, the decision was made.

Soon after the first scouts of the enemy were seen. The army would not be that far behind them. The day was wearing away, but before it was done battle would have been joined and a victor decided.

Haldring echoed his thoughts. "It will not be long now," she said quietly.

25. The Blood of Heroes

Brand watched as the enemy came into view. He was alert, but showed no sign of alarm. He may as well have been studying the sky for hints of tomorrow's weather as watching two thousand men march toward him, their swords eager for his blood. Thus the commander of an army must appear, or one man in a duel with another. Confidence was an act. Lack of fear in the face of danger was stupidity.

The enemy ran scouts before it. They were on the road, wary and watchful. They crossed the open farm lands and forest to the side. If they found sign of the passing of fifty horsemen earlier, Brand saw no indication of it. Taingern and Shorty were skilled warriors. They would have gone wide, beyond the range of footmen. That was one of the reasons why Brand sent cavalry, if fifty mounted men could be called such.

He was used to greater armies than these, to forces of tens of thousands and to ranks of spearmen and archers, but not to higher stakes. The outcome would alter the lives of an entire people. And just now, he knew that the success or failure of Taingern and Shorty would determine who won the day. They were the unpredictable in the battle to come. It was always so in any conflict. The masses did the job expected of them while the few who surprised often turned the tide. A skilled general waited for those moments and took advantage of them.

The enemy rumbled to a stop hundreds of paces away. This was a dangerous moment, because all depended on them coming forward. Brand did not want to delay battle.

That would give Unferth time to send more forces against him. He needed a victory now, clean and quick. If the enemy did not attack, he must attack it. This he would do, if he had to. But better they came to him, tired from marching and overconfident of their numbers.

Nothing happened. The moment was passing, and the longer they delayed the less likely they would attack.

"Why do they hesitate?" Haldring asked.

"I don't know, but if they do not come of their own volition, I will lure them."

"How?"

"Watch, and we shall see what sort of man commands the enemy."

Brand signaled for Sighern to come forward with him. He ordered also that his roan mare be brought forward and a horse for his banner bearer. This was done, and they trotted toward the enemy.

"Hold the flag high," he instructed Sighern. "Let them see it clearly."

As the two riders approached there was movement and commotion in the enemy ranks. These would be Callenor soldiers to a man, but they knew the banner of the chieftains of the Duthenor. It had flown in victories against them in days of old. And they knew also the stories of its origin. It was one thing to hear that Brand had returned, the rightful chieftain. It was another to see him in person, heralded by such a flag.

Two riders approached from the enemy. One would be its general, the other was his own banner bearer. This banner was white also, but upon it was the black talon of a raven: the mark of Unferth and a symbol the Callenor held as dear as the Duthenor did the dragon.

The two groups did not meet in the middle of the space between the armies. They merely came forward part way before their hosts to speak with their opponents, albeit

213

over a distance that required shouting. This was good to Brand's mind, because he wanted his words heard by all the enemy and not just the general. This would help to influence them.

Brand knew the general. He had met him once, long ago as a child. He was one of Unferth's trusted retainers.

"Greetings, Ermenrik," Brand proclaimed. "Have you come forth to offer your surrender?"

The other man laughed. "I think not. I offer you the chance to surrender instead. You are outnumbered near two to one."

Brand grinned. "I am not a fool, general. There is no surrender for me. Unferth wants me dead. That is the simple truth. So, why do you hesitate to carry out his orders? Are you scared of the rightful ruler of the Duthgar? Could it be that since last we met, I have grown from a boy into a warrior and you have fallen into decrepitude? You don't look so young, anymore."

The other man did not laugh at that. He had been called a liar in front of his men. They knew as well as he that Unferth wanted Brand dead. And though they were the enemy, it was because Unferth was their lord rather than that they were bad men. They liked the truth, and justice, as much as the Duthenor.

"You are not the rightful lord, boy. The world turns and the chances of fate give as well as take. Unferth is king of the Duthgar, and I do his will. But this is my promise to you. If you surrender, I *will* take you to him. Mayhap he will show you mercy."

"Interesting words, Ermenrik. The words *chances of fate* mean different things to us. To you, that *chance* meant wealth and ease and a life of comfort. To me, it was the murder of my parents." Brand paused, allowing his words to have weight, and then he continued. "And tell me, Ermenrik, were you there that night? Were you one of the

214

ones that killed a man and his wife? Murdered them? Is their blood on your hands?"

Ermenrik tightened his grip on the reins of his horse. "Enough!" he yelled. "I have not come here to bandy words with an exile and outlaw." He turned his horse and rode back toward his host, but Brand was not done.

"If you will not speak because my words cut, murderer, then how will you dare face me with blades of steel? You are a cur, a lapdog to a traitor unworthy of the men he rules. A king, he calls himself? He is no more than a pig in a muddy sty with a crown of filthy straw."

Ermenrik did not slow the pace of his horse or offer a reply. But his back stiffened and Brand knew his words had struck home. He looked across at Sighern, and saw the boy's eyes were wide. Then he turned his own mount and returned to the army.

Haldring met him. "Well," she said. "You know how to stir the pot when you want to. You've made him mad enough to attack us just by himself, I think."

Brand winked at her. "Words make sharper weapons than steel. Now, let's just hope he's not smart enough to wonder why I provoked him."

Brand dismounted and asked a warrior to lead his and Sighern's mount to the rear of the army. Then he turned to the front once more and studied the enemy.

There seemed to be a debate of some kind, for there were several figures gathered round Ermenrik, and there was much gesturing. But whatever the conversation entailed, orders were soon given. The men about Ermenrik dispersed, and the army began to move.

The Callenor came forward, a shrill horn blaring wildly, and the clamor of sword on shield came with them. Brand had achieved his aim. Now, he must hope that his tactics proved successful.

His own army was silent. The Duthenor did not bother to make noise or blow horns to scare the enemy. They trusted to their steel and the skill of their arms instead. And yet there was nervous tension within them that must be released.

The enemy ranks came close now, gathering into a trot as they came.

"The dragon!" cried Brand.

The Duthenor had been waiting for this. It was the battle cry that their ancestors had voiced, and they took it up.

"The dragon! The dragon! The dragon!"

Arrows were loosed from both armies. They flickered and slivered through the air. Brand gave a command, and the men raised their shields. The volley of arrows failed. Neither side had many bowmen.

Next, the long spears were thrown. This had less effect than the arrows. It was by sword and shield and the hearts of men that this battle would be won or lost.

Brand waited. He stood in the middle of the front rank. He was both a target for the enemy, and a rallying point for his own men. Of Ermenrik, he saw no sign.

The shield wall felt strong about him, and Brand breathed deep of the air. The noise of the trotting enemy was loud now, their cries fierce, the whites of their wide eyes gleaming.

The two forces came together in a roaring crash. Swords flashed. Shields resounded. Men cried and screamed and yelled. Like an ocean wave smashing onto the shore the enemy swarmed and crowded, seeking to move further, deeper.

The Duthenor were forced back a pace. Then two. Haldring, locked in close by his left side, killed a man with a sudden jab. Brand flicked his blade at just the right moment and tore open the throat of a burly warrior, his red beard bristling beneath his helm. Blood soaked it now.

The dead men fell. More died around them. Others took their place, coming forward through the ranks to fill the gap.

Slowly, the wave of enmity lessened. The Callenor came on, but the Duthenor held them back. The initial momentum had been diffused. This gave heart to the Duthenor but stole it from the enemy.

But the battle was far from done. The enemy had claimed no swift victory as they hoped, but their numbers were yet the greater.

The man to Brand's right fell, an axe forcing its way through his helm to bury itself in his skull. Brand cut the attacker's hand off as he tried to pull back the axe. The man wheeled away, screaming as he disappeared into his own ranks. He would not live unless a healer tended him swiftly.

A warrior pushed forward into the empty place in the line beside Brand, filling the gap. Behind, the shadow of the Dragon Banner fell over him. Sighern was where he was supposed to be, marking the place where Brand stood. And the enemy came against him, again and again. Callenor warriors almost seemed to fight among themselves to reach him, as though there were a prize for killing him. And well there might be. Unferth might have offered one. But this was for the good. The focus of the attack was on him, and where he stood. But this was the strongest part of the shield wall. If it held, and it was so far, the rest was safer.

A horn blew at the back of the enemy ranks. There was movement among the Callenor, and spearmen came forward. Ermenrik was trying something new.

Through the ranks they came, and men gave way to them. They reached the front, spears lowered, and thrust forward. The jabs were fast, and they could be delivered with more power than a sword thrust. Yet they were less agile.

"Forward one step!" Brand commanded. His call was taken up and repeated along the ranks of his men. They shuffled forward, and pressed the spearmen back.

But the spearmen were not done. The maneuver had taken them by surprise, for they required more room than swordsmen, and they were crammed. But they regrouped and pressed forward again, and this time it was the Duthenor line that buckled in several places.

A spear rammed at Brand's foot, and he lowered his shield to block it. At the same time another warrior drove his spear at Brand's face. He twisted, and the long blade smashed into the side of his head. The Helm of the Duthenor rang, and Brand stumbled and fell to the ground. In a frenzy, the enemy pressed forward to try to kill him.

Haldring threw herself down before him, her own body protecting his and her shield held before the both of them. And then Sighern leaped forward without a shield. In his left hand he still held the banner, but in his right he gripped a blade and it flashed and stabbed furiously.

A spearpoint gashed the boy's right side, but then Brand surged up again. Haldring rose with him. Together they reformed the line, allowing Sighern to move back.

Brand retaliated. He was upset at himself for his error, and angry that two people might have died to save him. He thrust his shield at the enemy, and the silver blade of his ancestors flashed and killed.

The Callenor stepped back before him, and Brand shouted. "Forward two steps! For the dragon!"

All along the line the shout went up, and the Duthenor tried to surge. In places the Callenor line rebuffed them, but in others it was pushed back two paces. And then, seeing their line fall back in many places, even those lengths of the Callenor line that had held their ground fell back to form one line again.

From behind him, Brand heard a message relayed by a warrior. "Brand! The enemy is sending a force to attack our left flank!"

Brand could not look back, but he raised the tip of his sword high to signal that he had heard. It was what he had feared, for the enemy's greater numbers allowed them to attempt it. But there was nothing he could do, not directly, and he knew the men on the left flank would form a shield wall and hold firm. As best they could.

He gambled, and shouted another order. "Forward march! The dragon attacks!"

All about him, up and down the line, the Duthenor and Callenor strove against each other. The spearmen were falling back, the tactic proving unsuccessful, and swordsmen replacing them. But if now the Duthenor could gain momentum and break the enemy, the attack on their left flank would falter. Yet it was a roll of the dice, and he knew it.

What would have happened, Brand did not know. But he knew he was right to place trust in Taingern and Shorty, for even as the Duthenor rallied to his call and tried to press forward, he sensed the battle shift.

There was turmoil in the enemy ranks. A commotion grew in the rear and spread. Above even the shout and din of battle he heard a swift thunder of hooves and knew that the fifty horsemen he had sent out had finally attacked. Their timing, or rather the judgement of the two men that led them, was perfect.

The thrill of battle surged through him. The chance of victory fed it. "Attack!" he roared. "Attack!"

And the Duthenor pressed forward. Their shields barged against the enemy's shields, their swords stabbed

219

and their throats voiced their battle cry: *For the dragon! For the dragon! For the dragon!*

The Callenor were caught between two forces. They were tired, surprised and badly led. Panic ensued.

The Duthenor rolled forward, killing quickly. At the rear of the Callenor force, they tried to rally, for the initial thrust of the horsemen dissipated as they wheeled away and circled back to attack again. But now the panic from the front of their ranks caught them and their morale broke.

Some tried to flee the field, others to rally together. Some were slain fighting, others as they turned their backs to run. It became a rout and the blood of the Callenor flowed.

A group to the left managed to flee the field, but the bulk of the enemy were hammered between the separate Duthenor forces. Fully half their number were killed before they surrendered, throwing down their swords.

Brand gave swift orders. The Duthenor surrounded them, but stopped killing. Ermenrik appeared. He had not dropped his sword, as well might be expected. There could be no surrender for him. Only overdue justice, and he knew it. He harangued his warriors, urging them to fight, but they ignored him.

"Silence!" Brand yelled, and Ermenrik ceased, the sword still in his hand.

Brand strode toward him, his own bloody sword still in his hand. Others came with him. But when Brand spoke, he raised his voice so all the Callenor heard his words.

"Warriors of the Callenor! Your surrender is accepted. You will suffer no further hurt, but you will leave your swords on this field and return to your own lands. This you will swear, and then you will be free to go. Do any think these terms unjust and refuse them?"

There was silence. What Brand did was a risk, but at heart the Callenor were no different to the Duthenor. Honor mattered to them, and he believed they would be true to their word. Not only that, word would spread and the opposition he may face in future battles would more easily surrender and have less reason to fight.

Brand turned to Ermenrik. For this man, justice must take a different form. He was a murderer. But indecision wracked him. Should he kill him now, or put him on trial?

Ermenrik seemed calm, but without warning he leaped forward. Steel rang on steel as Brand deflected his blow. But then the enemy general swung wildly, and having failed to kill Brand he struck at Haldring who was close by. She blocked his strike, but staggered back under the weight of it. Again he struck, but she recovered and flicked her blade at his leg, opening an artery in his thigh. It was a killing blow, but as she moved back out of the way she stumbled over the body of a slain Callenor soldier behind her and Ermenrik's sword ripped into her throat between helm and chainmail.

It was Ermenrik's final move. Brand's sword half-severed his neck and Sighern smashed his blade against the general's helm. The man's head lolled to the side at an unnatural angle and he fell to the ground, one leg kicking.

Brand rushed to Haldring. Blood spurted from her neck, and she had fallen to the ground, her hands futilely trying to stem the pouring out of her lifeblood. One moment Brand looked, fear chilling his heat, and then he acted. Swiftly he grabbed the pole from Sighern and stripped away the Dragon Banner.

He must stop the flow of blood, or she was dead. He knelt by her side, pressing the white cloth into the wound. In moments it was bloody, and she looked up at him, the light fading from her blue eyes.

"Live!" he breathed.

She seemed about to speak, but then she gasped and died. His hands were covered in her blood. He bowed his head, tears running down his cheeks. He did not move, still pressing the cloth against her wound, but the blood had ceased to flow for her heart had stopped beating. But Shorty and Taingern were suddenly there, and gently they raised him up and eased the now bloody banner from his hands. It fell to the stained grass.

Brand's gaze dropped to Ermenrik's corpse, and he kicked it. The dead body moved, and then fell back, lifeless once more.

Rage infused Brand. Why did the good die while evil prospered under the sun? But kicking a dead man was no answer. Instead, he wept, and two armies watched him.

The sun hung low now on the horizon. Fittingly, it was a scarlet sunset, a ruin of scattered clouds colored as though by blood. But there was more blood on the grass of the Duthgar than blazed in the sky.

All around was death, and the smell of death, and the low rays of the sun, red through a growing pall of smoke, shot through everything with an eerie light.

Crows and hawks and ravens gathered. Animals that scavenged haunted the forest edges. But they would not feed off the dead. The smoke grew stronger, and the roar of fires louder. Brand had ordered timber collected and the bodies of the dead soldiers burnt on massive biers, one for the Callenor and one for the Duthenor. It could be done swiftly, and it would prevent the spread of disease.

The surrendered Callenor had left, marching west into the setting sun and toward their own lands. Brand and a few others stood now before Haldring's grave. She was the only one who had been buried, and a cairn of small rocks marked her resting place. Words had been spoken, memories shared, and her sword driven into the cairn as a sign that here rested a great warrior. It was the Duthenor way, and though over the years the sword would rust and time destroy it, while it lasted none would take or touch the blade.

There was a stir in the small group. "Who is that?" one of the warriors asked.

They turned and looked where he gestured behind them. From the south came a person, a lone figure shuffling toward them purposely along the road whence the Duthenor themselves had earlier come.

26. Old Mother

Brand watched the figure approach. If the remnants of a battlefield disturbed whoever it was, they gave no sign. Instead, they moved ahead purposefully, oblivious to all that was around them, one step after another straight toward him.

The breeze that had blown through the fighting died with the sunset. The air was still now, and heavy with acrid smoke. It drifted sluggishly over the ground like fog, obscuring the newcomer now and then until the person drew close.

The walker was aided by two walking sticks, one in each hand, crafted of some dark timber. These she used to help her, for Brand saw now that it was a woman, and she moved quickly despite whatever frailty required use of the sticks in the first place.

She drew close, and finally came to a stop. Brand sensed Sighern stir beside him. He no longer carried the banner. It had been reattached to the pole and set in the ground. It may not be clean anymore, but the blood of a hero was a better emblem than a dragon.

"It's the marsh witch," Sighern said, and he made to move forward to greet her.

Brand clamped a hand down on his shoulder, and kept him in place. Sighern seemed confused, but Brand was growing certain. He had already lost one that he liked today; he would not lose another.

He stepped forward a pace, and spoke. "Greetings, old mother. Did you change your mind and come to help?"

She shuffled a step closer on her walking sticks.

224

"Aye, lad. I did, but it seems I'm too late. The battle is fought and won."

"It's never too late," Brand answered. "Come to the light, and leave evil behind."

The old witch looked at him quizzically for a few moments, as though puzzling something through.

Brand, too, was making up his mind. The witch had the gift of prophecy, and she had said they would never meet again. Yet here she was, or one that looked like her but was not. One that had been hunting him.

They moved at the same time. Brand drew his sword, and it caught the red rays of the dying sun. The two walking sticks of the witch became swords, and her body shimmered and transformed.

She was the witch no more. The guise was gone, the strands of magic that formed it loosed. What stood before Brand was a Halathrin warrior.

He heard shouts of *elf* as the two blades flashed toward him, but he was already moving. Yet even so he barely avoided them. The elf warrior was fast, and Brand knew he would have been dead had he not been suspicious.

Their blades flickered and crashed together. There was recognition in the elf warrior's eyes: at first touch he knew Brand's sword had been wrought by his own kind, and it surprised him. Mortals possessed few such weapons. But it did not cause him to falter. His twin blades were in constant motion, testing, cutting, flicking and thrusting. He moved with sublime grace, but speed and power went with it.

Few could have stood against him. Or none. But Brand was no ordinary warrior. His skills had been honed in a crucible of necessity and danger that others would not have survived. But he *had* survived, and learned.

Brand swept his blade at the elf's neck, but at the last moment flicked his wrist and thrust. This threw off his opponent's deflection and nearly killed him. It would have killed anyone else, but the elf merely rocked back out of the way and drove in again, faster and deadlier than before.

Brand was pushed back. He gave ground grudgingly, and tried to find the warrior's state of mind: stillness in the storm. But it mostly eluded him. Too much had happened today, and there was a cold anger within him that would not give way.

The elf pushed him back further, and Brand swung to the side, being careful not to be predictable and retreat in the same direction all the time. He studied the elf as he blocked and parried and swayed. The creature *looked* like a Halathrin, but was not quite the same. Brand had met immortals before, and they never had such pale skin nor eyes that lusted after battle and blood as did this one. But they were possessed of magic that allowed them to assume guises.

What other magic did his attacker possess? Brand allowed himself to calm as he retreated. He still could not assume stillness in the storm, but he was closer. The cold fury that troubled him receded, and by just defending he allowed himself some opportunity to think. The elf would soon use whatever other skills he had. The longer this went on, the greater the danger to him. Even if he killed Brand as he wanted, how then would he escape an army?

The answer was clear. He would assume another guise in the turmoil and try to escape that way. But if then, why not sooner and during the battle?

Brand fixed his gaze on him, and he swerved once more as he retreated. This time he thrust forward with his blade even as his feet shuffled backward. Again, he nearly struck the elf, but his opponent recovered quickly. One of the black swords swept at Brand's neck while the other jabbed at his groin.

226

Stumbling, Brand fell back. The elf drove at him in a fury of blades, but Brand had feigned his imbalance. His own sword arced through the air in a beheading stroke, but the elf was no longer there. With blistering speed he ducked the blade, rolled away and came to his feet once more, black blades circling the air before him.

"A valiant attempt, mortal. But you are no match for my kind."

Brand grinned at him. "In my experience, warriors who start a conversation during a fight are frightened of losing. They need to try to talk themselves into the fact that they're better."

The elf did not answer, but the killing light in his eyes shone brighter and he darted forward, almost too fast to see. He moved as though he had no bones, only sinuous muscles that coiled and struck like a darting adder.

Their blades flashed and clanged again. Brand would rather have deflected than blocked, but his opponent was too good. He was forced off balance all the time, cramped in his movements and his own attacks mostly anticipated. He had never faced so skilled an opponent, and it was a battle he wondered if he would lose. Nor could he expect help. It was a one on one fight, and no one would dishonor him by changing that.

If he were to win, he must at least survive a while longer, but this was increasingly hard. His enemy was running out of time, for the army, though spellbound by the duel, was beginning to form a circle around the combatants. The elf had to win and escape soon, or he never would.

The elf drove him back, his cold eyes burning with battle lust, his every move smooth, graceful and deadly. In his hands, the two dark swords wove a spell of sharp-edged death, yet Brand held them off and launched a counter-attack. He was tired of retreating.

With swift movements of his own, if not quite so graceful, his pattern-welded blade arced silver fire through the gathering dusk, cutting, slashing and jabbing.

The elf reeled away, only to attack again, but Brand harnessed his anger and leaped to meet him. Hot sparks flew from the blades and cold metal shrieked. A moment they stood thus, almost uncaring of defense as they each strove to kill, and then the elf nimbly leaped back.

He stood there, his swords held loosely in his hands, barely seeming to draw breath while Brand panted. And then he grinned, his pale face white in the gathering dark, but a streak of red ran across his cheek where the tip of Brand's sword had marked him.

Brand knew what would come now. He had been waiting for it, though what form it would take and what would best combat it he did not know. He drew a deep breath and lifted the tip of his sword a little higher.

When it came, it still surprised him. The elf just stepped away from himself. There were two of him now, both black-clad, garbed in silver armor, pale eyes burning with battle lust. But each image held only one dark sword.

Which was real and which illusion? Brand was not quite sure, even though he had been watching closely. This he knew though: the elf would not wait.

Brand sent out a tendril of his own magic to the image on the right. It was the one that he thought may have been the elf himself. But he did not wait to be attacked by either. Instead, he dived to the right and rolled, moving first to take the initiative and coming to the side of the righthand image so that they could not both advance on him and attack at the same time.

He surged to his feet, his sword weaving before him. To the side, Shorty and Taingern advanced. It was no longer a one on one fight. But he doubted they would reach either image in time.

Swift as jagged lightning, both elves sprang for him, but the second was hindered by the first, and the tendril of Brand's own magic sensed the real from the illusory.

He darted to the side again, as though ignoring the closer illusion and moving to combat the second. But at the last moment he ducked a vicious strike from the closest image that would have beheaded him and stabbed his Halathrin blade up into its body.

Brand drove the blade with all his might, surging up from his bent legs, thrusting also with the strength of his arms and angling the point of the sword to reach beneath the ribs and pierce the heart.

He knew instantly that he had chosen the correct target. His blade struck no image but a real body. Even elvish chainmail parted when struck by the point of a Halathrin sword driven by the full might of a skilled warrior.

The sword sheared through armor and clothes, through flesh and blood. It drove up, higher and higher, lifting the elf off the ground. There he hung a moment, the fury in his eyes washed away by surprise. Blood fountained from his mouth, and he died.

Brand kicked the corpse off his blade. He swung to see the other image, but it drifted away even as he watched like a whisper of mist vanishing into the air.

He turned back to the dead elf. Pale skin shriveled. The eyes burned away. Its whole body, armor and swords as well, disintegrated and seeped into the very soil as though made of some dark water that soaked into a subterranean chamber of the earth, far, far beneath the sight or reach of men.

Brand stood there, leaning on his sword in great weariness. It had been an endless day, but he had survived, if changed and only just. The battle was won, but the war was yet to come, and the magician that sought his death was a power in the world not to be dismissed or forgotten. He would try to kill him again, and Brand knew now that freeing the Duthgar was but a secondary thing. Whatever power the magician served was of the Dark, and there lay a greater peril to the land than ever Unferth could dream to be.

Epilogue

Char-harash, Lord of the Ten Armies, Ruler of the Thousand Stars, Light of Kar-fallon and Emperor of the Kar-ahn-hetep dreamed.

And his dreams were of battle and dark magic.

From the north swept an army of Letharn. Rank after rank of infantry marched. From the east came an army also, this of cavalry and chariots. Before both forces advanced the wizard-priests of the Letharn. With them they summoned lightning that leaped from the sky at their gesture and tore the earth asunder. When they raised their hands, the solid ground heaved as though it were an angry sea.

Battle raged. Sword clashed against sword. Horses neighed and men screamed. Magicians opposed wizard-priests and the world spun in smoke and fire while the sky darkened and chaos reigned.

Out of the chaos drove a spear. Char-harash cried out in pain. It took him in the stomach and spilled his entrails into the trampled dust.

No. He *had* cried out in pain. And then came the great dark. He knew it for what it was. Death. The gateway to the realm of the gods. He embraced it, for he was a god himself.

He hesitated. No. It was not so. He fought it, for he was not yet a god. He fought to live, but pain engulfed him. He felt the spear drive deep toward his heart, felt it pull out again, heard his moan as death took him.

Yes. That was long ago. The great dark still surrounded him. Entombed. Chanted over by his magicians. He heard the echo of their ancient spells even now. Or was he still being interred?

No. Eons had passed. The stars had shifted in the sky. Or was his last breath still fresh upon his resin-embalmed lips?

The dark hid things from him. But not all. Slowly he began to wake, and he called one of his kind to him. Horta, a magician of his own line. He was a magician also. Charharash. The God-king.

And soon he would wake and tread the earth once again. Let his foes fear him.

He dreamed no more. Dreams were for men. He was to become a god, and he would not dream but rather send nightmares to his enemies.

Thus ends *The Pale Swordsman*. The Dark God Rises trilogy continues in book two, *The Crimson Lord*, where Brand must face the usurper, his army, and discover more of his true adversary.

Amazon lists millions of titles, and I'm glad you discovered this one. But if you'd like to know when I release a new book, instead of leaving it to chance, sign up for my newsletter. I'll send you an email on publication.

Yes please! – Go to www.homeofhighfantasy.com and sign up.

No thanks – I'll take my chances.

Dedication

There's a growing movement in fantasy literature. Its name is noblebright, and it's the opposite of grimdark.

Noblebright celebrates the virtues of heroism. It's an old-fashioned thing, as old as the first story ever told around a smoky campfire beneath ancient stars. It's storytelling that highlights courage and loyalty and hope for the spirit of humanity. It recognizes the dark, the dark in us all, and the dark in the villains of its stories. It recognizes death, and treachery and betrayal. But it dwells on none of these things.

I dedicate this book, such as it is, to that which is noblebright. And I thank the authors before me who held the torch high so that I could see the path: J.R.R. Tolkien, C.S. Lewis, Terry Brooks, David Eddings, Susan Cooper, Roger Taylor and many others. I salute you.

And, for a time, I too will hold the torch high.

Appendix A: The Runes of Life and Death

Halls of Lore. Chamber 7. Aisle 21. Item 426
General subject: Divination
Topic: The use of magic and talismans
Author: Careth Tar

In the south of Alithoras, west of the lands of Azanbulzibar and the barrow mounds of the Shadowed Wars, which the immortal Halathrin call Elù-haraken, dwell a strange people.

They name themselves Kar-ahn-hetep, which means "children of the thousand stars" in their ancient language. But the long ages since their days of glory, and the short memory and fast tongues of men have reduced this to "Kirsch." Yet the wise know their true name, and the remnant of their race that still survive cling to it – and also to their old ways of magic.

The land of the Kirsch was once fertile, but the eons have altered the climate. It has become arid. These people existed in the time of the Letharn, and well before them, and inhabited one of the few lands not overrun by that conquest-hungry race. The inhabitants were fierce fighters. They were also numerous. And the great distance from Letharn strongholds was an additional defensive advantage. But mostly, their survival and indeed aggression toward the Letharn sprung from this: the

Kirsch practiced arts of powerful magic unlike that possessed by others.

Briefly, this is the nature of their magic arts. It centers around a belief in the primordial powers that form and substance the universe. This is what we would term ùhrengai. From this primordial force, two alternate forces arose. Again, what we recognize as lòhrengai and elùgai. But after that their beliefs diverge.

We, as lòhrens, use the one power. Elùgroths use the other. The Kirsch, on the other hand, use both – but they do not believe they access it directly. Instead, they employ talismans to focus their thought. Also, and importantly, they believe that agencies intervene in this process on the magician's behalf. This is often thought to be the spirits of the dead and other forces of nature, call them gods if you will. All of these act as conduits between themselves and the primordial power.

An example of this is the practice of divination.

The chief means of foretelling among the Children is the casting of the Runes of Life and Death. These are bones. Sometimes animal in origin, sometimes (and preferably) human.

Human finger bones are favored for a specific reason. The more so if they are obtained from a person of power. Human bones, especially from a powerful person, increase the accuracy of the foretelling because the agency constrained to act on the magician's behalf is more puissant. Thus, the finger bones of dead magicians are highly sought after. This gives rise to graverobbing, and in turn elaborate means of disguising tombs to thwart

236

exhumation. Also, it generates distrust among their society. Magicians hate (and fear) one another, always seeking to kill lesser rivals and protect themselves from greater.

The runes consist of ten bones. Each has two paired runes cut into them and colored by blood, two aspects of the same concept or force. By reading which opposite of a paired rune falls, and how the bones scatter in relation to each other, the future is told. Sometimes, a bone will not land squarely on one side or the other. This signifies doubt.

It is customary to shake the pouch that contains the runes ten times before use in order to prevent conscious tampering with the divination. It is also a tradition not to withdraw ten bones at once, this being considered to signal the highest ill-fortune should it occur by accident.

These are the ten runes and their double meanings, as translated from an ancient text.

Hotep: change – quiescence

It is the nature of the world that things change. Nothing is still. All things exist in a state of flux. The stars move in the sky. The wind blows across desert sands, shifting grains that once were boulders. Flowers bloom, and then in turn wither. This is change, and even the bones of the earth feel it. Yet there is that to humankind which is not material. It is of the spirit. And the spirit of man seeks quiescence. The wise know that true quiescence is the acceptance of change. The foolish seek always to grasp at starlight.

This then is the moral: when change is afoot, seek to be centered and accepting. Look for the opportunity that transformation will bring. If there is no apparent change, beware. Danger approaches!

Karmun: death – life

All things born of the earth return to dust. Only ideas are eternal. Yet an idea is nothing without a living mind to give it shape and purpose and voice. Death is not to be feared, nor embraced. It must be accepted. It, too, is an idea. In a living mind it can be fed by fear until it grows into a great, slavering beast that chases us without cessation. Or it can be accepted, its power used instead to nurture understanding of the beauty of transience.

This then is the moral: death is always close. Seek not to escape it, for in doing so you will run toward it. Rather, the wise accept it, and give themselves true life.

Harak: war – peace

War can exist without peace. But peace cannot endure without war, or the threat of war, because always there will be those that seek to steal, or enslave, or conquer. War also gives birth to invention. Yet too, it kills the young and the strong and those that one day may otherwise have achieved greatness. But this also is true. War brings vigor to the nation, training the strong in mind and body, giving them discipline and skill. Peace allows the weak to prosper. This in turn makes a society susceptible to those that would bring war. And yet, above all, it is in the heart of most people to seek peace. Yet the leaders of nations, though few in number, bring the many to battle.

This then is the moral: war and peace are two sides of the one coin. The wise prepare for war when peace reigns, as also they prepare for peace when war strides across the land. Only fools expect one state or the other to prevail without cessation.

Rasallher: mountain peak – valley

High atop the mountain, a man looks down and surveys the majesty of the world. "It is beautiful," he says. That same man, days before, looked at the mountain peak from the valley beneath its shadow. "How beautiful," he said. "What a creation of majesty!" The mountain and the valley are the same. The man is the same. Only his perspective has changed. It is no different with mountains than anything else. A man may invest his fortune only to lose it. But having lost it, he may say "such is life. I will rebuild my empire." Or he may take his own life. It is perspective only.

This then is the moral: in dealing with friends, family, warriors, rivals, other empires, put yourself in their shoes.

Discern their perspective. Understand them. Then you can better predict what they will do. And also, in this manner, you will learn of yourself.

Hassah: water – dust

Of dust, the earth is made. To dust, all life returns. Nothing is so barren as the dry sands of a desert, yet even in the arid waste life blooms. How so? The gift of water. When it rains life springs to action. A great race commences. Live. Breed. Send offspring into the world. Then comes again the time of sleep. Deep in the soil life burrows and protects itself. There, dormant, it waits through the long years of drought. Until the water comes again. Then once more the great race commences.

This then is the moral: even the witless seed and the dumb animal knows when to act and when non-action is required. The wise man follows nature's example. Act when it is propitious to do so. Hold back, wait, show patience when it is not. In this way, the wise turn the cycles of nature and the tides of human affairs to their advantage.

Durath-har: earth – air

Of the earth, life is born. It nurtures plants and animals, which in turn nourish man. Yet it is from the air that rain falls and through the sky that the sun shines. Without which no life can prosper and all the land would be barren as it is in a cave. And even as the earth is still, unmoving and unchanging, the air flits and drifts and grows hot and cold, ever transmuting. Yet what is earth by itself, or air on its own? Nothing. Nowhere places void of life.

This then is the moral: all forces on earth and heaven meet, and in that meeting opportunity is birthed. Rain gives rise to new growth. Heat withers grass and tree and shrub, but the desert flowers bloom where once the grass grew. Until the grass rises in its turn and smothers the land once more. Seek to anticipate the cycles of life and the hearts of men. When the cycle shifts, opportunity has already passed.

Orok-hai: the hanged man – the fugitive

Men are hanged in the empire for certain offences. Yet it is human nature to want to avoid penalties for crime. Some, though, on being caught will admit their guilt. Are these wise men or fools? Is it better to admit guilt and die with a satisfied conscience than to try to hide a crime? And what of the criminal who escapes, yet repents, and later does good in the world? Yet also there are those that are caught, admit their guilt, but remain unrepentant. The heart of a man is a dark place, a mystery greater than the thousand stars.

This then is the moral: in dealing with people expect that which is unexpected. The condemned may fight all the harder despite knowing they cannot win. Or the victorious tyrant may be magnanimous. But if you study them, learn how they have behaved in the past, and then you will better know how they will react in the future. Some men were born to be hanged.

El-haran: the wanderer — the farmer

In the heart of people is a desire to see new things. When the ibis gather and of a sudden flock north, do we not wish to go with them? The call of strange skies, the lure of the next hill, the next valley, the next wood or the taste of a new spring is strong. Such things sing to us and fill our hearts. Yet also something else takes root in our soul. The love of the land to which we are born. It is in our blood. We feel it in our feet as we tread the soil. It is in the familiar air we breathe, and being deprived of this land our spirit weakens even as a man falters that struggles to catch his breath.

This then is the moral: the hearts of people are divided. They will sometimes say one thing, yet do another. At one moment they are kind, at the next vexatious. A thief may do a noble deed, and an emperor steal from the poor. Such is the dichotomous nature of humanity. But people act under the influence of their internal impulses or external stimuli. The wise man studies these internal and external rhythms in their associates and enemies. Therefore, they can better predict how a person will react under what forces.

It is a fact universally known to mankind that eagles soar in the sky, wheeling, circling, riding the waves of air with nobility. But the sparrow is a creature that chatters away in shrubbery. It is plain. It is the least beautiful of birds. It gathers in flocks for it is timid and there is safety in numbers. Therefore, the eagle is admired and the sparrow a pest. Yet, is it not also true that the eagle is an opportunistic feeder that hunts or scavenges carrion as circumstances dictate? Is this then more noble than a sparrow? Is the eagle to be admired more because of its size? Is the sparrow lesser because it congregates as a community?

This then is the moral: all creatures and things have their place under the sun. Beware of false assumptions, unearned grandeur, reputations and the prideful opinion of others. Watch, learn, study and draw conclusions based on fact and untainted opinion. Test your discoveries against reality. This is the path to wisdom.

Urhash-hassar: multiplicity – nadir

Life teems in soil, air and water. Yet catastrophe comes in its turn through flood, drought, earthquake and sickness. Disaster razes life and destroys worlds. Yet from calamity new life rises, different, stronger. What then is the normal state of affairs of humanity? Is it multiplicity? Shall we spread over the earth, leveling forests, drying swamps, harvesting river and sea until the teeming waters are emptied and the tread of our boots tramps all the world? Or shall we in turn succumb, our bones and flesh nourishing the soil for new life? In days of old it is rumored civilizations existed before us. The tales tell that they were stricken down. And well may we wonder if they in their turn heard rumors of those that went before.

This then is the moral: it is foolish to believe in gain without loss and endless growth. It is not the way of nature. Yet also it is foolish to believe in defeat and oblivion. The wise man hopes for one and strives to prevent the other. The sage accepts all fates, and thereby rises above them. That person can smile in the face of nadir and feel the sadness of multiplicity – yet is chained by neither.

Appendix B: Encyclopedic Glossary

Note: the glossary of each book in this series is individualized for that book alone. Additionally, there is often historical material provided in its entries for people, artifacts and events that are not included in the main text.

Many races dwell in Alithoras. All have their own language, and though sometimes related to one another the changes sparked by migration, isolation and various influences often render these tongues unintelligible to each other.

The ascendancy of Halathrin culture, combined with their widespread efforts to secure and maintain allies against elug incursions, has made their language the primary means of communication between diverse peoples.

For instance, a merchant of Cardoroth addressing a Duthenor warrior would speak Halathrin, or a simplified version of it, even though their native speeches stem from the same ancestral language.

This glossary contains a range of names and terms. Many are of Halathrin origin, and their meaning is provided. The remainder derive from native tongues and are obscure, so meanings are only given intermittently.

Often, Duthenor names and Halathrin elements are combined. This is especially so for the aristocracy. Few other tribes of men had such long-term friendship with the immortal Halathrin as the Duthenor, and though in this relationship they lost some of their natural culture, they gained nobility and knowledge in return.

List of abbreviations:

Cam. Camar

Comb. Combined

Cor. Corrupted form

Duth. Duthenor

Hal. Halathrin

Kir. Kirsch

Prn. Pronounced

Alithoras: *Hal.* "Silver land." The Halathrin name for the continent they settled after leaving their own homeland. Refers to the extensive river and lake systems they found and their wonder at the beauty of the land.

Anast Dennath: *Hal.* "Stone mountains." Mountain range in northern Alithoras. Source of the river known as the Careth Nien that forms a natural barrier between the lands of the Camar people and the Duthenor and related tribes.

Aranloth: *Hal.* "Noble might." A lòhren of ancient heritage and friend to Brand.

Arell: A famed healer in Cardoroth. Companion of Brand.

Arnhaten: *Kir.* "Disciples." Servants of a magician. One magician usually has many disciples, but only some of these are referred to as "inner door." Inner door disciples receive a full transmission of the master's knowledge. The remainder do not, but they continue to strive to earn the favor of their master. Until they do, they are dispensable.

Asaba: *Kir.* "White stone – marble." A disciple of Horta, but not of inner door status.

Azanbulzibar: A fabled city in the far south of Alithoras.

Baldring: *Duth.* "Fierce blade." Once a lord of the Duthenor. Father of Galdring.

Black Talon: The sign of Unferth's house. Appears on his banner and is his personal emblem. Legend claims the founder of the house in ancient days had the power to transform into a raven. Disguised in this form, and trusted as a magical being, he gave misinformation and ill-advice to the enemies of his people.

Brand: *Duth.* "Torch." An exiled Duthenor tribesman and adventurer. Appointed by the former king of Cardoroth to serve as regent for Prince Gilcarist. By birth, he is the rightful chieftain of the Duthenor people. However, Unferth the usurper overthrew his father, killing both him and his wife. Brand, only a youth at the time, swore an oath of vengeance. That oath has long slept, but it is not forgotten, either by Brand or the usurper.

Breath of the dragon: An ancient saying of Letharn origin. They believed the magic of dragons was the preeminent magic in the world because dragons were creatures able to travel through time. Dragon's breath is known to mean fire, the destructive face of their nature. But the Letharn also believed dragons could breathe mist. This was the healing face of their nature. And the mist-breath of a dragon was held to be able to change destinies and bring good luck. To "ride the dragon's breath" meant that for a period a person was a focal point of time and destiny.

Brunhal: *Duth.* "Hallowed woman." Former chieftainess of the Duthenor. Wife to Drunn, former chieftain of the Duthenor. Mother to Brand. According to Duthenor custom, a chieftain and chieftainess co-ruled.

Callenor: *Duth.* One of several tribes closely related to the Duthenor. This one inhabits lands immediately west of the Duthgar.

Camar: *Cam. Prn.* Kay-mar. A race of interrelated tribes that migrated in two main stages. The first brought them to the vicinity of Halathar, homeland of the immortal Halathrin; in the second, they separated and established cities along a broad stretch of eastern Alithoras. Related to the Duthenor, though far more distantly than the Callenor.

Caraval: *Hal. Comb. Duth.* "Red hawk." A childhood companion of Brand.

Cardoroth: *Cor. Hal. Comb. Cam.* A Camar city, often called Red Cardoroth. Some say this alludes to the red granite commonly used in the construction of its buildings, others that it refers to a prophecy of destruction.

Careth Nien: *Hal. Prn.* Kareth ny-en. "Great river." Largest river in Alithoras. Has its source in the mountains of Anast Dennath and runs southeast across the land before emptying into the sea. It was over this river (which sometimes freezes along its northern stretches) that the Camar and other tribes migrated into the eastern lands. Much later, Brand came to the city of Cardoroth by one of these ancient migratory routes.

Char-harash: *Kir.* "He who destroys by flame." Most exalted of the emperors of the Kirsch, and a magician of great power.

Conmar: *Cam.* An alias of Brand.

Dernthrad: *Duth.* "Head shield – a helm." A farmer of the Duthgar.

Dragon of the Duthgar: The banner of the chieftains of the Duthenor. Legend holds that an ancient forefather of the line slew a dragon and ate its heart. Dragons are seen by the Duthenor as creatures of ultimate evil, but the consuming of their heart is reputed to pass on wisdom and magic.

Drunn: *Duth.* "Man of secrets." Former chieftain of the Duthenor. Husband to Brunhal and father to Brand.

Durnloth: *Duth. Comb. Hal.* "Earth might." Young sheep herder of the Duthgar.

Duthenor: *Duth. Prn.* Dooth-en-or. "The people." A single tribe (or less commonly a group of closely related tribes melded into a larger people at times of war or disaster) who generally live a rustic and peaceful lifestyle. They are breeders of cattle and herders of sheep.

249

However, when need demands they are bold warriors – men and women alike. Currently ruled by a usurper who murdered Brand's parents. Brand has sworn an oath to overthrow the tyrant and avenge his parents.

Duthgar: *Duth*. "People spear." The name is taken to mean "the land of the warriors who wield spears."

Elùgai: *Hal. Prn*. Eloo-guy. "Shadowed force." The sorcery of an elùgroth.

Elù-haraken: *Hal*. "The shadowed wars." Long ago battles in a time that is become myth to the Duthenor and Camar tribes.

Elùgroth: *Hal. Prn*. Eloo-groth. "Shadowed horror." A sorcerer. They often take names in the Halathrin tongue in mockery of the lòhren practice to do so.

Ermenrik: *Duth*. "Tallest tree in the forest." Trusted servant of Unferth.

Galdring: *Duth*. "Bright blade." A lord of the Duthenor. Son of Baldring.

Garamund: *Duth*. "Spears of the earth – trees." An old warrior of the Duthenor.

Gingrel: *Duth*. "Yellow river – a river mined for gold." A Callenor vassal to Unferth. Given lordship of a hall by the usurper.

God-king: See Char-harsh.

Grinder: A man-like creature of Duthenor legend that haunts fells and fens. Said to be born of a lightning strike in swamp water, but there are other tales of his origin. He hates men, and hunts those who stray into his shadow-haunted lands. Reported to shun weapons, but to kill by the enormous strength of his arms alone.

Halathar: *Hal.* "Dwelling place of the people of Halath." The forest realm of the immortal Halathrin.

Halathgar: *Hal.* "Bright star." Actually a constellation of two stars. Also called the Lost Huntress.

Halathrin: *Hal.* "People of Halath." A race named after an honored lord who led an exodus of his people to the land of Alithoras in pursuit of justice, having sworn to defeat a great evil. They are human, though of fairer form, greater skill and higher culture than ordinary men. They possess a unity of body, mind and spirit that enables insight and endurance beyond the native races of Alithoras. Said to be immortal, but killed in great numbers during their conflicts in ancient times with the evil they sought to destroy. Those conflicts are collectively known as the Shadowed Wars.

Haldring: *Duth.* "White blade – a sword that flashes in the sun." Sister of Galdring. A shield-maiden.

Harad: *Duth.* "Warrior." An old farmer, and husband of Hromling.

Har-falach: *Kir.* "Ruler/heavenly/mystical falcon." One of the lesser gods of the Kar-ahn-hetep. Often depicted as a man with wings and the head of a hawk.

Harlach: Etymology unknown, but not considered to be of Duthenor origin. An ancient witch of Duthenor and Camar folklore whose life has spanned hundreds, perhaps thousands, of years. Reclusive, often wicked and according to some legends the mother of a monster that roams the night hunting and killing men.

Hathalor: *Kir.* "Tresses of the sun – a lion's mane." One of the lesser gods of the Kar-ahn-hetep. Often depicted as a man with a lion's head.

High Way: An ancient road longer than the Duthgar, but well preserved in that land. Probably of Letharn origin and used to speed troops to battle.

Horta: *Kir.* "Speech of the acacia tree." It is believed among the Kar-ahn-hetep that the acacia tree possesses magical properties that aid discourse between the realms of men and gods. Horta is a name that recurs among families noted for producing elite magicians.

Howe: A large mound of turfed earth, usually covering a stone structure, that serves as a tomb.

Hromling: *Duth.* "Frost foam – snow." An old farmwife, spouse of Harad.

Hruidgar: *Duth.* "Ashwood spear." A Duthenor hunter.

Immortals: See Halathrin.

Kar-ahn-hetep: *Kir.* "The children of the thousand stars." A race of people that vied for supremacy in ancient times with the Letharn. Their power was ultimately broken, their empire destroyed. But a residual population survived and defied outright annihilation by their conquerors. They believe their empire will one day rise again to rule the world. The kar-ahn element of their name means the "thousand stars" but also "the lights that never die."

Kar-fallon: *Kir.* "Death city." A great city of the Kar-ahn-hetep that served as their principal religious focus. Their magician-priests conducted the great rites of their nation in its sacred temples.

Kar-karmun: *Kir.* "Death-life – the runes of life and death." A means of divination that distills the wisdom and worldview of the Kar-ahn-hetep civilization.

Kirsch: See Kar-ahn-hetep.

Laigern: *Cam.* "Storm-tossed sea." Head guard of a merchant caravan.

Letharn: *Hal.* "Stone raisers. Builders." A race of people that in antiquity conquered most of Alithoras. Now, only faint traces of their civilization endure.

Light of Kar-fallon: See Char-harash.

Lòhren: *Hal. Prn.* Ler-ren. "Knowledge giver – a counselor." Other terms used by various nations include wizard, druid and sage.

Lòhrengai: *Hal. Prn.* Ler-ren-guy. "Lòhren force." Enchantment, spell or use of mystic power. A manipulation and transformation of the natural energy inherent in all things. Each use takes something from the user. Likewise, some part of the transformed energy infuses them. Lòhrens use it sparingly, elùgroths indiscriminately.

Lord of the Ten Armies: See Char-harash.

Magic: Mystic power. See lòhrengai and elùgai.

Norhanu: *Kir.* "Serrated blade." A psychoactive herb.

Olbata: *Kir.* "Silence of the desert at night." An inner door disciple of Horta.

Pennling Path: Etymology obscure. Pennling was an ancient hero of the Duthenor. Some say he built the road in the Duthgar known as the High Way. This is not true, but one legend holds that he traveled all its length in one night on a milk-white steed to confront an attacking army by himself. It is said that his ghost may yet be seen racing along the road on his steed when the full moon hangs above the Duthgar.

Ruler of the Thousand Stars: See Char-harash.

Runes of Life and Death: See Kar-karmun.

Shadowed wars: See Elù-haraken.

Shemfal: *Kir.* "Cool shadows gliding over the hot waste – dusk." One of the greater gods of the Kar-ahn-hetep. Often depicted as a mighty man, bat winged and headed. Ruler of the underworld. Given a wound in battle with other gods that does not heal and causes him to limp.

Shenna: *Kir.* "Royal rectangle." A kind of cartouche.

Shenti: A type of kilt worn by the Kar-ahn-hetep.

Shorty: A former Durlindrath (chief bodyguard of the king of Cardoroth). Friend to Brand. His proper name is Lornach.

Shurilgar: *Hal.* "Midnight star." An elùgroth. One of the most puissant sorcerers of antiquity. Known to legend as the Betrayer of Nations.

Sighern: *Duth.* "Battle leader." A youth of the Duthgar.

254

Sorcerer: See Elùgroth.

Sorcery: See elùgai.

Stillness in the Storm: A mental state sought by many warriors. It is a sense of the mind being detached from the body. If achieved, it frees the warrior from emotions such as fear and pain that hinder physical performance. The body, in its turn, moves and reacts by trained instinct alone allowing the skill of the warrior to flow unhindered to the surface. Those who have perfected the correct mental state feel as though they can slow down the passage of time during a fight. It is an illusion, yet one that offers a combat advantage.

Taingern: *Cam.* "Still sea," or "calm waters." A former Durlindrath (chief bodyguard of the king of Cardoroth). Friend to Brand.

Thurgil: *Duth.* "Storm of blades." A farmer of the Duthgar.

Tinwellen: *Cam.* "Sun of the earth – gold." Daughter of a prosperous merchant of Cardoroth.

Unferth: *Duth.* "Hiss of arrows." The name is sometimes interpreted to mean "whispered counsels that lead to war." Usurper of the chieftainship of the Duthenor. Rightful chieftain of the Callenor.

Ùhrengai: *Hal. Prn.* Er-ren-guy. "Original force." The primordial force that existed before substance or time.

Wizard: See lòhren.

Wizard-priest: The priests of the Letharn, who possessed mighty powers of magic.

About the author

I'm a man born in the wrong era. My heart yearns for faraway places and even further afield times. Tolkien had me at the beginning of *The Hobbit* when he said, ". . . one morning long ago in the quiet of the world . . ."

Sometimes I imagine myself in a Viking mead-hall. The long winter night presses in, but the shimmering embers of a log in the hearth hold back both cold and dark. The chieftain calls for a story, and I take a sip from my drinking horn and stand up . . .

Or maybe the desert stars shine bright and clear, obscured occasionally by wisps of smoke from burning camel dung. A dry gust of wind marches sand grains across our lonely campsite, and the wayfarers about me stir restlessly. I sip cool water and begin to speak.

I'm a storyteller. A man to paint a picture by the slow music of words. I like to bring faraway places and times to life, to make hearts yearn for something they can never have, unless for a passing moment.

Printed in Great Britain
by Amazon